THE COTTAGE BY THE SEA

KERI BEEVIS

Boldwood

First published in Great Britain in 2024 by Boldwood Books Ltd.

Copyright © Keri Beevis, 2024

Cover Design by 12 Orchards Ltd

Cover Photography: Shutterstock

A CIP catalogue record for this book is available from the British Library.

Paperback ISBN 978-1-83533-582-6

Large Print ISBN 978-1-83533-578-9

Hardback ISBN 978-1-83533-577-2

Ebook ISBN 978-1-83533-575-8

Kindle ISBN 978-1-83533-576-5

Audio CD ISBN 978-1-83533-583-3

MP3 CD ISBN 978-1-83533-580-2

Digital audio download ISBN 978-1-83533-574-1

Boldwood Books Ltd
23 Bowerdean Street
London SW6 3TN
www.boldwoodbooks.com

This one is for my Long Melford family
Cousins, Beth and Ruth
And in memory of Auntie Irene

PART I

Something wicked this way comes.

— WILLIAM SHAKESPEARE

1

NORFOLK, ENGLAND

My name is Harper. I'm an author of romance novels. Now trying to write my own love story.

Too cheesy?

Harper Reed backspaced, deleting the opening sentence of her online dating profile, and took a generous sip of wine as she considered again what to write. Megan's words rang in her head: *Be honest. Dress it up a little, but be you.*

Her best friend had met her husband online a couple of years ago, and she had been full of advice. Harper knew Megan was right, but still she was self-conscious. Words were her day job and she wrote two novels a year, so why was creating an online dating profile so bloody difficult?

Maybe because she'd had to battle her nerves to sign up.

She had never done this kind of thing before. Of course she had dated, but not in a long time, and things had changed a lot in the last ten years. This online way of meeting people was completely alien to her. She had been introduced to her husband, Charlie, at a barbecue of a mutual friend. Now it seemed the internet and social media was the main way people met.

The wine was going down too fast and guilt stabbed at her as she reached for the bottle to top up her glass. Even setting up a profile had required the crutch of alcohol, so she dreaded to think how her nerves would hold up if she went on an actual date.

A year ago, she wouldn't have even contemplated doing this, but things changed. Megan was right. A further twelve months had passed and she was existing day to day in this big house, all alone. It had been her sanctuary, but also her prison, and she had to find a way to move forward, aware that she needed to start living again.

The first step she had taken was to get a dog. A cute black cocker spaniel called Bailey, who had found himself in the shelter she used to volunteer with after his elderly owner died.

She had felt a connection with him the moment they met, perhaps because of the circumstances of how he had ended up homeless, and it felt like they were choosing each other. It wasn't until he had come home with her that Harper had realised just how quiet and empty the house had become, and how much she needed him there.

Having the commitment of another being to look after also got her outside each day, where she could feel the fresh air on her face and see other people. It had been so easy to stay indoors, cocooning herself away from the rest of the world, and it didn't help that she worked from home. Before Bailey, she had no reason to leave and the longer she had stayed inside, the more difficult it had been to step foot out of the front door.

It was early days with him – he had been here just six weeks – but already he was giving her a purpose to get up each morning. And while her belly had been jittery with nerves the first few times they'd ventured out, her confidence was steadily growing. She no longer tensed if she saw someone heading towards her, knowing they might stop to chat.

From talking to strangers who wanted to pet her dog to online dating seemed a big step, but Harper knew she had to bite the bullet. She and Charlie had always planned to start a family; it's why they had left London and moved to Norfolk, and it was why they had bought this big house. Despite everything that had happened, she still wanted that dream. Although she had pushed everyone away, she realised she didn't want to be alone. She wanted to fall in love again, just as she wanted the sound of children's laughter echoing around the walls of the house. She wanted – no, she needed a second chance.

The dating site she was registering with was called IntoYou and it was one of the more reputable companies that charged a fee, aiming to match those who were serious about finding the right one. It was where Megan had met Tom and she had highly recommended it.

Deciding to return to her icebreaker intro when she could think of something that sounded better, Harper skipped ahead to the next section.

What Qualities Are You Looking For?

Another loaded question. Did she really know?
She typed even as she was running the answer through in her head.

Kindness. Honesty. Respect. Someone who knows that laughter and a sense of humour are important.

That had been her and Charlie in the beginning. Teasing

each other out of a bad mood, finding the same things funny. And she had always got a kick from knowing that when her husband laughed, she had been the one to put the smile on his face. She had thought they still had that to the very end, but when she looked back now, she could see how the humour had gradually disappeared from their lives.

As for the kindness, honesty and respect, they came top of the list for her, and having had and lost them, she understood just how important they were.

Fresh doubts crept in. Could she really go through with this?

She was painting a confident picture and no potential suitor would realise it was all smoke and mirrors, that, truthfully, she was a pathetic mess. That until recently she had struggled to leave the house.

Ignoring the kneading ball of panic in her stomach, she went to the next section.

Location, sexual orientation, age, and dependents were easy and she box ticked. It was her marital status that threw her.

Widowed was an option, but she was reluctant to select it. What if it put men off?

Harper was thirty-seven and had already buried her husband. An awkward conversation topic from the word go, especially given the circumstances. She desperately wanted to start fresh and would rather not discuss any of what had happened unless she had reached a point where she was comfortable with someone. Even then it would be difficult.

She decided against ticking the box, instead selecting single.

It wasn't really a lie. She was alone.

The 'do I want children' question also made her pause. Would her eagerness be off-putting?

Screw it. She didn't want any time-wasters. She ticked the yes box, knowing that if she was asking for honesty, she had to be truthful back.

She returned to her icebreaker, taking a large sip of wine, acutely aware it was her shop window. Her one chance to sell herself, and that she had just 400 words.

God, that sounded awful. It made it seem like she was an item for purchase.

It was true though. It was technically a meat market, no matter how it was dressed up. Everyone was shopping for flesh.

She tried to think of something witty, aware people liked funny. Although she hadn't had much humour in her life over the last two years, she had once been the girl who could make people laugh.

Not any more though. Instead, she imagined the sassy lead character from her bestselling novel, *Not Another Love Story*. Natalie Jones was headstrong, passionate and had a dry, self-deprecating sense of humour. She was how Harper had been before she had lost her confidence. Could she conjure her up?

How would Natalie write an online dating profile?

It was a tall ask. *Not Another Love Story* had been published almost a year before her world had fallen apart, and although Harper had tried her best to reinvent the character, she knew her recent work was lacking that magic touch. She had been going through the motions and suspected her agent knew it too. The sales for her newer releases hadn't been great and her royalties were no longer covering the bills. If it wasn't for Charlie's will and the life insurance, she would have been struggling for money.

Earning her keep was now a matter of pride. She had once been a full-time writer, paying her own way, and she needed to get back to that. If she could pull herself out of this slump and start living again, she hoped she would find her mojo.

But to do that she had to first write this damn intro.

She frowned at the screen of the MacBook before trying again.

Writer, daydreamer, dog mum. Terrible cook – seriously, I burn pasta. I like people-watching, the feel of the sun on my face, the cold side of the pillow, and orange Smarties. Favourite food – Mexican. Last film I cried at – *Marley & Me*. Guilty pleasure song: 'Footloose'. What's yours?

That was better. She could always come back and tweak it at a later date.

Finally, it was time to upload her photo.

The idea filled her with dread, but Megan had told her that without a picture, no one would message her. It made sense, Harper guessed. She wouldn't want to start talking to someone with a view to becoming romantically involved if she didn't know what they looked like.

Megan had already chosen a photo for her. A picture she had taken of Harper about a year ago when she had visited for the weekend. It was one of the rare ones where she was smiling and seemed genuinely happy.

Still, she worried, should she pick something else. Perhaps one that was more recent.

Not that she had anything newer. A different photo would involve taking a selfie, and gamely she picked up her phone, clicked on the front camera. The face staring back at her was sickly white, the dark circles under her eyes accentuated, and her blonde hair hanging limply around her face. Shuddering, she backtracked to the home screen, thinking better of the idea. Styling her hair and putting on a bit of make-up might make a difference, but she didn't have the inclination. Megan's photo it would be.

Harper uploaded it from the email her friend had sent her, then reread the answers on the dating form. Butterflies swarmed in her stomach as the cursor hovered over the create button on the screen.

Once she had clicked it, her profile would be live. Available for everyone to see. Was she really doing this?

Drawing in a breath, she rolled her shoulders back to try to ease the tension out of them.

She had to. If she wanted to get the future she craved, she needed to start living again.

Be brave.

As she pressed the button, joining the thousands of other members who were looking for love, she reminded herself it was just an app and she was in control. No one could message her unless she had hearted their profile. It would all be okay.

After all, what was the worst that could happen?

2

It didn't take long to get a match.

The idea of IntoYou was similar to Tinder, but instead of swiping, you hearted the profiles the app showed you. Once a user was hearted, they were able to send a direct message.

Initially, the hearting bit had intimidated Harper. It was just weird reading someone's information and looking at their photo, then letting them know she had liked what she had seen.

Everyone is doing it, Megan had assured her, saying she would get used to it. And she was right. It was a strange process, but over the following days, familiarity with the site, and knowing that every other user was doing the same thing, made it that little bit easier.

Still, Harper was tentative with her hearts, studying each profile carefully, and perhaps taking the whole process far more seriously than she should. She had received a number of hearts herself, but there was no one she wanted to talk to. Either they didn't have a profile picture or the information they gave suggested they wouldn't be a suitable match.

Almost a week after she had registered, two of the profiles

she had hearted messaged her, and while one fell by the wayside quickly – a good-looking guy with zero conversational skills, who kept making dirty innuendos, making him seem less attractive by the second – she had more success with the second one.

Adrian was thirty-eight and worked in IT, and his photo showed him to be boyishly attractive, with dark hair and an appealing smile. She had exchanged a dozen or so messages with him on IntoYou before handing over her phone number, where the conversation had moved over onto WhatsApp, and they had spent a couple of days of messaging before he had asked her if she fancied meeting for a drink.

Pushing herself to be brave, she had accepted.

Now, the following day, as she stood in her bedroom assessing her reflection in the full-length mirror, she wanted to be sick.

What the hell had she been thinking? In exactly one hour, she was supposed to be walking into a pub for a date with a man she had met on the internet. Was she insane? She couldn't go through with this.

The date had been on her mind pretty much all day, to the point that she couldn't concentrate on writing, managing only seven hundred of her usual three thousand-a-day word count, and she had ended up taking Bailey for a long walk to try to calm her nerves. It had worked, albeit briefly. Now her panicked brain was going into overdrive.

What if he sees me and is disappointed?

What if I see him and he isn't who he claims to be?

What if I clam up and we sit there in awkward silence?

What if I have a full-blown panic attack?

She was about to WhatsApp Adrian and back out when Megan FaceTimed her to wish her luck.

'I'm not going. I can't do this.'

'Harper. Stop and take a few deep breaths.'

'It's too soon. I should never have signed up to the site.'

'You're just having a moment,' Megan told her. 'And that's okay. Of course you are going to be nervous. This is a huge deal for you. But I promise you that once you've done it, you will be so proud of yourself.'

'You don't know that,' Harper argued. 'What if I have a panic attack and make a fool of myself?'

'You won't, but even if you do, it will be okay. Everyone gets a little scared doing this sort of thing, even if they don't show it. Adrian will be nervous too. You've got this, Harper. I promise you. You're doing really well. This is just one more little step to conquer.'

Megan was always so rational, and listening to her explain how it was normal to be anxious helped to ease some of the tension. She reminded Harper that there was no commitment. That it was just two people meeting for a no-strings-attached drink and she could bail at any point. It was going to be okay. She hadn't failed so far. She could do this.

'I want you to message me when you get home, okay?' Megan instructed. 'And even if you are getting along really well, I want you to promise me that you won't invite him back or get in his car, or agree to go home with him.'

Harper bubbled with nervous laughter. If Megan thought sex was on the cards, then she was woefully off track. Even if she hit it off with Adrian tonight, nothing was going to happen. Not until she was comfortable and ready, and given that she hadn't been intimate with anyone since Charlie, that was a while off.

Still, she appreciated her friend spending time talking to her and calming her down.

It was the one thing she had found difficult when they had made the move from London, leaving Megan behind.

It had been Charlie's idea to relocate to Norfolk. On his visits to the county, he had done a recce of the area, finding their house, which was just outside the village of Salhouse. It was an older-style detached property with generously sized rooms.

At first, Harper had been unsure. Her whole life was in London and she was used to the hustle and bustle of a city. Was she ready to give it all up for a move to the countryside?

Charlie had been persuasive, though. He had been reading all about the benefits of living in Norfolk. The lower crime rate, a more relaxed pace of life, and if they wanted to start a family, this was the place to do it.

The house was a place they could put their stamp on and they had the money to do so, thanks to a generous inheritance left to Charlie from his wealthy late grandfather. It had been a bone of contention with Charlie's dad, Cosmo, that the estate had been split equally between them.

Not that Charlie didn't work hard to make his own money. He was employed by a hotel chain based in London, but much of his time was spent on the road, travelling around the portfolio of properties his company owned, where he liaised with the hotel managers over maintenance and budget.

A couple of the hotels were based around East Anglia, he had pointed out in favour of the move, with one in Norfolk itself, so it would make things easier for him. Meanwhile, Harper's job as an author meant she could work from anywhere.

Eventually, she had relented, and for a while they had lived the dream, making the move out of London and building their new home together. And yes, Charlie had been right. Norfolk was a lovely place, but his job meant he was often away overnight. In London, Harper hadn't minded so much, but their new home was remote and she noticed his absences more.

In a bid to meet new people, she had tried to get out and

about, joining a local community page on Facebook and introducing herself as new to the area. As a result, she'd ended up with most of her evenings filled. She had signed up to the gym, joined a running group, then a book club, volunteered for a small animal rehoming charity and taken a yoga class. It was at yoga where she had first encountered Alicia, a slightly younger, confident woman with a similar sense of humour, and for a while Alicia had helped fill the hole of Megan not being there.

Though not any more. Alicia was gone too. Now it was just Harper, and sometimes it felt like Megan was the only person left in her life.

After Charlie had died, Harper had put all activities on hold while she grieved. There were other friends she had made, and many of them reached out to her to offer their condolences, but it was all so awkward, and they weren't people she had formed enough of an attachment to that she felt she could ask for help. Instead, she had holed herself up in the house alone – the worst possible thing she could have done, as it gradually ate away at her confidence, and when she didn't return to book club or to the animal shelter, or any of the groups she had joined, over time everyone stopped contacting her.

Move back to London, Megan had urged on more than one occasion.

As if it would be easy to just up roots and leave.

After Charlie's death, everything had become too much effort, too overwhelming. Harper hated that she had given in to the grief and depression, allowing herself to sink so low that she had at one point become borderline agoraphobic. But she was fighting her way back to the surface. The last couple of times Megan had come to stay, they had ventured out of the house, spending time around other people, and now Harper was actively pushing herself to claim her life back. Tonight she was taking her biggest step.

After saying goodbye to her friend, she smoothed her hands over the skirt of her dress and appraised herself again in the mirror.

Her reflection showed she was just a normal woman going out for a drink. Still, she worried now if the dress gave the wrong signal. Was the V neckline a little too deep? Perhaps she should go for something less figure-hugging.

For a moment, she was tempted to change back into her jeans, keep it casual. After all, she was only going to a pub. But then she studied herself again and realised she was overthinking everything. There was no sign of cleavage and the green dress skimmed her knees, bringing out the colour of her eyes. It wasn't overtly sexy, but it was both feminine and flattering, and her make-up was kept simple, her hair loose; a few curls styled into her natural waves. Nothing looked over the top.

Satisfied that she looked okay, she spritzed on perfume she hadn't wore since Charlie's death – the familiar scent evoking memories both tender and painful. Finally, with minutes to spare, she forced earrings into lobes that hadn't quite closed – a pair of demure diamond studs that were a long-ago Christmas gift from her late parents – and slipped her feet into the one decent pair of heels she owned. They had been sitting in the bottom of the wardrobe since the funeral and although they added inches to her five-foot five frame, they felt unfamiliar and did nothing to steady her trembling legs.

At this point, she would give anything for a glass of wine, but she knew she couldn't have one, as the Black Dog Inn where they were meeting was a fifteen-minute drive away.

Megan had told her to make sure she was the one to choose the venue, and to pick somewhere familiar.

Truthfully, Harper had struggled to think of a place. She barely went out these days, let alone to the pub, and she didn't fancy going to anywhere she had ever been with Charlie or Alicia. This was supposed to be a fresh start, not a chance to stir up memories.

Eventually, she had settled on the Black Dog Inn, remembering she had gone there for lunch with Megan the very first time Megan had caught the train up to Norfolk. The pub was only two miles from the station, set beside the River Yare in the suburb of Thorpe St Andrew, and Harper remembered it had a large car park, waterside views and friendly staff.

Downstairs, she made a fuss of Bailey and promised him she wouldn't be gone long – it was just one drink, right? – then, fighting every instinct to call off the date, she forced herself to leave the house, switching on the outdoor light on her way out, knowing that despite the balmy early September temperature, the nights were already drawing in and it would be dark when she arrived home.

By the time she reached the pub car park, butterflies were swarming in the pit of her stomach and she was shaking so badly she wasn't sure if she could actually get out of the car.

What had she been thinking? This was a terrible idea. Megan was wrong. She wasn't ready.

Even as Harper cursed her, a sheepish little voice in the back of her head reminded her that Charlie had been gone for two years.

This was never going to be easy, but if she wanted another shot at life, she had to move on.

The parking spot she had picked faced the door of the pub and she wondered if Adrian was already inside. It was a few minutes before they were due to meet. Had he decided to get here early so he could get the lay of the land, maybe choose a table, so he was prepared for their first meet? Or perhaps he was running late and wasn't even there yet? If she sat here long enough, would she see him heading towards the door? That would buy her some time to decide whether he looked genuine.

Maybe he was doing the same as her, sitting in his car and waiting to get to see what she looked like.

The thought initially unnerved her further, but then the prick of guilt had her reaching for the door handle. She might be terrified, but she also didn't want to be the person who stood someone up. She had left it too late to cancel, and besides, she was here now. She had to push through with the date.

Still, as she forced herself to approach the pub, remembering Megan's words that if things felt off or it was just too difficult, she only had to stay for a short while, her belly was fluttering and her tongue was stuck to the roof of her mouth.

The door-knob slipped against her clammy palm as she twisted it open, entering the familiar space, which was quieter than she expected, with only a handful of people at tables and a couple waiting as the barmaid poured their drinks. Harper had assumed that because it was a Friday evening the pub would be crowded, but today had been warm and she could see through the open back entrance that the beer garden was full.

Fewer people was definitely better, and she stepped up to the bar, looking around anxiously for Adrian, unsure if she was relieved or disappointed when she didn't spot him.

Feeling the weight of someone watching her, she glanced at the man behind the counter who was staring at her.

Briefly, her cheeks heated. Jesus, she must be sticking out like a sore thumb. He wasn't even hiding the fact he was looking at her. Did he know her?

As she looked back at him, a rabbit caught in headlights as she searched her scrambled brain, trying to decide if there was anything familiar about him and coming up blank, he arched his eyebrows in question.

What the hell did he want from her? And then it dawned.

He was waiting for her order.

Had he asked her what she wanted to drink? Suddenly she wasn't sure, but it would certainly explain the questioning look he was giving her.

'Um...' Unsure if she should wait for Adrian or order a drink, she stuttered before falling silent, and a frown creased his brow.

'Is everything okay?'

She heard him now and he was looking at her concerned, as if there was something wrong with her.

Jesus. She couldn't even hold it together in front of the bartender.

Speak, for God's sake.

'Yes, fine,' she managed, finally loosening her clumsy tongue. 'I'm meeting someone. A date. We haven't met before, so I don't know if he's here yet.'

'I see. So would you like a drink while you wait?'

The bartender seemed faintly amused by her information dump. He was a lot younger than her, maybe early twenties, and Harper's cheeks heated, realising he didn't need to know any of what she had just told him, that he wasn't interested in the ramblings of a thirty-seven-year-old basket case of a woman waiting for her internet date.

She was about to order a glass of white wine when she heard someone behind her.

'Harper?'

The voice was hesitant and she spun around, finding herself face to face with a man she immediately recognised as Adrian. He looked just like the pictures on his dating profile, which was a relief, and her nerves eased a little.

'Hi. Adrian.'

She thrust her hand at him as he leant in to kiss her cheek, and there was an awkward moment as they both laughed nervously before backing away, neither kissing nor shaking hands.

'What would you like to drink?' he asked, quickly moving on.

'I can get them,' Harper offered. 'I was actually about to order a glass of wine.'

'I've got this round. White or red?'

'Umm, white. Sauvignon Blanc if they have it,' she told him. 'Please,' she added, remembering her manners.

This round indicated that Adrian thought they would be staying for a second one and she tried to decide how she felt about that as the bartender poured their drinks. The fact he didn't want to cut the evening short suggested his first impression of her was a positive one and it had Harper considering her initial reaction towards him.

Physically, he was attractive. Dark hair, tall and broad-shouldered, and he had a nice smile. He was dressed in jeans and a short-sleeved grey shirt, looking stylish yet casual, and she had to admit that on first appearance he reminded her of one the male leads she wrote about. Of course, they had only just met, so time would tell whether they were compatible personality wise.

After paying, Adrian handed her the wine, then raised his pint of lager in a toast. 'Here's to IntoYou for introducing us.'

As they clinked glasses, Harper couldn't help but smile. Their date was off to a promising start.

She followed him as he led the way to a table towards the back of the pub. Cosy and more intimate, away from the other drinkers.

'So, is this your local, then?' he asked as they took seats opposite one another.

'Not really. I've been here before though, and it's nice.' He didn't need to know about her non-existent social life. 'What about you?'

'A few times, though not in a while.'

He had been happy enough letting her pick the pub. Megan had said that was a good sign and it showed he was respectful that their first date should be on Harper's terms.

She soon learnt he had other positives. He was an easy conversationist and asked plenty of questions, seeming genuinely interested in getting to know her and keen to hear about Bailey and how she had rescued him, as well as revealing snippets of his own life. And he had a self-deprecating sense of humour, which she appreciated.

Initially, she was nervous, but the evening was flying by, and what Harper had previously pictured being one drink turned into three, though the following ones were soft, as they were both driving.

Adrian had already told her the basics, so she knew he had never married, but now she learnt why. That it had been a combination of being work-focused and never meeting the right one. As he told her that, he seemed to be watching for her reaction, a slow smile spreading across his face and making his eyes crinkle at the corners when he added, 'Now I'm making more of an effort to find her.'

When her stomach fluttered again, it had nothing to do with nerves.

Of course, it was only their first date so she shouldn't jump ahead, but this was all really promising.

She had envisioned the whole online dating thing being a lot tougher, so it was a pleasant surprise just how easy it had been, and by the time Adrian walked her out to her car, she was relaxed in his company.

'I've had fun tonight,' he said, lingering close by, his hands in his pockets as Harper clicked the fob at her Volkswagen.

'I have too,' she agreed, keeping her tone light.

'So, would you like to go out with me again?'

She paused, opening the door and turning to face him, smiling and secretly delighted that he had asked. 'Yes, I would like that.'

'Good.'

That was when he caught her off guard, leaning in quickly to kiss her, seizing the moment when her lips parted in surprise to push his tongue into her mouth.

The move startled her and her first instinct was to push him away.

Whether it was the pressure of her palms against his chest or her murmur of shock, he sharply backed up, hands raised in apology. 'I'm sorry. That was too soon.' He slipped his hands back in his pockets, looking sheepish as Harper's heart raced.

'Yes,' she managed, crossing her arms defensively and not adding that the last person to kiss her like that was Charlie. Maybe she was overreacting, but she wasn't used to things moving this fast.

'I overstepped and I really am sorry. I didn't mean to make you uncomfortable.' Adrian paused and she could feel him willing her to look up. When she did, making eye contact with him, his contrite smile turned into a sly grin. 'You just looked so kissable. I really do like you.'

His words thawed her a little, her heartbeat quickening at the tiny kick of excitement knowing he found her attractive. After Charlie had died, she had given up on herself and had lost all confidence. Knowing that she was pushing the buttons of this very good-looking man was giving her a long-overdue ego boost. And aside from surprising, the kiss wasn't unpleasant. Yes, it was too soon, but it showed her the potential of what was to come if they continued to see each other. Something she still wanted to do.

'It's okay. I just need to take things slower.'

She hadn't told him about Charlie yet. He knew she had once been married, but immediately assumed it ended in divorce. Something she hadn't bothered to correct him on. Eventually, she would tell him, but not on their first date.

'Understood. And I am sorry. It won't happen again. Not unless you want me to kiss you.'

They parted on good terms, Harper relieved and happy the date had gone well, but now exhausted and eager to get home to her dog.

* * *

Half an hour after walking through her front door, she got a WhatsApp message from Adrian, checking she had arrived home safely.

She replied to confirm she had, and thanked him for a lovely evening.

He responded with a smiley-faced emoji and a kiss.

The following day, he messaged to ask her if she still wanted to meet up again – yes – and as she had picked the venue for their first date, she told him to choose this time. He surprised her by suggesting they stick to the same pub. The Black Dog was fine with her, as it was comfortable and familiar.

They made plans to meet later in the week and she spent the rest of the day with a foolish grin on her face, unable to stop thinking about him.

When Megan had proposed the idea of joining IntoYou,

Harper had been convinced it wouldn't work, but all it had taken was one date to find someone she was compatible with.

She had heard so many horror stories over the years about online dating, but this had been straightforward. Adrian seemed genuinely nice and was really easy to get on with. And he appeared to really like her.

The feeling was mutual.

Finally, her luck was changing.

3

It was Sunday morning and the sun was warm enough for Harper to enjoy her first cup of coffee in the garden. According to the forecast on her little portable radio, it was going to be a warm one, which didn't surprise her as the sky was already a cloudless vivid blue.

It was perhaps the weather that was putting her in such a good mood, and the infectious music the DJ was playing helped, but deep down she knew the reason she couldn't stop smiling was down to her date. It hadn't even been a day and half since their first date, but Adrian was already messaging her a fair bit, and she was looking forward to seeing him again later in the week.

As if on cue, her phone buzzed and a good morning text pinged up on the screen.

This was all going so well. She hadn't expected to click with someone so easily.

Megan was right, and Harper had admitted so when they had spoken after her date. Joining a dating site had been a smart move; it was already doing wonders for her confidence. She couldn't remember the last time she had woken up so happy.

Well, actually, that was a lie. It was before Charlie's accident. Every morning since his death, her first conscious thought was that she was a widow, before remembering everything that had led to that outcome. So it was a pleasant surprise that the last two days had started more positively.

Of course she had thought of Charlie, remembering he was no longer here and the circumstances of the car accident that had killed him, but beyond that had been a glimmer of positivity. A hope that perhaps she could find her way out of this dark place.

As she shaded her phone with one hand and replied to Adrian, she was tempted to ask him if he fancied meeting up for a walk that afternoon. Why wait until Friday to see him?

She had already planned on taking Bailey somewhere different today. The forecast was for uninterrupted sunshine and, given they were already into September, this might be one of the last nice weekends weatherwise before the nights really drew in. So far, they had stuck to local walks, but Bailey deserved new smells and experiences, and going further afield would be good for Harper's confidence.

It would be nice to spend this gorgeous day with Adrian too. It would be relaxed and casual, giving them a chance to get to know each other better. Harper had been thinking about going to one of the parks in Norwich, but perhaps they could head to the beach instead. The coast wasn't far from where she lived, and she hadn't been since Charlie was alive.

The idea of breathing in the salty air and the warm shifting sand catching between her toes was appealing and she was suddenly filled with an overwhelming urge to go. She had always loved the beach, the infinity of the sea and calming sound of the waves lapping against the shore.

Acting in the moment and outside of her comfort zone, she made the suggestion, then the nerves kicked in as she waited for Adrian's response. The blue ticks on WhatsApp told her he had read the message and she could see he was typing, but then he stopped and disappeared offline.

She was a fool and sickness churned in the pit of her stomach.

What the hell had she just done? This wasn't her. She didn't usually behave spontaneously. It was totally out of character. They had only met for the first time on Friday night and now she wanted to see him just two days later. It was too soon.

Stupid, Harper.

The next ten minutes dragged and she was convinced she had blown everything as she tried to resist repeatedly checking her phone for a response and failing miserably.

What an idiot. Everything had been fine and she should have left things how they were. Especially as they already had plans to meet up.

When her handset vibrated on the table, the noise making her jump, she snatched it up cautiously, both dreading and eager to read Adrian's reply.

> I would have loved to, but I'm really sorry, I'm down in Essex visiting an old school friend. Looking forward to seeing you on Friday though. xxx

Okay, that wasn't too bad. Yes, she was disappointed she wouldn't get to see him, but she hadn't messed up. And of course he was going to have Sunday plans; she hadn't given him any notice. The three kisses at the end of his message also made her a little giddy. Until now, he had used the occasional one to end his messages, but he wouldn't put three unless he liked her, right?

Realising she was grinning inanely at her phone, foolish heat crept into her cheeks. She was acting like a teenage girl and needed to pull herself together.

Still her smile remained and she was determined to enjoy her day with Bailey, even if Adrian wouldn't be joining them. Perhaps the park would be the better option as it was just the two of them. The beach would probably be busier given it was a nice day, and she was still building her way up to crowds. She didn't want to take on too much too soon.

Her phone vibrated again as she loaded the car with stuff for Bailey and fastened him into the back seat, and butterflies fluttered when she checked her messages to see that Adrian had sent her a selfie. He was smiling broadly for the camera, looking confident and devilishly handsome in a dark T-shirt. The attached caption read *Wish I was there*, followed by another three kisses.

Harper replied back, *Me too*, and boldly added kisses of her own.

As she pulled out of her driveway and onto the country lane, she decided on a whim that she would go to the coast after all. Maybe Gorleston. It wasn't too far to drive, and this was a new chapter for her. A chance to start over. She didn't need to wait for Adrian to be with her to face a crowded beach. She could handle it on her own.

Still, familiar nerves crept in as she neared the coast, and she fought the urge to turn the car around. She could do this.

It was a gorgeous day and she was determined to enjoy it as much as Bailey, knowing that if she did, it would be a huge step forward for her.

Here, the parking was free but the spaces were in demand. She managed to find one, then after taking a moment to reassure herself and calm her nerves, she let Bailey out of the car. Already, he was sniffing the ground inquisitively, his tail thumping in excitement at the new experience.

They were just like everyone else there. The people around them had no idea what she had been through or how terrified she was to be there. She would walk with her dog and she would play with him on the golden sand, and they would be normal. Just having a good time.

Drawing in deep breaths and painting a smile on her face, they headed down to the promenade. Bailey had to stay on his leash until they had passed the tennis courts, but then Harper set him free, hurling the red ball she had brought, genuinely delighted as he chased after it by the shoreline, for a moment startled, but then fascinated by the sea.

After that she was invested, forgetting about her fear as she experienced what appeared to be Bailey's first ever beach trip. As he had been surrendered to the animal shelter, she didn't know his full history, but she was sure he had never seen the sea before. They played on the sand and he ran his legs off as he charged after the ball, then she paddled while he bobbed against the waves, literally swimming doggy paddle.

By the time Harper was ready to head back to the car, her boy was exhausted and she had forgotten to be afraid.

She had done it.

What might seem petty and ridiculous to some was a huge deal to her. She was learning to live again and today she had proved to herself it was possible.

Walking back along the promenade, a damp Bailey leading the way with his ball proudly in his mouth and his tail wagging furiously, she couldn't help smiling.

She had really enjoyed today and caught up in her happy bubble, she almost missed the young family about to pass them by. Mum pushing a pram and dad carrying a sleepy-eyed toddler. Both parents were chatting animatedly, but their conversation abruptly stopped as the man locked eyes with her. He looked shocked.

'Adrian?' Harper blurted his name, at first confused. 'What are you doing here?'

She came to a halt and Bailey didn't miss the opportunity to plonk his bum down, appreciating the chance to rest his tired legs.

Adrian had told her he was in Essex, and for one stupid moment she wondered if the woman with him was the friend he mentioned he was visiting. Perhaps, for whatever reason, they had decided to come here instead. But then her mind was quickly switching through the gears, confusion giving way to suspicion, and then disbelief as he rubbed the toddler's back and she clocked the gold band on his wedding finger glinting in the sunlight.

He definitely hadn't been wearing that ring on Friday night.

The heat of humiliation flooded her face, as she understood she had been duped. Worse than that, he had made her an unwilling partner in his extra-marital activities.

How dare he?

'Adrian?' the woman he was with – no, not just woman, his wife – repeated. She appeared to be waiting for an explanation as to who Harper was, and while her gaze flickered between them inquisitively, her brows drew together in what looked like annoyance.

Did she suspect who Harper was? Worse still, did she know her husband was on a dating site?

Adrian recovered quickly. 'Harper, what a surprise. I didn't expect to see you today.'

No shit.

'Harper,' his wife repeated, her tone cool. 'I don't believe we've met.'

'I'm sure I've mentioned her before, darling,' Adrian interjected, keen to cut Harper off before she could respond. 'She's one of my clients. I've been doing some work for her firm.'

She wanted to speak up, to correct him, but anger choked her, the words refusing to come. He had lied to them both.

'It's good to see you,' he smiled. 'Enjoy the rest of your weekend.'

He was already leaving, tugging his wife along with his free hand, keen to get away from Harper so she couldn't expose him.

It was so wrong. He had two young children. One was still a baby, for Christ's sake. Harper didn't want to break up a family, but his wife deserved to know the truth. He was actively looking to meet other women, and Harper would bet her house she was not the first one to fall for his bullshit. She felt physically sick for the woman.

'Actually,' she called after them. Adrian's shoulders tensed as his wife glanced back, eager to hear whatever it was she had to say. 'I'm not one of your husband's clients.'

'Oh,' was all she got in response, as the woman waited for her to continue.

'Harper. Don't.'

Adrian's words were laced with a warning. But what could he seriously do? He wasn't the injured party here. Besides, Harper had nothing to lose.

'Adrian contacted me on a dating site. IntoYou,' she said, ignoring him, her stomach heavy as his wife's face fell. Determinedly, she pushed on. 'We met for the first time on Friday night. I promise you, I thought he was single.'

'I bloody knew something was going on.' The wife slapped him across the cheek and, shocked, he took a step back.

'Jenny! Stop it. She's lying.'

'You said you had to work late on Friday,' Jenny accused.

'I did work late. Damnit. Don't listen to her. She tried to come on to me at work and didn't like it when I knocked her back. This is some petty type of revenge.'

It was bullshit and Harper suspected that Jenny knew it. Still, she looked to Harper for confirmation.

'I'm telling you the truth. Look on the dating site. You'll see his profile. And check his WhatsApp messages.'

'You bitch.' Adrian's face twisted with fury and for a moment Harper wondered if she should have played along.

No, screw him. He didn't get to treat people like this.

Although she was still angry with him, she was desperately sorry for his family. Being cheated on was really shitty and Harper wanted to tell Jenny she understood her shock, but she knew the woman was probably just as mad with her right now, even though she had done nothing wrong.

'I'm so sorry,' she said, in way of parting, yanking at Bailey's lead. Now she had said her piece, she was eager to get away. As she quickly made her way back along the promenade, she could hear Jenny yelling, and then the toddler bursting into tears.

She had done the right thing, hadn't she?

For a moment, Harper wasn't so sure. She was blinkered, after all.

The anger she had been holding on to evaporated suddenly, leaving her feeling guilty and foolish. Surely there had been signs. Had she really been stupid enough to miss them?

Back in the pub car park, Adrian had suddenly come on too

strong. At the time, she had forgiven him, still exhilarated by how well their date had gone and putting it down to the fact he must really like her. Now she understood that he had probably hoped a night of sex was on the cards.

Perhaps she should be flattered that he thought she was worth putting in the effort of a second date, but instead her cheeks burned and tears threatened. He had played her and she had been stupid enough to fall for every lie that came out of his mouth. He must have thought she was such an easy target.

She was so caught up in feeling sorry for herself, she wasn't paying attention as she crossed the promenade, heading towards the steps that led up into the car park.

Someone yelled, but their warning was too late and before Harper could register anything, she was knocked flying off her feet.

4

Harper is playing on the beach with her dog when I spot her, throwing a ball towards the incoming waves and smiling in delight as the animal charges into the water to retrieve it. And I can't help but consider this as another sign that she is supposed to be in my life.

I had recognised her immediately, even with her honey blonde hair tied back in a loose ponytail. That pale blue sundress she has on – the one with the spaghetti straps that are begging to be ripped – is what she wears in the photo on her IntoYou profile.

I had forgotten how pretty she is, but there is something more there now. A sadness that can't be shifted. It's even there in her smile, and her sea-green eyes are haunted, reminding me she has experienced things she will never forget.

If you had asked me about her before, I would have told you she is a looker, that she is absolutely my type, but I knew she was unobtainable. I would never be able to have her in the way I wanted. But now things are different, and this new vulnerability she wears as a cloak is intoxicating. I would have walked away. I did walk away. But the universe works in mysterious ways, placing her in my path, and now I *am wondering if fate is really a thing, and if Harper Reed is supposed to be mine.*

There is no one I have to answer to. I am the master of my own future. How bittersweet it would be to have her. Everything would be coming full circle.

Of course she doesn't see me. I am just another face on the crowded beach. Still, the flicker of hope melts into bitter disappointment as she glances my way before heading back up to the promenade, the wet dog shaking disgusting germs everywhere.

She doesn't recognise me at all.

In a way, that makes it easier to follow her. I am just another casual beachgoer heading back to his car, and I am only a short distance behind her when she abruptly stops.

'Adrian?'

If I pause, then it will be too obvious that I'm being nosey, and I know all about discretion, so instead I keep my head down, slowing my pace as I cross to the other side of the walkway.

I can still hear enough of the conversation to understand there is a love triangle going on.

The man, Adrian, has a family, and Harper wasn't expecting that. She looks bewildered and so upset, and I am waiting for her to flee. What I don't expect is for her to throw Adrian under the bus, telling his wife exactly what he has been up to.

Adrian, of course, is furious. It seems to me he deserves to be brought down a peg or two. Harper's response was ballsy and my appreciation of her grows stronger, as does my intrigue. Who could have guessed that beneath her quiet personality lurks a little bit of fire?

Yes, she is upset, but it's better that Harper found out the truth. A man like Adrian doesn't deserve a woman like her.

I am tempted to follow the family, find out where they live, and dish out a little retribution on Harper's behalf, maybe slash Adrian's car tyres, but it doesn't look like they will be moving any time soon.

The wife is livid and the kids crying as Adrian tries to smooth over his cheating with a bunch of bullshit lies.

Instead, I continue after Harper, wondering if I should speak to her. This might be a good opportunity to say hello and check she is okay. I could always tell her what I witnessed. Maybe she will be vulnerable enough to let me be a shoulder to cry on.

As I work the idea through in my head, I hear a yell and look up to see a cyclist who is travelling too fast along the promenade. It's too late to do anything and, a second later, the cyclist, his bike and Harper all crash to the floor.

It's the perfect chance to intervene. Play the hero for Harper and get chatting to her.

Seizing the opportunity, I stride towards the scene.

5

The next few moments were of panic and confusion, of Bailey yelping, then of sharp pain, and Harper didn't realise that she was sat on the ground, her limbs tangled with metal, until the man started yelling at her.

'You stupid cow. Look what you've done to my bike!'

She double blinked, for a moment struggling to focus, before pulling him into her line of vision as he ripped his helmet off. He was a vision of middle-aged Lycra: a scrunched-up face, red with fury, and tufts of grey hair sticking up from his head, and already back on his feet while she was still on the ground. It took her a moment to register what had happened, that they must have collided.

The realisation brought with it a jolt of pain. Her leg was on fire and hurting like hell, and she gritted her teeth against the wave of nausea, scared she was going to pass out. The man was still shouting and she couldn't think straight with all the noise.

'Stop yelling at me. Please.'

She didn't think she had spoken the words aloud, but his bluster briefly paused and he looked indignant. But then he started again, sounding livid that she dared to interrupt him, before telling her she was to blame for the accident and that she had to buy him a new bike.

Was he serious?

Okay, so she hadn't been paying attention, but the collision was as much his fault as hers. Besides, she couldn't see any damage to his precious bike. She was the one who had come off worse, and had he hurt Bailey? She had heard him yelp.

Looking around for him, she saw he wasn't with them, realising she must have let go of his lead.

'Where is my dog? Bailey? Where is he?'

Harper could hear the alarm in her voice as she tried to push the cycle away, annoyed that the man wasn't helping. Instead, he kept shouting over the top of her, unconcerned that Bailey was missing. She needed him to stop so she could think straight and try to get to her feet.

'Hey, dude. What's your problem?'

The new voice distracted shouty cyclist man, giving her a moment of respite as he tried to justify himself, and Harper glanced up to see a small crowd had formed.

'Don't you "hey, dude" me. She caused this. She owes me for a new cycle.'

'She's the one sitting on the ground bleeding,' the guy who had spoken pointed out. 'Stop worrying about your stupid bike.' He looked at her now, concern etched on his face. 'Are you okay?'

She nodded, not entirely sure as she was still reeling from the collision. Her leg hurt like hell, but she didn't think she had broken anything. She just needed to find Bailey. 'I've lost my dog,' she told him, trying again to get up.

'Hey, wait. I don't think you should be moving.' He looked at the other people gathered. 'We'll help you find your dog. Right?'

'I don't give a shit about her dog!' the cyclist was quick to complain.

No one was taking any notice of him.

Instead, a female voice asked, 'Should I call the police, or an ambulance?'

'No, no ambulance,' Harper protested, her heart rate increasing. 'I'm okay. I just want my dog.'

The guy who had challenged the cyclist focused his attention on Harper. 'You're bleeding everywhere,' he commented, kind hazel eyes meeting hers as he got another man to help him lift the bicycle off her. 'At least let me get my friend to look at your leg. He's a doctor.'

'I need to find him.' Harper's chest was tight with panic, her voice high-pitched. 'He's a rescue dog. I haven't had him long.'

'Okay, tell me about him. What's his name?'

'Bailey. He's a black cocker spaniel.'

'Do you know which way he headed?'

'No, I didn't see.' Another wave of nausea threatened and she wasn't sure if it was from the pain in her leg or the fact that Bailey could be anywhere. 'What if he gets on the road or someone takes him?'

'We'll find him.' He sounded confident, which settled her a little.

'What happened?'

'Is everything okay?'

Two more men appeared, pushing their way to the front of the crowd, damp towels draped over their shoulders: a muscular, bare-chested man with a Tom Selleck-worthy moustache and his leaner-built friend, whose damp hair was curling as the sun dried it.

Sensing potential new allies, the cyclist, who had momentarily fallen quiet, tried again to point the finger of blame at Harper. 'Does my bike look okay?' he demanded.

Moustache man gave him an irritated glance before addressing the guy who had stopped to help her. 'What's going on, Damon?'

They knew each other.

As the cyclist started muttering under his breath, the curly-haired man dropped down to Harper's level to inspect her leg, and her helper – Damon – explained, 'We need to find her dog. He ran off when this twat hit her.'

'Hey,' the cyclist reacted, red-faced. 'She hit me!'

'No, you rode into her,' Damon told him. 'And you haven't stopped for one moment to check if she's okay.'

'What's your name?' the curly-haired man asked Harper, blue eyes locking on hers. Up close, she could see the dusting of freckles on his tanned face.

'Harper.'

'Hi, Harper. I'm Luke and I'm a doctor. Can I take a look at the cut?'

She was uncomfortable being the centre of attention. Her leg would be fine. She just needed to find Bailey then get the hell out of here. Maybe colliding with the cyclist was the universe's way of saying 'fuck you, Harper Reed' for what she had done to Adrian.

'It'll be okay,' she lied. 'I just need to find Bailey.'

'Your dog?' he confirmed, warm hands now touching her leg.

She must have looked worried because as she nodded in response Damon sought to reassure her. 'He knows what he's doing.'

The crowd around them was now starting to disperse, though one couple lingered.

'Chris and I will go and look for your dog,' Damon told her.

'And I think these people are going to help too.' He nodded to the couple, who confirmed they would, before glancing at the cyclist. 'Are you going to help us?'

The derisive snort and curse of swear words suggested not.

'Arsehole,' Chris, the moustached man, muttered, as the four of them headed off to find Bailey, leaving Harper with Luke and the cyclist.

'Don't worry. They'll find him,' Luke assured Harper. 'It's going to be okay.' Now he had spoken more words, she realised he had an Irish accent.

'Okay,' she repeated, unable to hide the tremor that it might not be. What if they didn't find him? What if she never got her dog back?

She tried to push the worrying thoughts away and focus on steadying her breathing. Luke was gentle as he inspected the cut and he checked with her that she hadn't banged her head. She suspected that he was picking up on her anxiety, as he made small talk, asking her about Bailey and if he went in the sea, telling her that he and his friends had decided to blow off the gym for a beach day. Harper knew he was being kind and trying to keep her distracted, and it was working, a little.

'Well, the good news is the cut's not as bad as it looks. You won't need stitches.'

It hadn't occurred to her that she might. Even the thought of going to hospital was enough to fill her with dread. She hadn't been in one since Charlie's death.

'I'll dress it, though. I have a first-aid kit in the car. Are you okay to wait here?'

She glanced over his shoulder at the cyclist, who had retreated to the other side of the promenade, where he was checking over his bike. He looked up and scowled at her and she suspected he wasn't ready to let things drop.

'I can come with you,' she told Luke, keen to get away.

He frowned. 'You should wait here. I'll be seconds.'

'I would rather come up to the car. I can walk.'

As though to prove her point, she started to clamber to her feet. It hurt and she fought to hide her grimace. She really didn't want him to leave her alone with the cyclist.

Clocking what the problem was, Luke relented, offering his hand to help her up.

Pain shot up her calf when she put pressure on her injured leg.

'Are you okay?'

Harper took a step forward and although it was uncomfortable, she was relieved that she was able to walk. 'I think so.'

'Here, hold on to me.'

He slipped his arm around her for support. The move was sudden and initially she wanted to recoil. She had become so unused to intimate human contact. Other than hugs with Megan when they met up, the only ones she got were from Bailey. The warmth and movement of another human body against her triggered her alarms.

Luke must have felt her tense because he didn't push her to move and asked again, 'Are you sure you're okay? Look, maybe it is best if you wait here.'

She really didn't want to do that. Instead, she focused on the path ahead, not wanting him to see how shaken she was. 'No, I'm good.' She just had to get up the steps and back to the car. Once there, she would let him dress her wound, then she needed to find Bailey and get the hell home, which she was sure she could do if she took it steady. Coming to the beach today had been a terrible idea and all she wanted was to get back to her safe space, where she could relax, shut the world out and not have to deal with people.

She tried to relax and let Luke help her, but as they reached the steps, her cyclist nemesis stepped into their path.

'Hey, I need your details before you leave. You have to pay for my bike repairs.'

'Please leave me alone.' Harper's tone was weary. She'd had enough for one day.

'You knocked me off my bike,' he persisted angrily.

'And you knocked *me* off my feet,' she pushed back.

'Well, you shouldn't have been in my way.'

'I'm pretty sure if you check the Highway Code, pedestrians have the right of way on a promenade,' Luke told him mildly. Despite his light tone, there was a firmness to his words. As the cyclist spluttered, ready to fire back, Luke added, 'Perhaps Harper should be asking you to cough up. Personal injury claims can work out costly.'

The cogs turned and Harper watched the cyclist weigh up his options. 'What are you, a solicitor?' he demanded.

'No. I'm a doctor.'

There was more grumbling, but the colour had drained from the cyclist's face. He hadn't anticipated being challenged or having things backfire on him. His gaze went from Luke to Harper, then back again, and he muttered a string of expletives.

'This bloody country is a joke,' was the last thing he said before he turned to walk away, pushing what still looked like a perfectly operable bike.

'Is it true what you said?' Harper asked Luke as she watched him go. 'Could I sue him?'

'Why? Do you want to sue him?'

It was a question she had asked more out of curiosity. 'No,' she admitted. 'I just want to go home.'

'You weren't in the wrong, if that's what you're worried about,' Luke told her. He helped her up the steps and into the car park.

'I'm down the end,' he said, guiding her, and she spotted the lights of the black Audi SUV as he clicked his fob at it.

For the first time, it occurred to her that she was putting her trust in a man who was actually a stranger. Because she had been told he was a doctor, she had automatically trusted him, but it could be a lie. After all, Adrian had easily managed to fool her.

The leaden ball in her stomach grew and sweat beaded on her forehead, clinging to the back of her neck. She glanced around the car park, not liking that it was relatively empty. There was another couple by a campervan, but it looked like they were getting ready to leave, and while there were plenty of people around them, down on the promenade and across the street, none of them were quite close enough to signal for help should she need it, unless she screamed really loudly.

But, even then, would it be enough?

She was overthinking things, her imagination going to the worst-case scenario, and she tried to relax. Luke had offered to fetch the first-aid kit while she waited. It had been Harper's idea to accompany him back to his car, keen to get away from the cyclist. He hadn't tried to lure her there.

Despite writing romance, she had always enjoyed reading true-life crime books. No wonder she was jumping to conclusions.

But Luke wasn't Ted Bundy or Fred West. He was here at the beach with his friends.

'Are you okay?' he asked again.

'I'm fine.'

Her reply was quick, her tone a little too breezy, and she wondered if he could hear the note of underlying panic, because he seemed to have a change of heart.

'Where are you parked?'

Harper nodded to her Volkswagen that they had passed a few spaces back. 'Just over there.'

'Why don't you wait at your car and I'll bring the kit over,' he suggested.

An infinitely better idea. Why the hell hadn't she thought of it?

'Okay,' she agreed, perhaps too eagerly.

He helped her to her car and she unlocked the door, lowering herself sideways onto the driver's seat, so her legs swung out.

'Better?'

She nodded, assuming he meant now she could sit down, but then the wink and quick smile he gave her as he left to get the first-aid kit had her questioning if he was a psychic and had read her ridiculous thoughts that he might have malevolent intentions.

When he returned with the kit and a chilled can of Coke – which he handed to her, ordering her to drink so it helped with the adrenaline rush – then cleaned and dressed her leg with the confidence and capability of a professional, she realised she had misjudged him. He was genuine.

His pocket started buzzing as he was packing the kit away and when he answered, she was able to gauge from his end of the conversation that he was speaking to either Damon or Chris and that they had found Bailey. Thank God.

Much of the remaining tension ebbed out of her, knowing that he was safe, and fifteen minutes later, she was reunited with her delighted dog and thanking the men who had helped her, before saying goodbye.

There were good people in the world, she reminded herself as she drove home to Salhouse, wincing a little each time she had to put pressure on her left leg as she changed gear.

What had started out as a good day had briefly turned into a terrible one, that would have had her hiding in the safety of her house again for the next year had it not been for Luke, Damon and Chris. The kindness they had shown her gave her encouragement to try again, and her mood was lighter as she pulled into the driveway, killing the ignition.

The buzz of a text came from her phone and, curious, she opened her bag to retrieve it. Megan was the only person she could think of who would message her, but her friend was usually busy with family on a Sunday.

She glanced at Adrian's name on the WhatsApp screen, a familiar sickness heavy in her gut. Why was he contacting her? Did he seriously think she ever wanted to hear from him again after the lies he'd told?

She was expecting contrition, possibly even a sob story to try to justify his actions. What she wasn't anticipating was the threat staring at her on the screen, and fear trembled through her as she read it.

> You stupid bitch. You have no idea what trouble you've caused. Word of advice. Watch your back. This isn't over.

6

After her disastrous encounter with Adrian, Harper decided she was done with online dating. She would love a chance to have a fresh start with someone new, but dating was supposed to give her a confidence booster, and instead Adrian had left her worried and afraid. The physical scars of that day had mostly healed, but the psychological ones remained. She had blocked him on her phone and also on the dating site after reporting his account, and she was tempted to delete the IntoYou app, knowing she wasn't strong enough to deal with any more disastrous dates. Instead, she focused on her dog and her book, ignoring all other distractions.

It was Megan who persuaded her not to give up. Although she had been shocked by Adrian's deception and the message he had sent Harper, she explained the experience had been bad luck. IntoYou wasn't free, which usually deterred the chancers and the cheats, and most men on there were seriously looking to meet someone.

Harper wanted to believe her friend; she really did – after all, Megan had kissed her share of frogs before finding her fairy tale with Tom. Still, it took her over three weeks before she dared venture back onto the site and a further ten days of tentatively exchanging emails with a few potential dates, before she plucked up the courage to meet with one of them for a drink.

Justin was nine years older and a teacher, and he was her opposite in many ways. According to his profile and the messages they had exchanged, he was adventurous and well-travelled, while, until recently, Harper had barely left the house. He was also heavily into sports that she knew very little about – cricket, rugby and sailing – and was a keen amateur photographer, spending a lot of time at the coast. Physically he didn't have the type of appearance that usually attracted her, but he wasn't ugly either, and his eyes seemed kind, as did his messages. But if she was being truthful, what really drew her to him was knowing he was a widower, having lost his wife to cancer eighteen months ago. If anyone would understand her experience, Justin would.

They arranged to meet in the Black Dog Inn five weeks to the day after her date with Adrian. Given how that had worked out, Harper had been reluctant to revisit the pub, convincing herself the place was now a bad omen, but, as Megan pointed out, it was convenient and familiar. Besides, the evenings were drawing in now as autumn firmly took hold and the pub had a well-lit car park. Safety took priority over fear of bad luck. Not that she was driving this time. After her experience with Adrian, her confidence had been knocked. To do this dating thing again, she required the courage of alcohol, and she had booked a taxi, having a generous glass of wine before leaving home.

Justin was in the pub already when she arrived and waiting at the bar, and the welcoming smile on his face when he saw her melted away most of her reservations. Asking Harper what she wanted, he ordered her a drink, served by the same bartender she had embarrassed herself in front of during her last visit.

If the bartender was wondering why she was here with a different man this time, he gave nothing away, and she guessed it probably wasn't uncommon in his line of work.

She thanked Justin for the glass of wine he handed her, and they took their drinks to a table at the side of the bar, next to the crackling fire.

Harper was grateful that they weren't sitting where she had with Adrian, while appreciative of the familiarity of the pub. As well as the bar staff, she recognised a few of the drinkers too. It was busier than on her last visit, probably because everyone was inside this time. But that was fine. It was a place where she knew the layout and the background music and chatter would help fill any uncomfortable moments of silence.

She established early on that she was not sexually attracted to Justin and sensed that he felt the same, but there was a connection between them. Perhaps it was because they were both widowed – despite her reticence, Harper had told him about Charlie – or maybe there was something else. She was comfortable in his presence and he was easy to talk to.

Still, she didn't know him well enough to let him give her a lift home, even though he offered, and shortly before closing, she ordered another taxi.

He insisted on waiting with her until it arrived.

'I had a nice evening,' he said, as they headed out into the cool night. 'But I will be honest with you, I don't think we have that spark.'

He was right, they didn't, but she appreciated the gentle smile that accompanied his words, softening the blow. Although the feeling was mutual, she still had an ego to protect.

As she nodded in agreement, he continued, surprising her. 'I enjoyed your company, though, Harper, and I would like to keep in touch as friends, if that's okay with you.'

It was okay with her. More than okay. With Megan so far away and Alicia out of the picture, she really liked the idea of having another friend close by.

'I would like that too.'

He left her with a chaste peck on the cheek, and she appreciated that, despite the lack of chemistry, he messaged her just as she was arriving home, to check she had arrived back safely.

There might have been a lack of attraction, but her confidence had been given a much-needed boost, and as she let herself into the house, kicking off her shoes, she realised how glad she was that she had been brave enough to try dating again.

She was pleased she had left the heating on, as the house was toasty warm, and, after letting Bailey in the garden for a late-night wee, got out the packet of herbal tea she had bought to help with her sleep. Something she had struggled with for a long time.

Things needed to change and she was taking positive steps. Bailey, the dating app, a hopeful new friendship with Justin, and now some self-care. Tomorrow, she decided, she was going to be brave and start packing up some of Charlie's things.

It would be ridiculous to some people, she supposed, that he had been gone for so long and everything was still how he had left it. And perhaps this self-healing wouldn't be taking so long if she had tackled the job sooner. Grief affected people in different ways, though, and until now, she simply hadn't been ready.

She was about to fill the kettle when barking came from outside, followed by a loud crash. Worrying that the dog had hurt himself, Harper rushed to the back door.

'Bailey?'

At first there was no response and standing on the step, she stared into the darkness as she waited anxiously for a sound, wishing she had sorted out the security light for the back garden.

The existing one had broken the summer that Charlie had died and she had never got around to getting it fixed.

Where was her dog? And what the hell had made the noise? Was someone outside?

She had no sooner called him again when the lump of black fur appeared. Although he started barking again, appearing a little agitated, he seemed unharmed, and she quickly ushered him inside, locking the back door.

Here in the countryside with no one else around, she was often lax with security. A bad habit as it wasn't necessarily safer than living in a city. The noise outside unnerved her. It had sounded like a plant pot falling, and yes, it was probably just a fox or similar, but it served as a reminder she should take more care, and needed to get the light sorted.

As the dog settled in his bed, Harper boiled the kettle and made her tea, taking it upstairs. After Charlie had died, she couldn't bring herself to continue sleeping in their marital bed. It held too many painful memories. The door to the master bedroom remained closed and she seldom entered, instead taking the room across the landing. It was still a decent-sized double, and overlooked the back garden, but it didn't have the benefit of an en suite or the added wardrobe space.

That was where she would begin tomorrow, plucking up the courage to go into her old room with bin bags. Once she had cleared out Charlie's things, perhaps she could redecorate the room and rearrange the furniture, then claim it back as her own.

For now, she went to the spare bedroom. Her iPad was on the bed and on a whim, she picked it up, logging on to the IntoYou site, seeing that she had alerts in her inbox. One was from Lee, a farmer who she had already exchanged half a dozen platonic exchanges with, while the other was new. A man named Gavin, whose handsome and brooding profile picture she had hearted a couple of days earlier.

She responded to Lee's question first, wanting to know what her favourite Tarantino movie was. A follow-up to a subject they had been discussing earlier. *Pulp fiction, of course*, she typed in her reply, asking what his was.

Gavin's message was brief and a little dull. *Hi, how's it going?*

Not too much she could do with that, so she told him she was good, and after a quick look again at his profile for a refresh and seeing that he had mentioned liking live music, she asked him who his favourite band was, in a bid to strike up a proper conversation.

Live music was something she loved. Well, *had* loved. When Charlie had been alive, they had regularly gone to gigs, from spit and sawdust pubs to see local talent, to huge stadiums to watch their favourite rock heroes. Of course, Harper hadn't been to anything since and the mere thought of attending a packed venue was enough to make her shudder.

This was all baby steps, she reminded herself. Okay, so she wasn't strong enough to do a gig right now, but it was something else she could build up to.

Waiting for a few minutes to see if Lee or Gavin were online to reply, she swiped through the profiles of other potential suitors, hearting a few she was happy to receive messages from.

Eventually, yawning, she decided to call it a night, setting her iPad down and getting undressed. She had just come back from the bathroom when another crash from outside had her jumping. She froze to the spot.

Downstairs, Bailey started going nuts again. This time, his barking was accompanied by a low growl, which did nothing to ease Harper's nerves.

Cautiously, she tiptoed across the bedroom to the window,

peeping through a crack in the curtains out across the garden. There was a faint light from the moon, but mostly it was just a mass of black shadows.

She had always felt safe living here, tucked away from the rest of the world, her home, her sanctuary. But for the first time, it occurred to her that if there was any danger lurking outside, she had no one here to help her. And if she ever found herself in trouble, there wouldn't be anyone around to hear her scream.

7

Walk away.

I tried. I promise you, I tried.

After that day at the beach with the crazy cyclist and that arsehole, Adrian, I concluded that Harper Reed might well be my undoing. I am normally a controlled man, but she pushes my buttons in such a way that I don't trust myself around her.

Maybe it's because of who she is, of what she represents. All I know is that since I saw her again, I haven't been able to stop thinking about her.

I can't afford to be rash, but unfortunately that is the effect she has on me.

It's why I sought out Adrian after Harper had left that day. He wasn't difficult to find, still bickering with his wife further along the promenade. She wasn't going to let his extracurricular activities drop any time soon.

If he had been a smarter man, I might have begrudgingly admired him simply for his boldness, but he wasn't. He had been sloppy and I'm glad he's been exposed. Besides, what he did goes against everything I believe in. I am a one-woman man. When I am with someone, I dedicate myself to them fully.

Adrian wouldn't understand that. I get why he wanted an opportunity with Harper, but he doesn't deserve her. And he hurt her. No one gets to upset or hurt my girl. She is mine alone.

See? I'm already referring to her as if she is mine. This isn't good.

It is because of emotions like this, letting them take over, that I followed Adrian's family home after they finally left the beach.

Old Catton is a nice suburb and the house that Adrian's family lives in is a neat newbuild.

The wife, Jenny I think her name was, wasted no time in packing, and her and the kids left the house again twenty minutes later.

I lingered around the property, scoping out the neighbourhood to make sure there were no cameras – I hate those bloody Ring doorbells – and checking escape routes. Adrian lives in a cul-de-sac, and I needed to know that if there was a commotion I could leave his house without attracting the attention of any neighbours.

Realising that his back garden backs onto woodland, I approached the front door and knocked. As I waited, I pulled the hood of my tracksuit top up, keeping my head down, then, when he answered, I charged at him, knocking him back into the hallway and kicking the door shut.

He never had a chance, the element of surprise allowing me to get in half a dozen punches before he could even try to defend himself, then, when he dropped to the floor, his hands raising to defend himself, I kicked the soft flesh of his belly.

Blood was gushing from his nose, dripping between his fingers, and he gasped for air.

'Stay away!' I snapped.

I wanted to go further. To tell him to leave Harper alone, that she didn't belong to him, but even in my rage, I knew it wasn't a good idea. I didn't want to risk bringing trouble to her door. That wouldn't be good for her or for me. Still, I gave him one more kick for good measure, before leaving the house.

It wasn't until I was back in my car, sensibly parked a couple of streets away, that I realised I had never lost my temper like that before.

I am a rational man. Okay, I have my vices, but everything I do in life is plotted out in fine detail and coolly executed. Even though I had been smart enough to check things out before attacking, my rage was blinkered, hot and uncontrollable, and that scares me to death.

As does the fact my obsession with this woman led me to her house tonight.

She is a siren, there in front of me when I try to escape her, reeling me in.

I have tried to walk away. After the beach, after what she drove me to do to Adrian, I understood she wasn't safe for me to be around. This woman is bad news, but she won't leave me alone. Lingering, taunting, blurring the edges of my mind. I can't think rationally when it comes to her, and my focus is clearly off, given the amount of noise I made, walking into flower pots and walls, even forgetting she had a dog.

I need to get a grip of myself. She is off limits for me.

Off limits. I consider my last thought, wondering why I have put this barrier up. No one gets to decide what I can and cannot have. There are no rules.

Maybe there is a way we can be together, and perhaps it's right that we should.

Have I been reading the signs wrong? Is the way to stop her haunting my dreams to make her mine?

8

After the disturbance outside, Harper had double-checked all of the doors and windows were locked before getting into bed. For a while, she had lain awake, worrying in case someone was outside, but when there were no further noises or disruption, her mind gradually settled and she convinced herself it had been an animal – maybe a fox or a muntjac – before sliding into a peaceful sleep.

By the time Saturday morning rolled around, the October sky a warm and sunny blue, the incident was barely on her mind, her focus having already shifted to the task she had set herself for the weekend, and she found herself staring at the master bedroom door, a roll of bin liners in her hand.

The plan to start sorting through Charlie's things had sounded good in her head, but she couldn't quite will her hand to open the door, and as seconds ticked into minutes, even Bailey, who had sat patiently beside her at first, was now slumped on the floor looking bored.

It had been maybe eight months since she had last stepped inside the room, time stretching, growing longer between each visit. In the early days after Charlie's death, she had no choice but to enter. Although she had slept on the sofa downstairs, all of her things were still in the bedroom they had shared. Things that she needed. Once she had taken them, though, the door had then been kept shut in a bid to hide away painful memories. Her visits had become sporadic, entering the room only when absolutely necessary and, over time, doing so had become more and more difficult.

It was an obstacle she needed to deal with, she knew that. Just as she knew she was being ridiculous. This was her bedroom and she had to claim it back. Just like she was trying to claim the rest of her life back.

She was actively dating, wanting to move on. If there was a point in the future where she chose to invite someone back home, what would they think, knowing she had a shrine upstairs to her dead husband? That the room was untouched from the day he had died?

Not that she would be inviting anyone back any time soon. It was still early days with the men she had been chatting to on IntoYou. She had exchanged further messages with Lee and Gavin this morning, both of whom had potential for a date, but that was it.

Someone called Brad kept requesting to send her a message, but Harper hadn't hearted him to allow access to contact her, and she had no intention of doing so, given that he hadn't even bothered to upload a profile picture. His details were scant too. His icebreaker was uninspiring, consisting of four simple words, 'Looking to meet someone', and there was no indication of his age or location, or anything else about him.

No profile photo meant no reply as far as she was concerned. It was wholly unfair that this Brad knew what she looked like, but wasn't prepared to reveal anything about himself, so she had rejected his requests, liking this new no-nonsense attitude she was adopting.

If only she could put it into practice now. March straight into the bedroom and get on with what had to be done.

She considered calling Megan, liking the idea of having someone with her, even if it was electronically, as she took this next step.

Her friend had been her life support since Charlie had died and Harper knew she would happily oblige, but that didn't stop this being something she wanted to do by herself. No, not wanted. She needed to do this alone to prove to herself she was strong enough. That she was slowly getting better.

She thought of Charlie and of the active social life they had led when he was alive, then allowed herself a moment to dream of the future she wanted, one where she had that life back and she wasn't so damned afraid all the time.

Closing her fingers around the cool handle, Harper pushed it down and open. Light spilled through the widening crack of the door as the sun beamed in through the window. Releasing a shaky breath, she sniffed at the stale air, trying not to stare at the bed she had once shared with her husband.

'One step at a time.' She murmured the words under her breath as Bailey pushed past her, tail wagging at all the new smells.

Harper entered the room after him, the bin liners clutched in her hand like a weapon. She needed to shut off her emotions and deal with this as swiftly as possible.

A pair of Charlie's reading glasses sat on the bedside table on the side where he had slept and the old T-shirt he had worn on his last night on earth was neatly folded over the chair in front of the dresser.

Sucking in a steadying breath, Harper forced herself further into the room. Everything was so silent and that only added to her nerves.

She needed music, she decided. Something loud and upbeat that would help her through this. The wall-mounted Echo speaker was covered in dust, but still connected to her home set-up, and the blue ring of light illuminated when she asked Alexa to find a rock station.

'Louder,' she ordered, as the infectious sound of Maximo Park filled the room.

If she could drown out everything going on in her head, focus solely on the music, she could get through this.

Tearing off a bin liner, she shoved the glasses and the T-shirt inside it. As Bailey sniffed around the room, she headed into the en suite bathroom, opening the bathroom cabinet. Deodorant and aftershave Charlie would never wear again went into the bag, then his toothbrush and favourite mouthwash, the shaving cream and razors that he had used every other day, his nasal hair trimmer and styling wax. He had been fastidious about his appearance. Maintenance and presentation was important to Charlie in all aspects of his life, and filthiness disgusted him.

Harper had always tried to meet his high standards, but since he had been gone, she had let both herself and the house go. What would he think if he could see the state of things now? The sink full of dishes she hadn't got around to washing up and everywhere in dire need of a dust. Then there was her appearance. Her blonde hair was full of split ends because it was badly overdue a cut, and her clothes were crumpled because she hadn't bothered to iron them.

She had made an effort for her dates, but at home, behind closed doors, she no longer bothered. Shame heated her face, knowing he would be appalled.

But then, even going the extra mile, she had never been quite enough for him.

Swallowing down on her bitterness, she moved back through to the bedroom with a fresh wave of determination, stripping the mattress and binning the linen, then throwing the framed wedding picture that sat on the dresser into the bag.

Underwear followed and then the drawer with his socks.

Something fell out of one of the balled-up pairs, clinking against the hardwood floor.

Harper saw a glint of silver as it disappeared under the dresser and she dropped to her hands and knees to retrieve whatever it was.

A key, she realised, fingers grappling under the unit and feeling the distinctive shape. She studied it, wondering what it was for. Possibly it opened a door in one of the hotels? Unsure, she slipped it into the pocket of her jeans, deciding to come back to it later, and tore off another bin liner.

In the wardrobe, she hauled out shirts and suits, the rack of ties. These she took more care with. They could all go to a charity shop. By the time she had finished with his clothes and shoes, she had six bin liners full. His cufflinks, watch and wedding ring she kept to one side. Although she didn't want them, she would take them to a pawn shop later.

Deciding there was no time like the present, she dragged the bags downstairs and went outside to load them into her car.

It was as she had just thrown in the last bag and was pushing the boot shut that she spotted the plant pot. It was one that sat on the side of the pathway that led to the back of the house, and it was lying broken on its side.

Was that the noise she had heard last night when Bailey was in the garden?

She looked at the dog now, as if he could give her answers. He had followed her outside and was waiting by the back door of the car, looking hopeful that they were going for a ride. He had only been in the garden so far this morning. Perhaps after she had taken Charlie's things to the charity shop, they could go down to Salhouse Broad. It was one of her favourite walks, and Bailey loved all of the different scents. It was a place where she could let him off the lead too and he could go in the water.

First, she wanted to clear away the broken plant pot. Her guess that it had been a fox was probably correct.

'We'll go in a minute,' she promised him, as he let out a whine.

It was as she was putting the shards of broken clay in the bin that she remembered there had been two crashes, and she wandered round into the back garden, looking for the source of the other noise.

When she found it, she frowned. The decorative cap that had sat on the corner of the patio wall was lying on the brick weave slabs. It didn't appear to be damaged, other than a small chip in the side, and she lifted it back into place. It had been loose for a while, but it was heavy, and there was no way a fox could have shifted it, and certainly not from the top of the wall.

So, what – or who – had been in the garden?

Despite the warmth of the bright day, a sliver of fear crept down Harper's spine.

From now on, she would make sure she kept all of the doors and windows locked.

The house had been many things to her over the five years since they had moved there. It had started out as a place of promise, before turning into a prison of loneliness, but it had also been her safe space.

The one thing she had never felt there was unsafe. Until now.

9

Although the cap from the patio wall lingered in her mind, Harper tried her best to ignore it. There was nothing she could do to find out what had happened, but perhaps she would get an alarm. And she would order a camera for the house, maybe a Ring doorbell, and get the back light fixed. Charlie had never wanted a door camera. He had claimed that the remote location of their new home made it safe, and over time, Harper had been lulled into a false sense of security.

Now she suspected his reasons had nothing to do with safety at all. No cameras as he didn't want Harper to see what he was up to on the occasions he was home alone.

Parking outside the charity shop, she lugged the bags of clothes inside, momentarily ignoring Bailey, who was whining on the back seat. Once she was rid of Charlie's things, she would give the spaniel her undivided attention, but first she had to do this.

She had expected to feel some kind of emotion, knowing Charlie's things were gone. A wave of sadness or perhaps relief. Maybe some kind of lightness. But there was nothing. Just numbness as she got back in the car. Charlie had been gone for two years, but still he held a power over her. She grieved for the husband she had loved, but also she despised him for what he had done to her and for all the unanswered questions she was left with.

No matter how hard she fought, would she ever be completely free of him?

Her mood was sombre as she drove back towards Salhouse, parking in the wooded clearing and heading onto the trail that led down to the broad, but Bailey, in that cute and enthusiastic way of his, gradually teased her out of it, his tail thumping hard and barking in delight when he realised where they were. It was hard not to break a smile as she watched him sniffing and peeing against every bush, his tail swishing back and forth. The beautiful autumn day helped. The leaves of the trees in the woods either side of them were a blaze of colours: golden and burnt orange and rusty shades of red. Some of them had already fallen, covering the ground in a patchwork blanket, while overhead the sky was a vivid cloudless blue, the sun burning bright.

As the path eventually opened into a grassy clearing, Harper could see the broad ahead, the water shimmering silver around the jetty that stretched out from the bank. There were a few people about, making the most of the weekend weather.

Knowing exactly where he was, Bailey rushed down to explore, while Harper wandered further along the bank, where a handful of boats were moored.

She had suggested getting a dog during her first year of marriage to Charlie, but he wasn't interested. He hadn't grown up in a pet-friendly household, so he didn't realise the joy they could bring.

Like her, he was an only child. His parents still alive and living in Oxford. She was no longer in touch with Cosmo and

Eunice, having been cut off within months of Charlie dying. She knew they had struggled with their son's loss. Charlie had told her there had been another son before him. One who was stillborn. As a result, Charlie had been the revered child in his mother's eyes. One who had wanted for nothing and who could do no wrong. His relationship with his father had cooled after the reading of his grandfather's will, and Harper suspected Cosmo and Eunice were bitter that Harper had been their son's sole beneficiary.

She had always suspected they didn't think she was good enough for Charlie, even though they had never said so. Though, in fairness, they probably thought no woman was good enough. They had always been coolly polite towards her, formal even, and she had dreaded the occasions when they came to visit or when Charlie had taken her to their stuffy, museum-like house.

Losing contact didn't bother her, especially given the circumstances surrounding Charlie's death. If anything, it made things easier.

'Harper?'

Hearing her name called pulled her sharply from her thoughts and she swung around, for a moment frowning at the man who was approaching her, before recognition dawned. 'Luke.'

The cute Irish doctor who had helped her at the beach.

Honestly, she was surprised she remembered his name, and he hers. It had been five weeks ago and only a brief encounter. The last place she had expected to see him was her local park.

He had a widening smile on his face as he neared, and a dog with him, she realised, seeing a scruffy little white terrier appear from the bushes.

'I thought it was you,' he told her, coming to halt in front of her. 'How's your leg?'

'It's okay, thanks,' she said, as a soggy Bailey joined them, delighted at the new canine company and introducing himself to the terrier by sniffing its bum. 'I've still got a bit of a scar, but it's mostly healed.'

'That's good,' he agreed. 'So, do you live around here?'

Harper nodded, but didn't elaborate whereabouts. She liked Luke, but she barely knew him. Instead, she asked. 'Do you?'

'Yes. Small world, eh?'

It was. What were the chances?

He must have noticed she was staring at his dog, because he added, 'Harper, meet Eric.'

'Hi, Eric.' The terrier was cute, though not the kind of dog she would have pictured Luke with. And it hadn't been with him at the beach. Maybe he had only just got it. 'I didn't know you had a dog,' she blurted.

A stupid thing to say, she supposed, as Luke's smile widened to a grin. She didn't know anything about him at all. Well, other than he was a doctor and he had nice eyes.

'Oh, Eric's not mine.'

'He's not? Whose is he?'

Luke glanced furtively around before his voice dropped to a conspiratorial whisper. 'I stole him from one of the boats over there.' He pointed vaguely towards where several vessels were moored along the water's edge, as Harper's eyes widened.

'You did what?'

'I think they've gone out somewhere, so they don't know.'

'You can't just take someone's dog,' she scolded, her tone high-pitched with shock and anger. Why would he possibly think she would be fine with this?

'Why not? He likes me.'

'You have to give him back.'

'But we've bonded.'

'Luke. This is not okay. You can't...' She trailed off, realising he was laughing at her now. 'You didn't really steal him, did you?' she asked, her eyes narrowing.

'No, he belongs to my neighbour. I've been looking after him while she's on holiday.'

'You idiot!' Harper smacked his arm.

'Hey, ouch. Okay, I'm sorry.' He grinned again. 'But it was worth it to see the look on your face.'

Yes, she had fallen for the joke, even though it was a dumb one. It was a stark reminder of how far she had distanced herself from everyday life that she no longer realised when someone was messing with her. How was she meant to get her life back on track when she couldn't even remember how to fit into normal society?

It was stupid really, and her reaction, she would later realise, was probably down to the trauma of finally clearing out Charlie's things, but in that moment, emotion consumed her, hot fat tears blurring her vision and spilling down her face.

Luke's eyes widened in horror, assuming he was the cause. 'Hey, I'm sorry. It was a stupid joke to make. I didn't mean to upset you.'

He hadn't, but she couldn't tell him that, as fresh grief at the finality of what she had done took hold and the words she tried to speak, wanting to assure him he hadn't done anything wrong, choked her.

'Harper.' He went to touch her arm, but she pushed him away, instead reaching for Bailey and fumbling to attach his lead. She couldn't stay here. This was mortifying.

'I have to go,' she managed through gulping sobs, stumbling back towards the trail that led to the car park.

Luckily, Luke didn't follow, and even more fortunately, given how popular the broad was, especially on a Saturday afternoon, she didn't run into anyone else on the trail. By the time she arrived back at her car, her tears had mostly stopped and the wave of absolute despair that had overcome her had morphed into embarrassment. Whatever must he think of her?

She resolved to never go to Salhouse Broad again. She couldn't risk ever bumping into him again. It would be too humiliating.

Her good mood had soured and back home she retreated to her living room, drawing curtains on the bright day outside, before curling up on the sofa, Bailey coming over and slumping down on the floor beside her.

What an idiot she had been to believe she could make herself better. She would stay here in the safety of the house where she couldn't make such a fool of herself.

* * *

It was Megan who eventually pulled her out of her funk. Her friend checked in with her a few times a week and her timing was fortuitous.

When Harper ignored her ringing phone throughout the rest of the day and most of the next morning, letting dozens of calls go to voicemail, she eventually received a WhatsApp message.

> I'm now going to video call you. If you don't pick up, I'm getting on the next train to Norwich.

She knew Megan well enough to realise she wasn't kidding, especially as she didn't normally hear from her friend on a Sunday, so she reluctantly answered the call when it came.

'What's going on?' Megan demanded. 'You look like hell.'

'I've been busy.'

'You don't look busy. Don't dick around with me, Harper. Why haven't you answered any of my calls?'

'I took Charlie's clothes to a charity shop yesterday.' Harper worked on keeping her tone steady.

Megan's anger evaporated. 'Oh, honey.'

Gradually, the whole sorry story came out, her cheeks burning as she recalled the incident with Luke down at the broad.

'He's not going to judge you,' Megan insisted.

Of course he would. He was going to think of Harper as the crazy woman who cried because she couldn't take a joke. She didn't point that out. It was over and she couldn't make the incident go away, but she would try to put it behind her.

'You've been doing so well,' Megan told her. 'And it's understandable there will be bumps in the road ahead. You just have to ride over them. Hopefully each one will hurt less.'

She was right. Locking herself away had been a big step back, but Harper could try again. There were two potential dates waiting for her to reply to their last messages on the IntoYou app. She just needed to pull herself together and take things slowly.

By the time she ended the video call, she was feeling a little bit better. As she went to delete all of Megan's previous call notifications, she spotted that she had a voicemail. Not from her friend. The Norwich number that came up was one she recognised, having called the charity shop before taking Charlie's things in, to check they would accept them.

Curious why they would be calling her, she listened to the voicemail they had left.

'Hello, this is Age Concern. You brought in some bags of clothes for us yesterday and we've been sorting through everything. We found a gold chain in the pocket of one of the pairs of trousers. I don't know if you realised it was there and if you want it back. Perhaps you could give us a call? We'll put it to one side until we hear from you.'

Intrigued, Harper called the shop to tell them she was on her way, then hurriedly cleaned her teeth and ran a brush through her hair, before slipping on her shoes and leaving the house.

She didn't own a gold chain and, other than his watch and wedding ring, Charlie hadn't been big on jewellery. Was it a gift he had bought her?

Or had it belonged to someone else?

The woman he had been having an affair with.

Harper's friend, Alicia.

So far, my attempts to talk to Harper are not going to plan.

I am putting a lot of effort in for this woman, and none of it is working.

My frustration is growing. I need to get a real conversation going.

She has always been an angel on a pedestal to me, coveted and admired, but out of my reach.

Until now.

If I am going to make her mine, I need to get to know her better. I need to know everything about her. Her likes and dislikes and, most importantly, I need to know what makes her tick.

That means I have to try harder to get her to engage with me.

Sow my seeds and I will reap my rewards.

She is worth the effort.

Harper had never suspected that Charlie and Alicia were seeing each other, and when the car accident happened, she didn't just have to deal with the grief of losing her husband, there had also been the shock of learning he had cheated on her with one of her closest friends.

Afterwards, when she looked back, she realised there had been signs in that last week; clues she should have picked up on. Alicia's relationship with her boyfriend had recently ended and she had been spending more time over at Harper and Charlie's house. Harper liked having her there. What had started off as a casual acquaintance through yoga had grown over the year she had known Alicia into something more. With Megan still in London, it was nice having another close female friend she could confide in.

But she remembered how one Monday afternoon she had arrived home from the supermarket to find Alicia and Charlie talking together in the kitchen. They had suspiciously stopped when she had entered the room, both of them looking flustered. Then Charlie had followed Alicia out of the house as she left, using the excuse he was taking the bin out, and Harper had seen them deep in conversation by Alicia's car.

It hadn't overly bothered her at the time. Her husband and her friend. She trusted them both and Alicia had never shown any interest in Charlie before. So, a couple of days later when Charlie had called her claiming he had been summoned urgently to the hotel in North Wales, she had believed him.

Little had she known Alicia had been in the car with him. Because she had died alongside him that fateful, earth-shattering day.

Just how long had they been carrying on behind Harper's back? She hadn't wanted to find out.

The humiliation of knowing they had played her for a fool burned deep, and fresh anger surfaced now as she looked at the delicate gold chain dangling from her fingers, as she sat in her car outside the charity shop.

It was quite distinctive, with its tiny blood-red heart pendant. It definitely wasn't Harper's, so it had to belong to Alicia.

Her former friend had liked wearing jewellery, and she had always favoured gold, but why was it in Charlie's pocket? Had it been put there for safekeeping, or worse, had it been meant as a gift?

The idea choked her that the man she had married, who had promised to love and cherish her, might have bought expensive jewellery for another woman.

How could she have been so stupid? How did she manage to miss all of the signs?

Her rage at the injustice of the situation had no outlet. She couldn't scream and shout at Charlie, as he was no longer here. And Alicia would never know how deeply the betrayal of their friendship had cut, because she had died in the car accident too.

Unlike Charlie, who had later passed away in hospital, Alicia had been killed at the scene.

Slipping the chain into her pocket, Harper started the engine.

This was yet another sign that she needed to move on. She couldn't keep allowing Charlie to have control over her life. It was ridiculous. He was gone.

Back home, she decided to take an assertive approach, opening the IntoYou app and proposing a meet-up to both Lee and Gavin, dismissing the niggle of guilt that she would be dating two men at the same time.

She reassured herself it didn't count. She wasn't in a relationship with either of them. It would just be a drink to see if there was any compatibility.

There was no immediate response from Gavin, but Lee came back to her fairly quickly, pleased with her suggestion. Not wanting to waste time, Harper proposed a drink in the Black Dog Inn the following evening.

It was fast becoming her date pub, she realised. The staff and the regulars were going to start recognising that she was always in there with different men.

* * *

Luckily, it was a different crowd when she showed up, and much quieter, perhaps because it was a Monday night. The female bartender smiled at Harper as she approached the bar.

A quick sweep of the room told her that Lee wasn't yet there, so she ordered a glass of wine, eager to take a couple of sips and calm her jittery belly. Just the one alcoholic drink, though, as she had her car with her this time.

This whole dating lark still scared her, even if the nerves

weren't quite as bad three dates in. At least she had been able to focus on work today and had achieved her daily word count.

She went over what she knew about Lee. He was a movie nerd – that had been his own term to describe himself – and she knew he was forty years old and divorced. He looked pleasant enough in his photo – dark cropped hair and even features. Time would tell if they hit it off.

Feeling her phone vibrate, she fished it out of her pocket, wondering if he was delayed, as he had said he was unfamiliar with the pub. It wasn't Lee's name on her screen, though. Instead, it was a WhatsApp from Justin.

They hadn't spoken since Friday evening, when he had checked she was home safe after their date, and she read his text now, seeing he was just checking in with her, and hoped she was okay.

Grateful for something to do as she waited at the bar, she messaged him back. She hadn't planned on telling him she was out on a date, but then he asked what she was up to and as they had decided to be friends, she figured there was no harm in telling him.

He reacted with a grinning emoji and a thumbs up, before pinging another message.

> Same pub? I hope it works out for you. You'll have to let me know.

Harper smiled, confirming that yes, she was in the Black Dog, and asked if he had any more dates lined up.

His reply came after a moment.

> Nothing for me. I'm having a boring night in, marking homework.

She started to type a response, a witty comment about how

they would both be giving grades tonight, when she felt a tap on the arm.

Expecting Lee, she turned, a smile on her face that froze and then dropped.

This was Lee, the same man she had been talking to on Into-You, but he had aged by about twenty or more years. The hair that had looked almost black in his photo was mostly grey with a good smattering of white, and his features, while still even, were fanned by heavy lines. There was no way he was forty. He was at least sixty. Possibly older.

'Harper, it's great to finally meet you. I'm Lee.' He leant in to kiss her cheek before she could react to stop him, leaving her in a cloud of overpowering peppery aftershave. 'Can I get you another glass of wine?' he offered.

There was absolutely no shame that he had met her under false pretences and, as she shook her head, managing to mutter a 'no, thank you,' she wondered if he planned to come clean about the deception.

The subject of age was going to be the elephant in the room if he didn't say something, which meant that Harper would have to. But how the hell was she supposed to bring it up without insulting him? Make a joke and ask him if he had borrowed Marty McFly's DeLorean to get here? She couldn't do that.

She would have offered to pay for his pint, as she had already ordered a wine, but she was so annoyed that he had lied to her, she decided she wouldn't be hanging around for more than one drink.

'Shall we sit over here?' Lee suggested, heading towards the table where Harper had spent her date with Adrian.

An ominous sign if ever there was one.

Perhaps she should just go and not give this man any more of her time. It would be the sensible thing to do, but her feet had already decided she was going to follow after him, and the next thing she knew, she was pulling out a chair to sit down.

'You're very pretty,' he said, grinning broadly at her. 'But then I already knew you were from your profile picture.'

'Um, thank you.'

This was just so awkward. How was she supposed to act like it was okay?

And how many other women had he deceived? Had they called him out on the lie, or just gone along with it?

'You look a little older than I was expecting, if I'm honest,' she told him, unable to stop herself. He was treating her like a fool.

His expression went carefully neutral and silence stretched between them as he stared at her. For a moment, Harper thought he was going to cling to denial, and she worried that he might turn aggressive with it, but then his mouth relaxed into a smile.

'I might have knocked off a few years,' he admitted. 'But you are so lovely, I had to get you to talk to me.'

It was a lot more than a few years, but she supposed at least he had admitted to the lie.

'So how old are you?' Not a question she would usually ask a stranger and her tone was blunt, but he deserved it.

'Forty-nine,' he told her, his gaze flicking away briefly as he said the number.

Another untruth and she raised her eyebrows as she stared at him.

'Okay, okay, I'm fifty-six.' He shrugged and took a sip of his beer. White foam coating his top lip. 'I don't get what the big deal is. Age is just a number. What difference does it make if I'm a bit older than you?'

He was still lying, but Harper wasn't going to push it. It was easy for him to say it wasn't an issue, and she wondered how he would have felt if the situation had been reversed. Still, she was here now and she made the effort to talk to him while she finished her wine. He wasn't a terrible conversationalist, but she struggled to get past his initial deception; trust understandably being a huge deal for her.

'Do you want another one of those?' Lee asked as she drained her glass.

'Actually, I'm going to head home.'

He looked disappointed at her answer. 'But the night's still young.' Apparently he was under the impression everything was going well.

'I'm sorry, but this is not working for me. I wish you well for the future, though.'

As she started to get up, Lee's tone turned bitter. 'It's the age thing, isn't it. I don't know what is wrong with some people. You have a shallow attitude.'

Tempted as she was to correct him, and point out it was the fact he had lied to her that was the problem for her, and that perhaps he was shallow not wanting to date women his own age, Harper decided it was easiest to walk away. She didn't want this to become a thing.

'I'm going to leave now,' she told him, making a last attempt to exit on pleasant terms. 'I'm sorry this didn't work out.'

Her effort was met with a scowl and he muttered something under his breath, which she was pretty sure included the word bitch, but thankfully he made no attempt to follow her.

It didn't stop her hurrying to her car and locking the doors once she was inside her Volkswagen. Not that she thought Lee posed a danger, but it was better to be safe than sorry.

Pulling into her driveway a short while later, she finally felt the release of tension in her shoulders, grateful that she had cut the date short. Maybe she would have better luck with Gavin. If he ever got back to her.

Sending a quick message to Megan to let her friend know she was home safe, as had become their normal routine, she got out of the car. She heard Bailey barking before she entered the house, and he was waiting to greet her as the door opened, but not with his rubber chicken in his mouth, as he usually did. Instead, he danced around her, barking again and whining, as if he was trying to tell her something.

He was probably just annoyed that she had left him alone, she assumed, heading through to the kitchen to fetch him a treat. Though, when she had arrived home from her dates with Adrian and Justin, he hadn't been agitated like this.

Still, she dismissed it, making a fuss of him as she gave him the treat, before opening the bottle of Sauvignon Blanc she had chilling in the fridge and pouring herself a glass. After Lee's deception tonight, she deserved it.

She let Bailey out into the garden, staying by the back door and sipping at her wine as she watched him disappear into the blackness. Moments later, his barking started again and this time he sounded really worked up.

'Bailey?'

When he ignored her, continuing to bark, she considered fetching the torch and going to find him, but then she remembered what had happened on Friday night after her date with Justin. The noises she had heard and the broken flower pot and the patio cap that had fallen to the ground.

'Bailey!'

Sudden goosebumps chilled her skin. Was someone in her back garden? Was that why Bailey was going nuts?

She should go outside and find him, but she was afraid. Just in case.

Just in case of what, Harper? What are you afraid of?

He was her dog. If there was a chance he was in danger...

Putting down the wine glass, she opened the drawer where she kept the torch, switching it on and heading outside, the beam cutting across flowerbeds and swiping past trees, yelling again for Bailey to come to her.

The black shadow came from nowhere, giving her no chance to react, and she screamed as it crashed into her. It took several moments, during which she was fairly certain her heart had stopped, before she realised it was Bailey.

Almost sobbing with relief, she caught hold of his collar, leading him back into the house and locking the door.

She stared through the glass into the darkness, wondering if she was being watched.

This was it. Tomorrow she was going to call someone about the light and buy the camera she had been thinking about. Whatever had upset her dog might just be a harmless animal, but her nerves were in shreds. She needed to feel safe in her home again.

After doing a downstairs room-to-room check, flipping light switches and checking locks, to give herself peace of mind, she fed Bailey another treat, gulped down the rest of her wine in a bid to relax the tension in her shoulders, then headed upstairs.

She felt the cool draught the moment she stepped onto the landing, quickly realising that it came from the main bathroom. The window was ajar, and yes, she had opened it after using the shower to clear the condensation, but she thought she had shut it before going out.

Trying to shrug it off, knowing she was still unsettled by Bailey's barking, which was why she was jittery, she closed and locked it before going into her bedroom.

Straightaway, she had a sense that someone had been in there. It wasn't anything obvious. The curtains were drawn, her make-up bag still on the dresser, everything just as she had left it, but the smell of the room was wrong. It was perhaps silly and she couldn't quite pinpoint anything at first, but all of her spider senses were tingling.

Then she spotted the top bedside table drawer was ajar. Had she left it that way?

Quickly, she went to the drawer, opening it, and her stomach somersaulted as she saw her journal was upside down. It was one she used as therapy, writing in it about how she was feeling, her despair at Charlie's betrayal and his death, and her tentative hopes for the future.

She always left it face up.

The idea that someone might have been reading her innermost thoughts horrified her.

As tension thrummed through her and her heart pounded, she did another room-to-room check of upstairs, her phone in one hand and a bottle of deodorant spray – the only thing she could lay her hands on as a possible weapon – in the other. It was only as she entered the master bedroom that she considered – too late – that perhaps she should have first called the police.

But would they come out for a scared woman? The house hadn't been wrecked. Nothing had been stolen. It was just an open window and a wrongly positioned journal. Oh, and a feeling she had. Don't forget that.

They would think she was mad.

And perhaps she really was, as she could see as she turned on the light that the master room was just as she had left it yesterday. The bed stripped and the dresser top empty. Ready now for her to decide how she wanted to redecorate it.

Still, she kept her finger on the nozzle of the deodorant spray as she checked the en suite and then the guest bedroom.

No one was upstairs and she had just lit up her house like the

Blackpool illuminations. For now, she made no attempt to turn any of the lights off, finding it comforting.

Perhaps she really was overreacting to everything and her writer's imagination was getting carried away.

She had almost talked herself into believing she was wrong, but then, as she walked back into her bedroom, she spotted that the pair of knickers she had kicked off earlier before stepping into the shower ahead of her date were gone.

12

How was Harper supposed to go to the police and say that someone had broken into the house and stolen her underwear?

It was embarrassing, especially as nothing else was missing.

After she had realised the knickers were no longer on the floor where she had kicked them off, she had checked the laundry basket. Then she had looked under the bed and in her underwear drawer, in case, for some inexplicable reason, she might have put them back in there. They were definitely missing.

Was this why Bailey had been agitated? Had he been trying to tell her someone was in the house?

Needing to talk to someone, she called Megan. It was almost midnight and Harper would forgive her friend for not picking up, but she couldn't just go to sleep.

She had Justin's number too but didn't feel she knew him well enough yet to trust him with something like this. Besides, she didn't want to tell him her underwear was missing.

When Megan's familiar voice came on the line, she relaxed a little.

'What's up? Are you okay?'

Her friend sounded worried, though also sleepy, and Harper quashed down the spike of guilt that she might have woken her.

'I'm sorry. I know it's late.'

'Is this something to do with your date? You said you were home.'

'I am and, no, this has nothing to do with that. I'll tell you about him another time. This is...' She trailed off. Megan was going to think she was nuts.

'What's wrong?'

'I think someone has been in the house.'

'What?' Megan's tone was sharp and Harper sensed she was suddenly a whole lot more awake. 'Who has been in the house?'

'I don't know.' Harper explained about Bailey's reaction when she arrived home and then in the garden, leading up to the open window, disturbed journal and eventually the missing knickers.

Megan listened, chipping in, at first urging her to call the police, berating her for investigating the house alone, but by the time the journal and underwear were brought up, she had fallen silent.

'Are you certain you closed the window?' she asked as Harper finished talking.

'Yes. At least, I thought I did.' Harper could hear the doubt in her own voice and knew it was possible she had forgotten, but it didn't explain the journal or her missing underwear.

She pointed that out now.

'I'm sure they will show up,' Megan told her, sounding far too blasé about it. 'I do stuff like that all the time. I'm convinced I left something in one place, then find, usually a day or so later, it's somewhere I would never have imagined.'

'You don't believe me.' Harper struggled to keep the disappointment out of her tone. She had hoped – no, expected – that Megan, of all people, would be on her side.

'I never said I didn't believe you. All I'm saying is that stuff like this happens, and often there is a rational explanation. Maybe Bailey took them.'

'Why would he do that? He's never done anything like it before.'

'There's always a first time and it makes more sense than someone broke into your house to steal your knickers.'

When Harper didn't respond, Megan added, 'Look, I want to know that you are safe. Of course I do. What I don't want is you worrying that something is wrong if it isn't.'

'So how do you explain my journal?'

'Is it possible it could have shifted when you closed the drawer?'

'The drawer was ajar,' Harper reminded her, the edges of her temper fraying. 'And it hadn't just shifted. It was upside down. I know when someone has moved something. I'm not stupid, Megan.'

'I know you're not.' Megan spoke in a soothing tone that Harper knew was supposed to calm her. Instead, it had the opposite effect, the earlier tension creeping back into her neck and shoulders, and her inner coil tightening when she heard whispering, realising that Megan was telling Tom about the call.

'I should go,' she snapped. 'Sorry I disturbed you.'

'Harper, stop,' Megan said, quickly coming back on the phone. 'Look, maybe I should come up and stay for a few days.'

'I don't need you to come and babysit me,' Harper was aware she was being ungrateful but she couldn't hold back. 'I know you think I'm falling apart. But I'm not. Someone was in this house.'

There was a moment of silence before Megan spoke, her words careful and her tone a little weary. 'Look, I want to help you, but I'm two hours away. I will come up to Norwich. The offer is still there, but I can't get there tonight. If you think you're in danger, then you need to call the police.'

'Never mind. I'll speak with you later.'

'Harper. Don't be like—'

Megan never got to finish her sentence as Harper ended the call.

She knew what had happened. She wasn't going crazy... was she?

Doubt crept in as she remembered back to those first few months after Charlie had died when she had been paranoid and delusional. Megan had made her talk to a grief counsellor and it had helped a little, but at that time she was already starting to find leaving the house a chore, so eventually she cancelled the sessions. Instead, she stubbornly dealt with things her own way, which was why it had taken so damn long for her to start the healing process.

Was it possible she was regressing? Had she imagined everything tonight? It had been Bailey's actions that had set her off, convincing her someone had been in the garden. Had she clutched at straws, creating her own narrative?

Okay, so perhaps she had forgotten to close the window, but the journal had been face up and she knew she had left her knickers on the floor by the door.

But maybe Megan was right. Had Bailey hidden them somewhere?

Unsure what was truth and what was not, far too awake to sleep, she pulled on her robe and headed back downstairs. Overthinking everything would drive her crazy. Instead, she decided she would try to use the time productively to write.

Bailey wandered through to her office as she was firing up her Mac, and she made a fuss of him, stroking his soft black ears, wishing he could tell her what had upset him earlier.

As he settled by her feet and let out a yawn, she opened the manuscript she was working on, aware she still had a way to go and mentally working out what her weekly word count needed to be to make her deadline. Her agent, Adam, had been flexible over the last two years, more than understanding of her bereavement, and working with her publisher to allow her extensions. She couldn't ask for another one. They were going to lose faith in her at some point.

Harper had always prided herself on her professionalism and she was embarrassed it had slipped, but it had been harder to write romance after discovering the lies of her own marriage. It made her feel like a fraud. She was approaching the end of her contract, with just one more manuscript to deliver after this one, and she really needed to pull this book out of the bag, somehow, and prove she was both reliable and still good enough to sell books, before negotiations began.

Tentatively, she typed a few sentences, frowning at them, then deleting and starting again. After staring at the screen for almost twenty minutes, frustration growing as the right words wouldn't come, she got up and went through to the kitchen to grab her wine glass and the bottle of Sauvignon.

Back at her desk, she filled the glass and took a few sips as she continued to stare at the screen, distracted when she saw her phone light up where it lay on the desk beside her Mac.

For a short while, she tried to ignore it, sipping more wine, attempting more words, deleting, retyping and refilling her glass, before she gave into temptation and snatched up the handset.

She had assumed it would be a message from Megan, knowing her friend didn't like to sleep on an argument. Not that they had really fallen out, but Harper knew she had been a bitch and was also keen to clear the air. She resolved to apologise in the morning, for now distracted by the alert on her screen.

Brad had requested to send her a message again, and this time she could see that his profile contained an image. Curious, she opened the IntoYou app, clicking onto his account.

He had updated his information. A full bio now, revealing he was thirty-seven, the same age as Harper, divorced, no children, and he was a firefighter. While his icebreaker started the same – looking to meet someone – he had now elaborated on it.

Here goes. I've finally plucked up the courage to properly fill this bit in. I went through a bad divorce a couple of years back and am now piecing myself back together. This online dating thing is completely new to me and a little bit scary.

Harper could relate to that and appreciated his honesty. Intrigued, she read on.

I enjoy cooking, and eating, of course. My friends are my family. They have been there for me through the toughest of times. I have a dog, Monty (he's a rescue hound, which are the best), and you have to love dogs or you and me won't work.

He had a dog and felt the same way about him as she did about Bailey. Her heart was already melting and Brad hadn't finished yet.

What else excites me? Getting to sound the horn. What fire-fighter doesn't love that? Oh, and I adore live music. Favourite gig: Muse, Shepherd's Bush, 2017.

She double blinked. Seriously? What were the chances of that? She had been at that concert with Charlie and Megan, and

Megan's then boyfriend, Jamie, and it was the best live gig she had ever been to.

His section telling her what he was looking for had her heart pumping faster.

Mutual respect and someone who is my best friend as well as a partner.

Everything she was reading – except the cooking bit, because she was rubbish at that – suggested they were on the same wavelength.

Eagerly, she clicked on the profile picture, not disappointed at the face staring back at her from the screen. There was no denying Brad was attractive. He had dirty blond hair and an infectious grin on his face, and blue eyes that rivalled Luke's, the doctor she had embarrassed herself in front of at Salhouse Broad.

Even though she was already regretting ignoring Brad, based on his original profile, her finger still hovered over the 'message accept' button. After her earlier encounter with Lee, could she trust any of the men messaging her? What if he wasn't who he said he was?

Eventually, curiosity won out. Brad was gorgeous, and she reasoned that the other men she had met had been as their profile pictures. She couldn't let the encounter with Lee derail her.

She clicked open the message, eyes widening when she saw he had taken the time to write a couple of paragraphs, instead of the usual, 'hey, how's it going?'

Hi Harper. You're the first person I have tried to contact on here. I only got brave enough to fill in my information tonight, so please forgive me if I get any of this wrong. It's my first experience of a dating site. I'm going to be honest, yours is the only profile I've seen that I've clicked with. We seem to share the same values and I like people-watching too. But, really, you had me at dog mum. What breed? My dog, Monty, is a sweetheart. He's a rescue, a real 57 varieties of Heinz hound. Oh, and don't tell anyone, as you'll dent my manly pride, but I cried at Marley & Me too.

So far, Harper's online dating experience hadn't been great, so she didn't want to get her hopes up and then have them dashed, but Brad was saying all of the right things.

Cautiously, she started to type a reply, then hesitated. Maybe she would be better to wait until the morning to respond. She didn't want to come across as overeager, replying in the middle of the night. Plus, she wanted to give some thought to what she should say.

Clicking out of the message, she saw that Gavin had been in touch too, finally replying to her question about whether he fancied a meet-up, telling her yes.

Truthfully, she was a little swayed by Brad's message and fast losing interest in Gavin, but she supposed she shouldn't be rash. Deciding to leave his message until the morning as well, she logged out of the app and turned her phone face down so it didn't disturb her.

Aided by another glass of wine, she returned to her manuscript.

Lee had been an unfortunate blip and perhaps it was his deceit, along with Bailey's barking, that had sent her imagination into overdrive. Was Megan right? Had she overreacted, looking for signs that were not there?

What that said about her frame of mind, she wasn't sure. Thank God she hadn't called the police.

The wine relaxing her, and the words finally flowing, she settled in for a night of writing, pushing her personal life to one side.

She wanted a fresh start and was determined to get one. Tomorrow, she would apologise to Megan, then respond to both Brad and Gavin.

Everything was going to work out okay.

13

It was the stupid dog who almost gave me away.

I hadn't cared about its barking while I was in the house, locking the animal in the kitchen to muffle the sound. It had been background noise. A little irritating, but not enough to distract me from my task of getting to know Harper better.

She was out on a date, in her new favourite pub, and the tracker I had put on her car would alert me when she was leaving to come home. Plenty of time for me to familiarise myself with her house, steal a key, hide a couple of tiny cameras, and to find out more about her and the little things that make her tick.

It's amazing how small they make spyware cameras these days and it's easy to tuck them away so they are unlikely to ever be found. Perfect for me to keep an eye on Harper while she is indoors.

Upstairs in her bedroom, I took my time, spraying her perfume into the air and breathing in the fruity scent, trying on the various creams and potions she uses. In her wardrobe, I riffled through her clothes, deciding which outfits I would like to see her in, then I spent time in the bathroom, putting her toothbrush into my mouth, wanting to taste her, sucking on it as if it was a lollipop as I emptied the contents of her make-up bag onto the counter.

She owns mostly subtle, understated tones of bronzes and pinks, and I made a note of that, as I need to know what she likes, but also what she doesn't. No whorish red for Harper. Not in the clothes she owns or the lipsticks in the bag. She is too soft for that. At least that is the impression she tries to give.

I like the demure ones. The vulnerable and the fragile. I know what lies beneath and it's my job to unleash it.

Red is my favourite colour and now I yearn to see her draped in it. Red is bold and passionate, and it intimidates. It seduces, burning fire bright, powerful and dangerous, but never boring.

She will wear red; I already knew that as I put everything back. When she is mine, I will dress her head to toe in the colour.

Running my finger against the blade of her razor, I watched the slice turn crimson with droplets of blood. The sting of the cut was intoxicating, and the metallic taste as I replaced the toothbrush in my mouth with my wounded finger was like coming home.

It was back in the bedroom, while searching through the drawers of the bedside cabinets, that I found the best prize of the night. A journal, in which Harper documented her struggles since the death of her husband.

The book was a treasure trove, showing me how the confident woman I remembered had become a broken bird. It gave me an insight into her everyday life, telling me how lonely she is, of the children she wants, and it revealed the spark of hope she has for the future as she tries to get her life back on track.

She is stubborn, a quality I appreciate, and her inner strength as she attempts to heal herself, even though she repeatedly fails, shone through in her words I read. Fragile is good, but weak is boring. Weak will give up and let you walk all over it. I much prefer a woman who challenges me.

I wanted to take the journal, aware that it has everything I need to reel her in, but she would know it is missing and that someone had been in the house. Instead, I devoured as much of it as possible, stopping only when I received an alert that she was leaving the pub.

Her date hadn't lasted long.

I quickly took photographs of a few key pages, before replacing the journal in the drawer. It was as I was about to head downstairs to let the noisy dog out of the kitchen that I spotted the knickers on the floor.

Scooping them up, I pressed the crotch to my face and inhaled, for a moment giddy with excitement. This was like foreplay, a prelude of what was to come, and the temptation to wait for her, to reveal myself early, was almost uncontrollable.

It wasn't the right time, though. I realised that. If she saw me in her house, she would freak. It was too great a risk and I knew I had to take things slowly and work at her speed.

Once she is mine and we are together, the wait will have been worth it.

I couldn't bring myself to put her knickers back on the floor, though, instead slipping them into the pocket of my jeans. A token prize for being a good boy. Something to fantasise to later.

Leaving the kitchen door ajar so the barking spaniel could figure his way out, I returned upstairs to the bathroom, climbing out through the window I had come in through, the one Harper had forgotten to close. It was to my good fortune there is a flat utility room roof below it, probably an extension at some point to the original house, making it easy to access.

People think they are safe living in remote areas, but their sense of false security is my gain. I have always liked the countryside. Fewer nosy neighbours to see you loitering and no one close by to raise the alarm.

Harper's car was already pulling into the driveway before my feet hit the ground.

I should have left then, but the temptation to stick around was just too great, and of course she let the idiot dog out again. Last time I ended up knocking things over as I fled. And tonight the silly animal almost gave away my hiding place. I honestly thought Harper was going to find me when she came outside with the torch.

Luckily, I got away and now I am back home, the pair of cotton knickers I stole from the house in my hand.

In the corner of the room my housemate, Samantha, looks up from where she is eating her dinner, her eyes narrowed in what looks like pure hatred.

She only moved in recently and is still getting used to my house rules. To say she doesn't like me much is an understatement.

I need a housemate. It's too much of a struggle to get by without one, but Samantha is getting on my nerves. Normally, I am picky about who lives here, but she caught me at a weak moment.

It's because I'm so occupied with Harper. My obsession has reached the point where I am struggling with everything else in my life, including Samantha. I really can't be bothered to make any effort with her, even if she is dressed in my favourite colour red.

'You're disgusting,' she snarls at me now, curling her upper lip in revulsion as I make a show of holding the gusset of the underwear to my face and breathing in the scent. She knows where my other hand is and I want her to watch.

Ignoring her, I remember the words I read in Harper's most recent journal entry.

Do we only get one soulmate? I thought Charlie was mine, but it turns out I wasn't his. What if he was it for me, though? My only chance. I loved him and now I hate him in equal measures. I am trying so hard to move forward, to find out if there is someone else out there, but what if I am wasting my time?

'You're not,' I murmur, apparently loud enough for Samantha to hear, given her raised eyebrows. I don't care, continuing to ignore her as I speak aloud. 'I'll be coming for you soon.'

14

Harper awoke the following morning to Bailey licking her face, and she had absolutely no recollection of what time she had fallen asleep on the sofa.

She remembered the incidents of the previous night and her conversation with Megan, then going downstairs to write, and the messages she had received from Brad and then Gavin. She recalled how the words had finally come, that she had been typing like a woman possessed, fuelled by the wine in her glass, but after that it was blank.

Her head was pounding, and easing open her eyes, she immediately winced at the light streaming through the crack of the curtains.

Unsure what time it was, she gently pushed Bailey away, and reached for her phone, which was on the floor beside the sofa, shocked to see it was gone 10 a.m. She never slept this late, and poor Bailey. No wonder he was licking her. He needed feeding.

Gingerly, she got up and went through to the kitchen, disgusted when she spotted the two empty bottles of wine on the worktop. No wonder she felt rough.

Letting the dog out to pee, she fixed his breakfast, then poured a glass of water and downed a couple of painkillers. It was a drizzly morning, fitting for October, and the trees at the bottom of the garden had shed several more leaves. While she watched Bailey romp about, Harper thought back to the previous night.

In the cold light of day, she was more willing to believe she had overreacted and let her imagination run away with her. She couldn't be certain that she had closed the bathroom window and Megan was probably right about Bailey taking her knickers. It was more likely than someone breaking into her house to steal them. Okay, so she couldn't yet explain the journal or the vibe she had felt, but there had to be a rational explanation.

Making a fuss of Bailey when he came back in and telling him what a good boy he was, she put the bowl of food down for him, then, after locking the back door, she went upstairs to clean her teeth and shower.

First task on her list this morning was to call Megan and tell her she was sorry for hanging up on her.

Luckily, her friend was gracious enough to accept the apology, hesitantly suggesting that perhaps Harper might benefit from going back to see a therapist.

Rather than point blank refusing, she pretended to mull over the idea, and after turning down Megan's offer again to come up to Norwich for a few days, insisting she was fine, Harper ended the call, promising she would touch base in a few days.

Last night might have been a result of her overactive imagination, but it had highlighted to her that she should be a little more cautious about her safety. If someone had been in the garden or the house, she had no backup plan and there weren't any neighbours close by that she could call on for help.

That was why, after making a cup of coffee and taking it

through to her office, she went on Amazon and ordered a couple of cameras, then arranged for an electrician to come out who could fit them and look at her garden light.

Keen to delay facing whatever rubbish she had churned out late last night, she avoided her manuscript, spending some time perusing paint colour charts and trying to decide what shade to paint the master bedroom.

Eventually, knowing she had to get some work done, she opened her MacBook, readying herself for a trainwreck of words. Instead, she was pleasantly surprised to find she had written twenty-two decent pages.

Remembering the saying, 'write drunk, edit sober,' she smiled wryly. Perhaps the wine hadn't been a terrible idea after all and she decided to capitalise on the moment, sitting down in her chair and continuing the story.

She worked for much of the morning, aware Bailey needed a proper walk, but unwilling to break her flow, especially when the words were finally coming to her easily.

Eventually, it was a WhatsApp alert on her phone screen that distracted her enough to stop. The name Bard flashing up, which confused her.

Curious, she opened it, shocked to see a string of back-and-forth interactions, the time stamp indicating that she had still been awake gone 3 a.m. As she read through them, her face heated, realising that Bard was actually Brad. She had given him her number.

And this wasn't cool and casual Harper talking to him. She barely recognised the confident and forward woman who had been messaging in her place.

At first, her words were coherent and decisive, but further down the WhatsApp trail, she could see misspellings and sentences that didn't make any sense.

Not that Brad seemed to mind. He had cottoned on that she was drunk, and judging by his responses, he found the whole thing highly amusing.

She reread the message he had just sent.

> Good morning. Hope your head isn't too sore.
> Just checking we are still on for tonight.

Had they made plans to meet?

She quickly scrolled back up the messages, this time paying full and thorough attention, realising that she had been the one to ask him out.

Why would she have done that when they had only just started talking? And why the hell had she given out her number so freely?

Because you were drunk, you idiot.

Curious how the conversation had begun, she clicked on the IntoYou app and read through the messages.

Brad had started it, contacting her again, with an add-on to his previous message.

> I hope this doesn't sound too creepy, but I think you're really pretty.

He had ended it with a blushing emoji.

Harper had seen it and, in her drunken state, had obviously decided not to wait until morning to reply.

> I think you're pretty too. Pretty sexy.

She cringed, knowing she would never usually say something like that.

Half afraid of what else she might have said, she read on,

shocked when she realised they had only exchanged half a dozen messages before she offered him her phone number.

Oh Jesus. What had she been thinking?

And what the hell must he think of her?

Probably that she was a sure thing, when, of course, she wasn't.

This was exactly why she had intended to wait until this morning. She had hoped to make a good impression.

Should she cancel the date they had arranged? She had only been out with Lee last night. Besides, Brad knew she had been hammered. Surely he would understand. It wasn't that a meeting was off the cards, but she would really like to find out more about him first, and let him get to know who she really was.

She tentatively replied to his WhatsApp.

> I am so sorry about last night.

There, she would just leave it at that and see what he came back with.

She was about to log off when she spotted he was online and had already read her text. Seeing he was typing, she decided to wait and see what he said.

> You have nothing to apologise for. I enjoyed talking to you.

Harper waited a beat, then responded, deciding honesty was the way forward at this point.

> But will you hate me if I say I don't remember any of it?

He started to type, then stopped, and there was a lengthy pause before he resumed.

Had she offended him?

The longer she waited, the more her paranoia grew. She didn't want to put him off, but if they were going to meet up, it had to be with a clean slate. She was not the person who had been messaging him last night, and he needed to understand that.

After what felt like forever, his message popped up.

> I get it, you were drunk. I've been there. What I need to know is do you regret messaging me last night?

How did she explain this? She concentrated on getting her thoughts straight in her head.

> Yes, because I was drunk and I wish that wasn't your first impression of me. But please know I had planned to reply to your message this morning. I liked what you said.

This time, his reply was instant.

> That you are pretty?

A winky faced emoji told her he was teasing, and she relaxed a little.

> Well, of course I liked to hear that.

She added a delighted emoji before continuing.

> But truthfully? I clicked with your profile too. And the message you sent me.

Brad's reply was instant.

You did?

She grinned at her screen.

Did you really cry at Marley & Me?

More typing.

I honestly did. Scout's honour

Before she could respond, another message pinged up.

So, about that drink. Are you going to give me a chance?

Harper hesitated, trying to find the right words for her reply.

I need you to know I am not how I was last night. I don't usually hand my number straight over, or say the things I did. I blushed this morning reading them. If we do meet, I need to take things slow.

Hitting send, she waited.

Slow is good with me. You will be my first ever internet date, so I'm a little nervous about this too. One drink. You can pick where we go. We can have a chat, no strings attached, and see how we get on. What do you think?

He was saying all of the right things. So far, Harper had been on three dates and none of them had worked out. Maybe her luck was about to change.

Deciding Brad was worth taking a chance on, she typed her

response.

> Okay, then. Tonight. One drink. Do you know the Black Dog Inn?

15

This time, before leaving the house, Harper was careful to make sure all of the doors and windows were securely locked. She wasn't going to leave anything to chance, even if she was now mostly convinced she had imagined the intruder.

Her belly was jittery with nerves as she left, telling Bailey to be a good boy and promising him she wouldn't be late, switching on the porch light, then locking the front door behind her.

It was a filthy night, the earlier drizzle now turned to pouring rain and as she hurried across the driveway to her car, it was difficult to dodge the puddles in the dark.

In another three weeks, the clocks would go back. She had never liked this time of year, finding the shorter days oppressive, especially when they were gloomy too. Since Charlie had died, it had been even more difficult, the darker days and miserable weather really affecting her mood, and she was dreading winter's approach.

Maybe if her date with Brad went well tonight, it would give her something to look forward to over the coming months.

It was this foolish hope that had the butterflies dancing in her stomach. She could have so easily blown things before they even started, and she was lucky he had been chilled about her drunken messages. Knowing he had an easy-going nature cranked up her expectations even further, but what if there wasn't a spark in real life?

Or, worse still, what if she liked him, but he wasn't attracted to her?

She tried to push the negative thoughts away as she drove to the pub, pulling into the car park and taking the nearest available space to the entrance. Clicking on the interior light, she smoothed nervous fingers over her hair and checked she hadn't got lipstick on her teeth, before making a dash inside. She was already a couple of minutes late and didn't want to keep Brad waiting.

Not that she should have worried as she could see upon entering that she was first to arrive. Tuesday evenings, it seemed, were even quieter than Mondays, though that was perhaps due to the weather. There were just a couple of tables occupied, and the young bartender who had served her on her first two dates appeared bored as he wiped down the countertop.

He glanced up as she approached the bar, looking pleased to see her, and Harper guessed the nights must drag when the pub was as empty as this.

'What can I get you?' he asked, showing no sign of recognising her from her previous visits, but that was hardly surprising. He must see a lot of faces.

Given her earlier hangover, she should really opt for a soft drink, but she was sick with nerves about meeting Brad. One glass of wine wouldn't hurt. She just needed to make sure she didn't open another bottle when she arrived home.

'A glass of Sauvignon Blanc, please.'

He nodded, eyes narrowing in recognition of her order, even

though he must serve dozens of glasses of the drink. 'I know you. You were in here last week, right? For a date?'

Embarrassed heat flooded Harper's face. 'Yes,' she managed. He must have overheard when she and Justin were introducing themselves to each other.

His smile widened to a grin and he winked at her. 'It went well then.'

Went well? He obviously assumed she was meeting Justin here again tonight. What the hell was he going to think when Brad showed up? Two dates in one week. Three if she counted Lee, but thankfully this bartender hadn't been serving last night.

'Actually, I'm meeting someone else,' she told him as he took a bottle of wine from the fridge.

'Another date?' he questioned, though his tone was casual and he didn't look up from the glass he was pouring.

She realised he wasn't judging her, just merely making polite conversation, probably for something to do. Still, feeling awkward, she fumbled getting her card out of her purse, her hand shaking as she tapped the contactless screen. 'Umm, yes.'

As soon as the words were out, she regretted them. She should have lied and pretended she was meeting a friend.

The bartender seemed like he would be happy to carry on chatting, but Harper had embarrassed herself enough. Thanking him, she took a big sip of wine before going to sit at one of the empty tables at the back of the pub.

While she waited for Brad, she pulled her phone out of her bag and fired off a WhatsApp message to Megan, letting her know she was out on another date and telling her she would message again once she was home. Noting the time as she put the handset down on the table, she realised that Brad was already ten minutes late. Not good with timekeeping then.

He hadn't messaged to say he was running behind, but the weather was horrible, and it was possible it had delayed him.

Patiently she waited, though a little self-conscious that she was sat alone. When her phone eventually beeped, she snatched it up expecting an update of where he was.

Instead, it was Megan. A thumbs up to confirm she had read Harper's message.

Where was Brad? They had arranged to meet at 7 p.m. and it was now gone twenty past. Opening WhatsApp, she could see he hadn't been online since 4.30 p.m.

Getting a little bit agitated, she sent him a message.

> I'm here in the pub. I'm sitting at a table near the back.

Previously, her messages had been read straight away, but this time she didn't get the double tick. It worried her a little and her mind started conjuring up all manner of scenarios. The rain was so heavy; what if he had been involved in an accident?

She had no way of knowing, so was left with no choice other than to wait. Her anxiety was building, though, the glass of wine she was nursing gradually getting emptier, and she kept obsessively checking her phone.

Her cheeks burned with humiliation as she snuck a glance towards the bar. The guy who had served her was going to be wondering where her date was. Why the hell had she told him she was here to meet someone new? Fortunately, he wasn't paying her any attention, instead chatting away to one of the customers who had gone up to be served.

By 7.30, the WhatsApp message still hadn't been read and she was certain Brad wasn't going to show. The table closest to her had just left, which meant there was only Harper and one other couple in the pub. Aware they kept glancing over at her, she kept her head down, scrolling through her phone, afraid they might try to talk to her.

What had happened? Brad had been so keen, talking her into meeting him when she had tried to back out this morning. She had really thought that this time would be different.

'I guess your date must be running *really* late.'

The voice startled her and she glanced up, seeing the bartender looking at her. He was clearing glasses from the table that had just left. Was that a smirk he had on his face? Did he think it funny that she had been stood up? Her cheeks burned with humiliation.

'I guess so,' she snapped, finishing her drink and reaching for her bag. 'Thanks for pointing that out.'

His eyes widened, realising he had offended her. 'Hey, I didn't mean anything by that comment. I'm sorry if you thought I did. You don't have to go because I'm an idiot who always says the wrong thing.' He looked genuinely worried he had upset her and she softened slightly, realising she was being oversensitive.

'It's okay. I think we both know he's not coming. I should go.'

'Let me get you another drink. On the house.'

'You don't have to do that.'

'I want to. Please. I'm really sorry.' He sounded so contrite now, she felt bad. He wasn't that old. Maybe in his early twenties. Was he worried she would make a complaint about him? It had been a stupid throwaway comment and she had overreacted.

'You have nothing to apologise for, unlike my date,' she assured him, forcing herself to smile as she cracked the joke.

'Please. I'll feel bad if you go. It's pouring with rain and you've turned out for nothing.'

'Okay,' she relented. 'Thank you.'

Truthfully, she just wanted to go home now, but she would take the free drink if it stopped him feeling bad.

'I'm Isaac, by the way,' he told her as she followed him over to the bar. 'Another Sauvignon?'

'I'm driving, so a Coke will be fine.'

He sneered at that idea. 'A mocktail then,' he insisted.

She didn't really want one, but shrugged. If it kept him happy. 'Okay.'

'What would you like?' he asked, handing her a drinks menu.

'How about you decide?' she smiled.

Seeming pleased with that idea, he grabbed a glass and started mixing and shaking, probably delighted to have something to do on such a quiet night.

As Harper watched him, her thoughts again turned to Brad, wondering why he had stood her up. He must have got cold feet. Maybe the more he thought about her behaviour last night, it made him realise he didn't want to meet up with her after all.

He could have told her though, instead of letting her turn out in the rain.

'Here you go.' The bartender set the glass in front of her with a wide grin.

Harper studied the orangey coloured drink with the frothy top. 'What is it?'

'A passionfruit martini – without the martini, of course.'

She took a sip, surprised by how good it was. And realistic too. 'There's definitely no alcohol in this?'

'Not one drop, I promise.'

'Thank you.'

She was about to take the drink back to her table when the bell sounded and the door opened. Both Harper and the bartender looked over to see who it was, and she knew Isaac was wondering the same as her. Had her date decided to finally show up? Fresh disappointment burned seeing it wasn't Brad. Instead, three men, caught up in animated conversation, strode into the bar.

It took a second to realise that she recognised one of them, as blue eyes locked on hers, and realising it was Luke, the cute doctor, she wanted the ground to swallow her up.

After embarrassing the hell out of herself in front of him on Saturday, she had hoped to never see him again. But no, here he was to add fresh humiliation to her evening.

'Harper. I didn't expect to run into you.'

No, Luke, I really didn't expect to run into you, either.

Seriously, what were the chances? They both lived in Salhouse and the Black Dog Inn wasn't even close to the village.

She managed a smile for him, as her cheeks continued to burn. 'Hi.'

As the bartender went to serve Luke's friends, he moved closer.

'Are you okay?' His eyes were narrowed as he studied her with both concern and wariness, as if he was afraid she was going to burst into tears again. 'I was worried about you the other day. I'm sorry I upset you.'

'You didn't.' Harper's tone was a little blunt, but she desperately wanted out of this situation and she still had the full glass of drink the bartender had given her. She couldn't just leave. It would be rude. 'You caught me at a bad time, that's all. It was nothing to do with you.'

'Okay.' He didn't seem convinced, even as he accepted her vague explanation.

'Are you having the usual, Luke?' one of his friends asked.

'Please.'

Harper hoped he might rejoin them so she could go back to her table, but instead he glanced around the bar, eyes meeting hers again.

'Are you here with anyone?' He was being polite. It was obvious she wasn't with the loved-up couple, and other than them, the bar was empty.

'No. I was supposed to be meeting a friend, but he... they can't make it.'

'I gave her a free mocktail to make up for him standing her up,' the bartender added, far too cheerfully, and Harper went back to wanting to throttle him.

'Right.' Luke fell silent for a moment. 'Well, you can join us.'

Harper's flush intensified. 'Honestly, I'm fine.'

'I can see that.' He smiled, and when she met his eyes again, she understood he wasn't offering out of pity. That helped her ego a little. 'Will and Mike, meet Harper,' he said, introducing her to the two men he was with. 'She's a friend of mine.'

A friend. He thought of her that way? They had only ever met twice and both times had been chance encounters when she wasn't looking her best.

'Would you like another drink?' Mike offered, she assumed out of politeness, as she still had a full glass. He looked to be the oldest of the three, his brown eyes crinkling at the corners and dimples cutting into his dark skin as he smiled at her. Harper instantly warmed to him.

'I'm good, but thank you.'

Deciding to put her last awkward encounter with Luke behind her, she accepted his invitation, and as the evening progressed, she was glad she had.

At first, she had worried she would be intruding, but Mike, and Will, who reminded her of Ed Sheeran with his pale complexion, pointed chin and mess of ginger hair, both made her feel welcome. They, like Luke, worked in the emergency department at the Norfolk and Norwich University Hospital, and they briefly touched on work, commenting on the rarity of being able to grab a drink together, due to their erratic shift patterns.

'This was a good choice,' Will said to Luke, confirming that Luke had been the one who had suggested the venue. 'I like it here.'

Harper didn't mention her phobia of hospitals, finding it ironic she was socialising with three doctors, and she inwardly cringed when Mike shifted the subject, asking what she did for a living, and she had to tell them she was an author.

It was stupid really, getting embarrassed about her profession. Being published had always been a huge dream for her and she had worked hard to make it a reality, receiving countless knockbacks before finally finding success. She loved that she got to write for a living and she was proud of her books, but revealing her occupation usually provoked one of two reactions. Either a moment of awe, acting like she was some kind of celebrity, or one of disbelief, as if she was making it up.

The social side of book writing had always been a struggle for her. Her books were the stars, not her, and she always worried that her readers would be disappointed when they met the person who had written them, which was why she kept publicity events to a minimum.

'You never mentioned she was an author,' Will chided Luke now, as he and Mike both viewed her with a new fascination.

'I didn't know she was,' Luke pointed out. 'We've only met twice.'

He didn't seem quite as starstruck as his friends, though he showed an interest, asking about her books, and Harper squirmed under the spotlight. They saved lives for a living, while she made up love stories. If they were going to compare who had the worthiest job, she wasn't going to win.

She politely answered their questions, but was relieved when the conversation moved on to other topics. All three of them were laid-back and fun to hang out with, and for a while she actually forgot about Brad and the fact she had been stood up.

By the time they got up to go, they were the last ones left in the pub and the bartender seemed pleased that he was finally able to close.

'Are you glad you stayed?' Luke asked, as he lingered by Harper's Volkswagen at the end of the night. The rain had finally stopped, though there was a lot of water on the road and puddles everywhere, and the temperature had dipped. The first really cold night of the year.

They had already said goodnight to Mike and Will, who lived in neighbouring villages to the west of the city and were travelling home together in Mike's car.

'I am,' she told him. 'Thank you for letting me join you.'

'No worries. At least it wasn't a wasted night.' He shifted his feet, hands thrust in his pockets to ward off the cold as he studied her, seeming to consider his next words. 'He's a dick, you know that, right? The guy who stood you up. It's his loss.'

Harper nodded. 'His loss,' she agreed lightly, unsure if Luke was just trying to be a friend or if there was something more going on here. She had caught him watching her a few times during the evening. Did he like her?

She considered him now, deciding how she felt about that.

He was very different to Charlie. Longer and leaner, and dark-haired, where Charlie had been fair. There was no denying he was attractive though, and he had killer blue eyes. An attractive mouth too. Wide and expressive, with lips that weren't too thin or too wide.

'Are you working tomorrow?' she asked, playing for time. She wasn't ready for him to leave yet.

He nodded, pulling his hand from his pocket to look at the

watch on his wrist. 'Yeah, in fact, I should get going.' One side of his mouth tugged higher than the other as he smiled at her, and a tiny spark of lust ignited in her belly.

Pull yourself together, Harper.

She tried to quash the sudden attraction, frustrated at where it had come from. 'Me too,' she agreed, opening her car door. 'Well, thanks again. I guess I might see you around.'

'Maybe,' he said, his smile widening to a grin. 'Goodnight, Harper.'

He left her then, crossing the car park to his Audi.

Trying to ignore the twinge of disappointment that he was gone, she got inside her car, turning on the engine and the radio for company.

Luke followed her out onto the road, staying behind her all the way back to Salhouse, and Harper found that she kept looking in the rearview mirror, waiting for him to turn off. It surprised her when he didn't.

She lived at the furthest point of the village, down a quiet country lane. If he was in the main village of Salhouse, as he had told her, then he would have had to turn off before now.

An uneasy thought crept in. Was he following her to find out where she lived?

On the one hand, it would be cute if he fancied her, but he had passed up on the chance to ask for her number.

No, she berated herself. There was nothing cute about it. It was creepy.

She was toying with driving past the turn-off into the lane that led to her house, but then she glanced in the rearview mirror again and saw his indicator flashing. There was one more turn-off and she watched as he took it, her shoulders sagging with relief.

What the hell was wrong with her? One minute she was enjoying his company, the next she thought he was stalking her.

Feeling a little foolish, she drove the rest of the way home, pulling into her driveway. Instead of killing the lights and engine, she stared at the house; blanketed in darkness apart from the welcoming porch light. For the last two years, this had been her hiding place from the world. Now she realised she was nervous about going inside.

Even though she had put the incidents from last night down to her overactive imagination, there had been the disturbances on Friday night, which she had yet to find an explanation for.

Rather than messaging Megan from the car, she decided to wait until she was inside, snatching her fob from the ignition and hurrying to the front porch, her key ready to jam in the lock. It took seconds, but felt like longer, and all she could think was what if someone was hiding in the bushes and suddenly grabbed her from behind?

They didn't and moments later she was in the house and locking the darkness outside, grateful she had left the hall light on.

Bailey came running to see her and she made a fuss of him, standing guard by the door and watching him with the torch as she let him out to pee. She then went room to room, checking everywhere was empty and that all of the doors and windows were locked.

Satisfied it was safe, she made a cup of herbal tea, changed into a pair of PJ bottoms and an old T-shirt, then checked her WhatsApp, frowning when she saw Brad still hadn't been online or seen the message she had sent. Had something happened to him?

Curious, she logged on to the IntoYou app and clicked his profile.

The site didn't allow a time stamp of when users had been online, but she read through their messages again, looking for any kind of clue for what he had changed his mind. He had seemed so keen.

He most likely had social media accounts, but she didn't have his surname and would never find him just by entering Brad. It said on his profile that he was a firefighter and she tried a few Google searches to see if anything came up, to no avail.

The only other information she knew about him wouldn't help. He had a rescue pup called Monty, he was divorced and he liked Muse. There was no way she was going to find him. He hadn't even told her whereabouts in Norwich he lived.

She was about to give up, when an idea occurred to her. She had the picture he had uploaded to IntoYou. Would she find him if she did a reverse image search?

Aware she was behaving like a stalker, but telling herself it was because she was concerned about him and not on a mission to try to prove that he hadn't intentionally stood her up, she saved his photo to her phone and searched the image on Google.

Two matches came up straightaway, for LinkedIn and Facebook, and she clicked on the latter, eyes widening when she saw his name wasn't Brad.

It was someone called Mason Cook. Wondering why the hell he had lied to her, she clicked on the rest of his photos, glad he was lax with his security and she could access pretty much everything. The photos were definitely him, there was no doubting that, and she was toying with messaging him and asking him why he had lied to her, when she spotted his location, her confusion growing.

According to Facebook, he lived in Canada. If that was really true, why the hell was he messaging her in Norwich?

Even as she started scrolling through his profile, the first trickle of unease was creeping up her spine. It was obvious he was Canadian from some of his updates, and he had dozens of friends commenting on his posts.

She had been a little slow on the uptake, but now she was starting to understand. Mason hadn't been messaging her at all. Someone had stolen his photo. She had been catfished.

It all made sense. 'Brad' had wanted to contact her, but she hadn't let him because he had no picture. That would explain why he had used someone else's.

And she had been foolish enough to fall for it, her head swayed by a good-looking man. It hadn't been just that, though. Brad's profile had reeled her in, again written after he had tried to message her.

Was it all bullshit? Had he made everything up to try to appeal to her? The rescue dog, showing the vulnerable side of himself as he dipped his toe into the world of online dating. It was almost a mirror image of her experience.

Who the fuck was he? And why had he lured her to the pub?

To be fair, the venue had been her choice, but why arrange to meet if he had no intention of showing up?

Harper considered the question for a few moments, at first drawing a blank, but then, like dominos, several thoughts hit all at once.

The knocked-over plant pot and decorative cap that had fallen from the patio wall.

Her paranoia last night that someone had been in the house.

What if Brad had wanted her out of the way so he could break in?

That last thought slammed into her, stealing her breath, and she started shaking uncontrollably. The idea was far-fetched and ridiculous, but it also made perfect sense.

He had pushed for the date, all the while knowing it would be impossible for him to show up.

Except there was no sign of a disturbance and nothing had been taken.

She was jumping to conclusions again, assuming the worst. She had been catfished, but it didn't mean there was a sinister agenda. The real Brad was probably some bored teenager or lonely middle-aged man having a bit of fun at her expense.

The vibrating of her phone made her jump and she snatched it up, seeing Megan's name and cursing that she had forgotten to update her.

'Hey,' she tried to keep her tone breezy as she answered. After her friend's reaction last night, there was no way Harper was telling her about Brad's fake profile.

'Is everything okay?' She could hear the frown in Megan's voice. 'You never messaged me. Are you still out?'

'I'm good. I'm fine. And I'm home now. Sorry, it slipped my mind.'

'You had a good time with this Brad then?' Megan asked.

'Not exactly. He stood me up.' Harper forced a laugh. 'It wasn't a wasted evening, though. Remember that cute doctor I told you about? Luke. The one who helped me that day at Gorleston?'

'Yes.'

'He happened to be in the pub with his friends. They invited me to join them.'

'And how did that work out?'

'Okay.' Harper shrugged, even though Megan couldn't see her reaction. 'We had a laugh and they were nice to talk to.'

'This Luke didn't ask for your number then?'

'No, it wasn't like that. They were just being friendly. Anyway, I think I've been rushing this whole dating thing and need to slow down.'

'You've hardly been rushing it,' Megan said sternly. 'And

you're doing so well. You can't give up now. This is a huge step forward.'

Harper understood. Her friend was concerned she might retreat into herself again. She was also right. The dating had helped Harper's confidence, even with the mishaps along the way.

With Brad, or whoever the hell he was, out of the picture, it just left Gavin who she was talking to. In his last message, he had agreed to her suggestion of meeting for a drink, but Harper hadn't got back to him. After ending her call with Megan, she replied to him now, suggesting a drink at the Black Dog whenever he was free. Hopefully, he hadn't become bored waiting for her to reply and met someone else.

Setting her phone down, she got ready for bed.

It was as she was trying to find a comfortable position, willing herself to fall asleep, that her mind drifted back to Brad and the photo he had stolen from Mason Cook.

She knew people catfished, often just for kicks, and that he was probably a stranger, but how had he known about the Muse gig at Shepherd's Bush? Had it really been a coincidence?

She thought back to Lee, Justin and Adrian. She and Lee had bantered online about their favourite movies, but although they had touched on music, she was certain they hadn't talked about the concerts they had been to. Same with Justin.

The date with Adrian had been over a month ago and at the time Harper had been so nervous, she struggled to remember what they had spoken about. But now she really thought about it, she was sure the topic of music had come up. He had asked her who her favourite band was and she had told him about the gig. She was certain of it.

After learning he had a wife and then the threatening message he had sent her, she had tried to push him from her mind, anxious not to bump into him. She had heard nothing since, eventually putting the message down to a knee-jerk reaction, but now she recalled his menacing words: *Watch your back. This isn't over.*

Had she misjudged Adrian? Was he behind the Brad profile? Had he set it up with the intention of getting her back?

It was a lot of trouble to go to just to lure someone to a pub.

And last night after her date with Lee, had her instincts been right? Had someone been in her house? The jury was still out on that one, but it couldn't be Adrian anyway. He didn't have her address.

He did know her date pub, though, and could have possibly followed her. And if he had done that, then what else did he have planned?

16

There are a lot of benefits to taking in a housemate, but right now the negatives are outweighing the pluses.

I honestly don't know why Samantha is here. I don't even like her that much. She is sulky and mouthy, and I just can't be bothered with her. As a result, I haven't shown her any of my usual hospitality.

She will have to go before Harper moves in, I know that. I only have space for one housemate at a time. Besides, Harper is too important. I can't wait to spend time alone with her. She is special and everything has to be just right. It's what she deserves.

At least I've made a breakthrough and she is now talking to me. I just need to build on our growing friendship and gain her trust. And sooner, rather than later. It's starting to bother me that she is talking to other men, that she is going on dates. She is mine and I don't want them tainting her.

My fake Brad profile has worked well for me and revealed truths about Harper that I know she would rather keep hidden. Last night, alcohol lowered her inhibitions, revealing she is not quite the prude she likes the world to believe she is. She is perfect and I can't wait to have fun with her.

Mason Cook's picture certainly served its purpose. I don't know him at all. When I steal photos, I play Six Degrees of Kevin Bacon, clicking through the profiles of friends of friends of friends until I find one that suits my needs and has lax security.

Social media is a goldmine and it's full of idiots willing to share every aspect of their life online. They tell me where they are and who they are with, let me know when their homes are empty, and, of course, they present me with a wealth of opportunities.

Harper has an online presence. She has to for her job, I guess, though she never shares anything personal. I am now in her book group under another one of my fake profiles. The friendly reader who is a huge fan of her work and has bought all of her books. There is no way she would ever figure out it is me, and it's another way for me to stay close to her.

It's a shame I couldn't turn up as Brad for our date, but if I had, it would have given the game away. He has been quiet for too long and it's time I bring him back into play. He needs to apologise to Harper for tonight, and seek her forgiveness. I have his story all planned. A car accident on the way to meet her and how he was taken unconscious to hospital.

That will tug on her heartstrings given how her husband died and she will give him another chance. I will use the opportunity to break into her house again with the key I secured last time. There were three spares hanging on a hook in the utility room and I doubt she will have noticed one is missing. Still, I have had a copy made and intend to return the original, just to be on the safe side. I also want to place a couple more cameras. Watching her in the house is becoming addictive and it's now one of my favourite pastimes.

I log on to WhatsApp on the phone I have been using for Brad, frowning when I open my conversation with Harper and see she has removed her profile picture.

It takes a moment for me to click, the apology I send her not delivering to her phone. I look to see when she was last online and note it's no longer showing.

That's when realisation dawns.

She has blocked me.

Quickly, I log on to the IntoYou app. My message trail with her is still there, but when I try to click on her profile, it won't let me.

Damn it, Harper.

I honestly believed she would give Brad a second chance, especially when she found out why he couldn't meet her. In fact, I was counting on it.

Now I have to start over, and stupid as it may sound, it's killing me that I can't access her profile. I know I still have the cameras and the tracker, but the profile was a way to communicate with her.

Who else is she talking to? Or what if it's no longer there? Maybe she's deleted it.

Frustration builds and I throw the phone across the room. As it smashes against the wall, Samantha flinches. She meets my gaze and instead of her usual sullen, angry expression, I see fear in her blue eyes.

A fizz of excitement heats my veins. So far she has been angry, demanding and disgusted, but this is the first time she has seemed scared of me.

Maybe she will serve a purpose after all. A distraction to help me clear my head. I need that. When I am thinking straight, I can figure out a way to get Harper back.

I get up from my chair and approach Samantha, delighted when she retreats, watching me warily.

'What are you doing?' She sounds worried.

'I think it's time we get to know each other a little bit better,' I tell her, raising my eyebrows suggestively, and I hold out a hand to her. 'Come here.'

I offer her a non-threatening smile, and let the lie of my next words roll off my tongue.

'I'm not going to hurt you.'

17

Harper spent much of the following morning wondering if she should contact the police, scared in case Adrian was carrying out a vendetta against her, but her lack of evidence stopped her. She was still undecided if anyone had been inside her house, though her underwear still hadn't shown up, but they were hardly likely to arrest him for catfishing her.

The fake Brad profile had unnerved her and she had blocked him on the IntoYou app, as well as on her phone, but she had no proof Adrian was behind it.

In the end, she decided she would be wasting their time and hers. She would chalk the Brad encounter down to an unfortunate experience and try to put it behind her.

The electrician showed up later in the afternoon, fixing the back light and putting up her cameras, and by the time darkness fell, Harper was feeling decidedly safer in the house.

Over the following days, she was careful to take precautions when she walked Bailey, careful to go out only in daylight hours and not to venture far from home. She also got into a routine of regularly checking the doors and windows were locked.

The only person she was still in contact with on IntoYou was Gavin, and she was tempted to close her account. She had reverse image searched his photo though, and he was who he claimed to be. He had taken his time coming back to her again, but when he did, he proposed meeting Sunday evening for a drink.

Harper hesitated before accepting, but eventually she agreed.

She would meet Gavin, she decided, and see how things went, then she would make a decision about whether to stay on IntoYou.

To prove to herself she was moving forward, not backwards, she spent the rest of the week focusing on work, adding a decent word count to her manuscript, and spending more time going through Charlie's things, packing up in boxes further items that could go to the charity shop, clearing the garage of his golf clubs and gym equipment, putting it all on Facebook Marketplace. She tried to be ruthless about holding on to any personal mementos. She still had the necklace the charity shop had returned to her, and decided that could go to the pawn shop with Charlie's ring, watch and cufflinks.

Now she only had one room left to do and that was his study, but it was a big job for when she had more time. When she was finished, she wanted all of his things out of the house.

It wasn't that she wanted to erase his existence. Whatever had happened between them, he had still been her husband, but she had their wedding album and her ring, and that was enough. She wanted to move on now. After learning that he had been cheating on her, she deserved a fresh start.

As Sunday approached, she grew nervous about her date with Gavin. He wasn't like the other men she had met and although she had given him her phone number, he hadn't made any attempt to contact her other than on the day of the date with a quick message confirming they were still on for a drink.

Part of her was surprised to get his text. She had been starting to wonder if he wasn't going to show. He seemed so laid-back about the whole thing and also appeared to be a man of few words. What if they didn't have anything to talk about? Harper tried her best to ask questions when she was on dates, but if Gavin gave her monosyllabic answers and didn't ask anything back, the date would become punctuated with awkward silences.

That fear lingered as she got ready for the date, her belly jittery as she left the house. She arrived at the Black Dog a few minutes early, heading straight inside. The pub was familiar to her now and the staff now felt like friends, even if she didn't really know them. She would order a drink and get herself settled and prepared before Gavin arrived.

'Harper?'

A man stepped in front of her as the barmaid offered her a welcome smile, and she double-blinked, for a second thrown by the close proximity, before she pulled his face into focus.

'Gavin,' she replied, recognising his face from IntoYou.

He had arrived early too, which left her a little flustered, catching her off guard as he leant in to peck her on the cheek, and she caught a waft of not unpleasant aftershave. While he ordered them both a drink, she took a moment to try to pull herself together, catching the eye of the male bartender, Isaac, who had made her the mocktail. He was serving another customer, so didn't speak, but he nodded at Gavin with a knowing look and offered her a friendly smile.

They took the drinks to a table at the back of the room and she drew in a steadying breath, opening with a couple of politely mundane questions, as they didn't have much conversation history, asking if Gavin had found the pub okay and whether he'd had a good week, relieved that in person he was chattier than online.

He was quite attractive with close-cropped hair and pale grey-blue eyes, though deep frown lines carving around his mouth and knitted between his eyebrows suggested stress, and he didn't seem to smile much. As he elaborated on his week, mentioning a run-in with his ex-girlfriend, Angie, that he then went on to describe in bitter detail, she realised the split hadn't been amicable and he certainly wasn't over it.

Not a good start.

Despite the sinking feeling in the pit of her stomach, Harper tried her best to guide his attention back to her and their date, offering information about herself when he didn't seem interested enough to ask. She wondered why he was on IntoYou. It was obvious he wasn't ready to move on.

Still, she stuck the date out for two drinks, a little flustered when she offered to get in the second round and he insisted on paying. She couldn't fault his generosity, but it made her uncomfortable. She liked to pay her way and always bought the second drink if there was one, not wanting to be in anyone's debt.

After her first glass of wine, she had opted for a Coke, unlike Gavin, who was drowning his sorrows in a second pint. He had said he was driving and she hoped it wouldn't push him over the limit. The alcohol was already making him melancholy and feeling sorry for himself.

'Do you have a busy week of work ahead?' she asked, trying to keep the conversation going as he fell silent, frowning at his drink.

She had managed, between his bitter moans about Angie, to ascertain that he was a plumber. If he knew what Harper did for a living, it was because he had read her IntoYou profile, though she seriously doubted he had, because he hadn't seemed in the slightest bit interested.

'Yeah, though it's hard to concentrate with everything going on. Did I tell you she still has half of my tools? The bitch took them out of my van and is holding them to ransom.'

'Oh,' Harper said, not wanting to ask why, her heart already sinking as she suspected she was about to find out anyway.

She concentrated on finishing her Coke while he told her, making a point of looking at her watch as he paused for breath.

'I should probably call it a night,' she told him, even though it had only just gone 8 p.m. She stifled a fake yawn. 'I have a busy week too.'

He didn't ask about it, instead scowling and seeming affronted. 'I was going to get in another round,' he said, sounding genuinely put out that she was considering leaving.

'I really should get home.' Harper offered him a pleasant smile, not wanting to end the evening on a sour note. 'It was nice meeting you,' she lied.

'So that's it?' Gavin demanded, his gaze darkening. 'You take advantage of my hospitality, get your free drinks, and then bugger off.'

Apprehension knotted in Harper's gut. She hated any kind of confrontation.

'I offered to buy the second round,' she reminded him. 'You insisted.'

'Because I figured we were going to make a night of it. Maybe head back to your place.' His voice had risen, his tone angry, drawing the attention of other drinkers.

Mortified, she knew she needed to draw a line under this now. 'I'm sorry you thought that. I don't go home with anyone on a first date,' she told him firmly, struggling to keep hold of her temper.

'So, you're a prick-tease then?'

Seriously? Where the hell did this guy get off?

'I'm leaving now. Goodnight.' Harper grabbed her bag and her jacket, not even stopping to put it on, aware she was shaking with anger.

A hand on her arm stopped her route to the door.

She smelt Gavin's beer breath before she turned to look at him, and she tried to sound authoritative as she told him, 'Let go of me.'

His eyes narrowed in response, but he made no attempt to do as she had asked, instead staring at her, and she didn't like the mean expression he wore.

'Is everything okay here?'

She realised that Isaac had joined them.

He asked the question to Harper, his attention on her briefly before he eyeballed Gavin.

'Yes, thank you. I was just leaving,' she told him, grateful he had intervened. She tried to pull her arm free, not liking that Gavin held on.

'Sir, I think the lady would like you to let her go.'

Gavin stared back at Isaac and Harper willed him to listen, really hoping this wasn't going to turn ugly.

'Isaac, is everything okay?' The female bartender had now joined them.

Issac nodded, before addressing Gavin again. 'Let the lady go.' This time, his tone wasn't so polite.

Gavin hesitated, but it seemed to finally dawn on him that he had an audience. A couple of men at another table appeared ready to step in.

'Fucking hoity bitch,' he muttered under his breath before releasing his grip. He kicked at the table where they had been sitting, his almost empty pint glass sliding off the edge and smashing to the floor.

One of the watching men was now on his feet, fists clenched.

'I think it's perhaps best if you leave,' the female bartender suggested, her tone firm.

'Don't worry. I'm going.'

Gavin scowled at Harper, shocking her by spitting on the floor in front of her.

Without a word, he left the pub, slamming the door.

Isaac followed after him to check he wasn't coming back, while his colleague checked on Harper.

'Are you okay, love?'

She nodded, relieved that Gavin had gone and vowing to delete the IntoYou app when she got home. She had thought she'd hit rock bottom with Lee and Brad, or whatever his name really was, but tonight was a new low, and she wasn't sure she could stomach any more dates after this one. 'I'm fine. I really appreciate you both stepping in though,' she said as Isaac rejoined them. The confrontation was over, but she couldn't stop herself from shaking. It was probably the adrenaline.

'Do you want to sit down for a moment?' the barmaid offered, noticing. 'I'd be shaken too if I was you.'

'I'm fine,' Harper repeated, forcing a smile, embarrassment now taking over from anger. Luckily, the other drinkers had all turned back to their conversations, but still, this was mortifying and she just wanted to leave. 'I'm going to head home, but thank you.'

'Okay, love. Isaac will walk you to your car. Just in case he's still out there.'

'Thank you.'

She was appreciative of the offer as they stepped outside,

realising that if Gavin was still in the car park, things could have turned nasty. Luckily, there was no sign of him.

'This is me,' she told Isaac with a smile, as she clicked her fob. 'Thank you for helping me. I really appreciate it.'

It had been brave of him, considering Gavin was bigger and probably stronger.

'No problem. Are you sure you're going to be okay?'

'I'll be fine now. Thank you again for everything.'

She watched him walk back inside the pub, before releasing a shaky breath, needing a moment before she started the engine. Plucking her phone from her bag, she sent a quick message to Megan.

> Date's over. Now heading home. Wait till I tell you about this one.

It wasn't until she was halfway home that Harper noticed the car behind her seemed to be following a similar route. There wasn't much other traffic on the roads, so it stood out, and her stomach tightened, even though she told herself she was being stupid.

Gavin wasn't following her. She hadn't seen a car leave the pub after her, though, if she was honest, in those first couple of minutes she hadn't really been paying attention.

He had already left though, so it wouldn't be him. This was simply another driver heading on a similar route.

Still, her apprehension grew as she took the turn into Salhouse village and the headlights followed.

When she indicated to turn into the lane that led to her house, she watched the car closely in the rearview mirror waiting to see if there was a similar amber flash.

When it didn't come, the tension eased out of her shoulders.

It was just after she had arrived home and was getting out of her car that she heard the rumble of an engine and spotted head-lights again, as the vehicle drew to a halt, blocking the entrance to her driveway. She heard the car door open and saw the shadow of a figure step out. Unnerved, she didn't stop to see if it was Gavin. There was no need for anyone to drive down this lane. There were no other properties and it was only really used as a cut-through by dog walkers.

As she reached the front porch, the sound of footsteps crunching on gravel sounded behind her, and she fumbled with her keys, her fingers shaking as she tried to find the right one. She didn't care who it was. She just had to get in the house and to safety. Once inside, she would ascertain if she was in danger and whether she should call the police.

Jamming the key in the lock, she heard Bailey barking, the noise not loud enough to drown out the sound of her thumping heartbeat. She had her fingers on the handle, pushing it down, when an arm suddenly closed around her waist, jerking her backwards against a hard body, her feet briefly lifting off the ground. Harper screamed, the sound piercing the cool night air for only a second or two before a hand clamped over her mouth, muffling the noise.

She didn't need to see him to know it was Gavin, the mingled smell of beer and aftershave making her want to throw up. Understanding just how much trouble she was in, she panicked, completely forgetting what she was supposed to do if attacked. She struggled against him violently, but he didn't release her, instead tightening his grip, his mouth close to her ear.

'Thought I was just going to walk away, did you, bitch?' he demanded, his tone aggressive and temper fuelled. 'You and I have unfinished business.'

As he pulled her towards the house, she understood he was planning on going inside. On the other side of the door, Bailey was going frantic, but that didn't deter Gavin. The spaniel would be no use anyway. His bark might sound ferocious, but he was a softie.

What the hell was Gavin planning to do? He had said unfinished business. Did he still think she owed him for the two drinks? She would gladly pay him back. Give him extra to go away. But she was certain he didn't want her money. He wanted her to owe him.

Fuck. Was he planning to rape her? Because that's what it would be. She would not consent to him. He would have to fight her every step of the way.

Her house was in the middle of nowhere, though. No one would be coming to her rescue. Somehow she had to get away from him and raise the alarm.

He briefly removed his hand from her mouth as he went to open the door, and she started screaming again. It was unlikely anyone was close enough to hear, but she had to try. As the door opened and Bailey came dashing out onto the porch, barking his head off, a memory surfaced. Remembering she was supposed to let herself go floppy, she dropped her weight, sagging in Gavin's grip so he struggled to drag her. From her position lower to the ground, she grabbed hold of his ankles, clinging on for dear life, hoping like hell she was doing this right.

It worked. He eased his grip slightly and Harper wriggled against him, managing to knock him off balance as Bailey danced around them, growling and barking. She managed to wrench herself free, but, unfortunately, he stood between her and the safety of the house.

Her car wasn't an option either, as her keys were still in the front door lock.

With no other choice, Harper ran for the road, unsure where

she was going. All she knew was that she had to either find help or somewhere to hide.

She almost made it onto the lane, but Gavin caught hold of her as she passed his car, wrestling her to the ground and slapping her across the cheek.

'No, please. Stop!' She would beg if she had to. This couldn't happen.

This time, he had hold of her hair, his fingers tangled against the roots, causing her to cry out in pain. As he dragged her back towards the house, the gravel cutting into her knees, Bailey tried to intervene.

Harper could tell from his intermittent growling and whining he didn't understand what was going on, only knowing she was distressed. She willed Gavin not to hurt the dog, but it seemed he was focused on her alone.

Her heart thumped, her breath coming in sharp spurts. The terror of what was coming if she couldn't find a way to stop him clogging her throat.

'Hey!'

The voice that called out sounded both shocked and angry.

It wasn't Gavin, and for a moment Harper wondered if she was hallucinating. But then she saw the flash of light and heard gravel stones kicking up further across the driveway.

'Get the fuck off of her.'

That was when Gavin released his grip, and Harper fell to the ground, for a moment too dazed to realise what was going on. As she lay face down on the driveway, Bailey rushed to her side, whining and licking at her cheek.

In the background, she could hear angry yelling, what sounded like a brief fight, then more crunching of gravel before the sound of a revving engine. By the time she had managed to roll over, someone was standing over her, and for a moment she panicked, certain it was Gavin, but then he spoke, and his voice was familiar.

'Harper. Are you okay?' She recognised the Irish accent. Luke?

No, that wasn't possible. He didn't know where she lived. And, okay, he was in Salhouse too, but what were the chances?

Still, it was his voice talking to her and as he dropped to his knees beside her, she recognised his face. The killer blue eyes were darker in this light, but it was still him.

'Don't move. Are you hurt?'

He reached out to touch her arm, his hand steadying and warm, and it kickstarted her brain, making her realise just how much she was shaking.

'No, I don't think so.' She barely recognised her own voice. 'Is he gone?'

'Yeah, he drove off. I'm sorry. I tried to stop him.'

Harper didn't care about that. She didn't want Gavin here. 'What are you doing here?' she asked. It was a stupid question given what had just happened. She was grateful Luke had shown up, even if the timing was coincidental.

'I was out with Eric and heard screaming.'

Which made sense, she supposed. She dismissed the tiny niggle. He was here and he had scared Gavin away. Right now, that was all she cared about.

'Do you think you can get up?' he offered, holding out a hand to help her.

Harper nodded. Her knees were grazed and stinging from where Gavin had dragged her across the gravel, but other than that, physically she was okay. In shock from what had just happened, but okay.

She let Luke help her into the house, not realising there was a second dog with them until she was sat on the sofa in the lounge. Of course, he said he had been walking Eric.

The terrier's presence was helping to settle Bailey, which was good. Giving him a distraction from what had just happened. Harper needed one of those too, and she tried to focus on Luke's calming voice and his steady stare, determined not to lose it in front of him. Not again.

She noticed his tight jaw and the reddening mark on his cheek.

'Are you okay?' she asked now, trying to ignore that by pinning her attention on him, she didn't need to deal with her own current fragility.

'Yeah, he got a punch in. Caught me off guard. I'm fine though. No bother. I'm more worried about you.'

'He didn't hurt me,' Harper lied, ignoring the sting of her cheek and the fact that her knees were cut open and dripping with blood. The wounds would heal. Right now, it was her psychological scars she was worried would haunt her. She wouldn't give into those though. Not while Luke was here. For now, she had to put on a brave face and try to hold it together.

He dropped onto the sofa beside her and looked at her gravely, pulling out his phone, as Eric chased around the room with Bailey, both still a little agitated, but distracted enough by the company to play.

'I need to call the police,' Luke said.

Reluctant as she was at the thought, not wanting to make a big drama out of what had happened, there was the risk Gavin might come back.

Knowing that, Harper nodded.

PART II

_____

Everyone is a moon and has a dark side which he never
shows to anybody.

— MARK TWAIN

18

TWO WEEKS LATER

The police took the attack on Harper seriously, arresting Gavin, and, after charging him with actual bodily harm, he had been released on bail awaiting trial, with the condition in place that he could not approach her.

Harper learnt that he had a history of violence against his ex-girlfriend, Angie, who had reported him on several occasions, though always backed out when it came to pressing charges. That wouldn't happen this time as the police had camera footage of the attack – thank God she had bought those – and she had already given a statement, agreeing she would testify in court.

Knowing that at some point she was going to have to relive what had happened to her made her sick to her stomach. Luckily, her physical injuries were mostly superficial and had almost healed, but the psychological scars would take longer. Megan had insisted on travelling up the following day, and Harper knew her friend was wracked with guilt for suggesting the dating site.

It wasn't her fault.

She stayed for the Monday night and offered to extend her

visit, but tempting as it was to say yes to the offer, Harper sent her home. She had allowed Megan to put her life on hold to look after her following Charlie's death. Now her friend was married and had her husband and job to get back to. It was time to be strong for herself.

Still, in that first couple of days alone, she struggled to leave the house again and poor Bailey had been deprived of walks, with only the garden for outdoor exercise.

This time, she recognised that she was retreating into herself and, having come so far with her confidence, knew she couldn't give in to her fear, but it had taken effort, and during her first time out she was constantly on high alert and skittish at every little noise.

Was she going to be on edge like this right up to the trial, scared that Gavin might break his bail conditions and attack her again?

She was determined to make him pay for what he had done, for setting her back, and she wanted to make sure he never attacked anyone else. Luke would testify too, and she knew he would be there to support her, just as he had that night of the attack.

It terrified her that if he hadn't shown up when he did, things could have escalated and the consequences would have been much worse. He had been a steady and reassuring presence, staying by her side as the police asked questions and, after they had left, making her a cup of disgustingly sweet tea and persuading her to drink every last drop to help calm down her adrenaline spike. He had sat quietly with her as she'd tried to hold herself together and, perhaps realising she was scared to be alone, insisted on spending the night on her sofa.

With hindsight, maybe she should have said no, but that first night, she had been a shaking mess and could barely think straight. It wasn't until after the police had left that she wondered if she should have said something about Adrian too.

The next morning had been a little awkward, perhaps because she still barely knew Luke and he had witnessed her at her most vulnerable. She had been uncharacteristically shy around him before he left. They had swapped numbers and he had said he would stay in touch, but, truthfully, other than the trial, Harper wasn't sure if she would see him again.

How wrong she had been about that.

The second time she had plucked up courage to leave the house to walk Bailey, they had bumped into him and Eric, and following that encounter it seemed their paths had crossed at regular intervals.

Not that she minded. Walking with Luke gave her confidence, and he was so laid-back and easy to talk to, she forgot to be afraid when she was with him. And Bailey and Eric were always pleased to see each other. Maybe Luke being in her life was fate.

Over the following days, they had settled into something of a routine. Harper's job meant she could be flexible, so they met around Luke's shifts at the hospital, the dogs playing while the two of them talked, getting to know each other better.

It surprised her to find out just how much they had in common. Similar musical tastes, and they liked the same TV shows. Luke preferred his food hot and spicy, as did Harper, and they shared a similar sense of humour. Somewhere along the line, the remaining traces of her anxiety melted away, and she found she looked forward to seeing him.

When he told her one morning that his neighbour would be returning from her cruise in a couple of days, she was crushed, finally realising just how much she had been taking his company for granted. Without Eric to walk, he would have no reason to meet up with her, and she didn't want him to disappear from her life.

She hadn't forgotten that night in the pub, and how, after he had walked her to her car, she had felt that spark of attraction. It was still there; perhaps if she was honest with herself, it always had been, and the more time they spent together, the more acutely she was aware of it.

After the night Gavin had attacked her, she had deleted the IntoYou app. There was no way she was going out on any more internet dates, not after what had happened. How ironic that after trying to meet someone online, she was growing fond of someone she had met in the real world. The problem was, she had no idea how Luke felt, and whether her feelings were reciprocated. He was always pleased to see her and seemed to enjoy hanging out, and sometimes she caught him watching her, a thoughtful look on his face, but he had never made any kind of move to tip their friendship over into something more.

Now, with Eric's owner returning home, she was going to lose him. Somehow she had to find a way to stop that happening. But how?

She could make a move on him, but if he rejected her... No, she wasn't ready for that humiliation.

Halloween was approaching and she knew they both liked horror films. She could propose a movie night. Something casual that didn't scream date.

'Are you working Thursday night?' she asked, the morning they met for his last walk with Eric, aware this was her final chance. She had been building up to asking, annoyed with herself at what a big deal she was making of it. Although she tried to keep her tone casual, she was aware of the tremor of nerves in her question. If he was on shift, then she didn't have a plan B.

'No, only during the day. Why?'

Harper jabbed the toe of her trainer at a stone on the track they were walking along, giving it her full attention, even though she was aware he was looking at her. 'It's Halloween.'

'Yeah, it is. You want to go trick or treating?' She could hear the smile in his voice.

'Haha. No, but I wondered if you fancied a scary movie marathon.'

He was still watching her and she was still refusing to look at him, aware of her face heating, despite the coolness of the morning. How pathetic. She was thirty-seven, not fifteen, and she couldn't even ask a guy out. But then life hadn't quite gone according to plan. She had anticipated being settled into her marriage with kids by this point, not left a widow by her cheating husband. Having to start again was hard.

'Are you going to make popcorn?'

She forced herself to meet his eyes. Cool pools of blue that were steady as they held her gaze, but one side of his mouth pulled up in a teasing smile.

'Do you want popcorn?'

'I'd rather have pizza and wine.'

Harper's heart did a little skip. Was that a yes? 'I can order pizza, or cook something if you prefer.'

'Pizza's fine. I'll bring the wine. And we get to choose the movies together. Deal?'

She smiled back. 'It's a deal.'

Knowing he had agreed had her walking on air for the rest of the day, nothing able to knock her happy mood, but as Thursday approached, fresh nerves kicked in. They hadn't defined what this was. What if he did just want friendship? He had never mentioned anything about having a girlfriend – or boyfriend, for that matter – but that didn't mean there wasn't one.

She remembered Adrian, who had conveniently removed his wedding ring.

No. Luke was not like Adrian. And as the pair of them were friends, he had no reason to hide anything from Harper.

When Halloween arrived, she fussed about, too distracted to write, so instead gave everywhere a tidy before overanalysing what to wear. She was tempted to ask Megan for her advice, wanting as much as anything just to talk to her friend and tell her about her growing friendship with Luke, but she was scared she might jinx it. If tonight went well, she would update her.

In the end, she kept things casual and comfortable. A pretty, long-sleeved cotton dress that skimmed her knees, and a pair of trainers.

They had agreed on 7.30 p.m., allowing time for Luke to grab a shower and change, and at quarter past, her belly churning with butterflies, Harper ordered the pizza. She had checked with him what he liked and had gone for one with plenty of chillies.

Five minutes before he was due to arrive, she received a message from him.

> Sorry, I'm still at work. We've had a nasty RTA come in. I'll keep you updated.

Her heart sank, but she reminded herself it wasn't Luke's fault. If he was helping the victims of a car crash, it was important he stayed. Still, she wished he was here and hated that she felt guilty for being disappointed. He was doing a job helping the public and dealing with life-or-death situations. When Charlie's accident had happened, Harper had wanted him to receive the best care.

Of course, that had been before she learnt that Alicia had been in the car with him.

Would that have changed the way she had felt?

Honestly, no. At the time, she had been in shock and unable to process everything. He was still her husband and he had been badly injured. The betrayal didn't hit her until after the first wave of grief, when she had been told there was no more they could do for him.

Thinking of Charlie now, she knew she had to get back to sorting out the rest of his things. Since Gavin had attacked her, her plans had been put on hold. She simply couldn't focus her energy on clearing out the study or decorating the master bedroom, not while she was trying to recover.

It had taken all of her effort to keep up a steady word count on her book, knowing she needed to hit a solid five thousand a day if she was going to meet her deadline. Her agent, Adam, had been in touch to ask how things were going and she had promised him she was on track.

As soon as the book was handed in, she would get back to the other tasks.

A smashing sound, like something breaking outside, pulled her from her thoughts and she glanced at the front door. Moments later the bell rang, distracting her, and the brief hope that it was Luke after all, even though that would be impossible, faded, as she remembered the pizza.

The notification that it was on its way had come through moments before Luke's WhatsApp message.

That was quick.

Ignoring Bailey's barking, she went to the front door, throwing it open, surprised to find the porch empty. Half expecting that the delivery driver had left the food and run, she stepped outside, glancing around for the pizza box. There was nothing there, though, and thinking about it, there had only been maybe fifteen seconds between the bell ringing and the door opening. That wasn't enough time for anyone to get back in their car and leave without Harper seeing them.

So, it wasn't the pizza, but it was Halloween. Maybe trick or treaters?

Except the house was too far out of the main village. Its isolated location had never attracted kids before. And again, if tonight was the exception, why weren't they stood on the doorstep waiting for treats?

Unsettled, she went back inside and locked the door, as Bailey paced the hallway agitatedly.

'Come on, boy,' Harper told him, going into the kitchen for his dog treats.

Instead of following, he let out a low growl at the closed door. One that had the little hairs on the back of her neck standing on end.

'Bailey!' She had barely spoken his name when the doorbell rang again, and she jumped, the packet of treats slipping from her fingers.

Bailey didn't seem to notice, too busy focusing on the door, growling again and his hackles raised. Harper's shoulders tensed as she froze, rooted to the spot. She was aware of the tension thrumming through her, as her stomach twisted itself in knots.

Who was outside and why were they ringing her doorbell again?

She didn't want to answer, but a second and then a third impatient ring, each one making her jump, told her that whoever was out there was unlikely to give up.

This time, she slid the safety chain across the latch with trembling fingers, before cautiously opening the door. As before, no one was there.

Her heart thumped hard. 'Hello?'

She waited for a moment, but no response came. In the dark

chill of the night, a spider weaved its web between the posts of the porch, the delicate silver strands illuminated by the overhead light. Beyond, the driveway was full of shadows and silence.

Well, apart from Bailey, who had pushed past her legs, his nose pressed up against the gap in the door, still growling, and desperate to get outside, which did nothing to help her nerves.

Pulling him away, she shut the door again, locked it.

This time, she hadn't even left the hallway. The ring of the bell coming almost immediately, suggesting that whoever was taunting her was hiding close to the door.

There were bushes either side of the porch, but there was no way she was going outside to investigate, and remembering how she had been attacked so close to the safety of the house brought back a slew of unwelcome memories.

Was it Gavin outside? If so, he was breaking his bail conditions.

She didn't open the door this time, instead raising her voice. 'This is a private property. I'm going to call the police.'

Again, no response.

Picking up her phone, she wasted no time dialling 999.

When she explained her situation, worried that it was Gavin Brooks, the operator told her to stay inside. A patrol car would be sent over.

For the next few minutes, there was silence. Bailey stopped growling and there were no more disturbances.

Uncorking a bottle of wine, Harper poured a glass. Just a small one. Something to help calm her down while she waited for the police. She had just taken a sip when the doorbell rang again, and her hand shook so badly, she spilt wine on the edge of her rug.

'Shit!'

Pull yourself together.

She was turning into a shuddering wreck.

Assuming it was the police, she put the wine glass down and went to the door.

As she was about to open it, she questioned the timing. Would they really get here quite so quickly?

Hating that all of the tension was back and her belly jittery with nerves again, she called out, 'Who's there?', the tremor evident in her voice. She was knotted so tightly, her sole focus on whoever was standing the other side of the door, that she didn't register until after the words were out that Bailey wasn't growling. He had followed her to the door, barking, but his tail wagging in anticipation, as though he knew there was no threat.

'I have a pizza delivery,' came the reply from the other side of the door.

Pizza? She had forgotten about her food delivery. Still, she was unsure, worried it might be a trick. She was afraid to open the door.

For a few moments, she froze, unsure what to do, then came an impatient voice.

'Do you want your food or not?'

Warily, she unlocked the door, not even opening it as far as the chain would stretch. Recognising the delivery uniform the man on her doorstep was wearing, she almost sobbed with relief.

He didn't look happy that she had kept him waiting.

'I'm sorry,' she apologised as he handed her the box.

As he went to walk away, a thought occurred to her.

'I don't suppose you've seen anyone else hanging around here?' she asked.

He shook his head, telling her, 'Nope,' and seeming eager to leave. She was probably holding him up.

'Okay, thank you. And sorry about before.'

As he walked back to his car, Harper quickly glanced around

the porch for any sign someone else had been there. Seeing nothing out of the ordinary, she shut and locked the door. Whoever it was had probably left when she'd told them she was calling the police.

The waft of pizza filled her nostrils as she carried the box through to the kitchen, and her stomach rumbled. Despite her shredded nerves, it seemed she still had hunger pangs.

She put the food in the oven to keep it warm for now.

As she wrung her hands together, hoping the police wouldn't be too much longer, she suddenly remembered the cameras that were now installed outside.

The one on her porch would show her anyone standing on the doorstep.

Why the hell hadn't she thought to check them before?

Probably because they had only been installed a couple of weeks ago, and she had so few visitors, there was seldom anything to notify her of. The app grabbed a recording if it picked up movement. So why hadn't it gone off this evening?

Wiping her clammy hands against her dress, she picked up her phone and opened the app. The last notification had come at 7.31 p.m. That had been shortly after Luke's message that he was stuck at work. But it hadn't picked up the pizza delivery guy.

Clicking the video, she watched the footage from that time stamp, every muscle tensing. The figure approaching the door was dressed all in black and as he looked at the camera she saw he wore a clown's mask. A gimmicky Halloween one with blue raised eyebrows and thick red smiling lips. Green tufts of hair stuck out either side, under what looked to be a tracksuit hood. If Harper had seen it in a shop, she would have thought it looked tacky, but worn on the face of the man standing on her doorstep, it was scary as hell. Especially when he started waving at the camera and she realised he held what looked like a large stone.

The next moment the screen went black, and she understood he had broken the lens.

An all too familiar fear choked her. This was no trick or treater; he was an adult. She could see that from the footage. He was tall enough to reach the camera above her door, and there were no kids with him.

Was it Gavin dressed up so she didn't recognise him? And was he still outside the house? Although the delivery guy hadn't seen him, it didn't mean he had left.

The doorbell rang again and she almost dropped her phone.

This time, it was the police. Harper was too scared to open the door and the PC directed her to the window, where she pulled back the curtain so she could see his patrol car and warrant card, before letting him in.

He looked young enough to be her son, but he was kind and thorough, taking her concerns seriously and making plenty of notes. He watched the footage of the clown with a frown on his face and asked her to send a copy of the video to his phone, then he looked all around the outside of the property and did a walk through with Harper, checking all of the doors and windows were secure.

'Whoever it was, has gone,' he assured her. 'I very much doubt it was Gavin Brooks. He would have to be very stupid to break his bail conditions. Unfortunately, Halloween brings out all of the pranksters. I imagine it was probably someone random trying to get a kick out of scaring you. I'll check in with Mr Brooks anyway, just to give you peace of mind.'

'Thank you. I appreciate that.'

'Do you have a friend or relative you could perhaps stay with tonight? It might make you feel safer.'

No, she didn't. Unless she checked into a hotel, she was stuck here, and she had no idea if Luke would be able to make it over.

The PC had checked the house, though, and if Gavin had been here, he was now gone. 'I'll be okay,' she assured him. 'I'm expecting a friend.'

He nodded and told Harper to call the emergency number if she had any further problems, and by the time he left, although still a little on edge, she was feeling calmer about things. She was convinced the clown was Gavin. He had tried to scare her, but now the police were going to visit him. It would all be okay.

Alone in the house again, she turned on the radio to ward off the silence. All of the curtains and blinds were drawn and she flooded the downstairs rooms with light.

She was tempted to message Luke and see if he was still coming over, but she didn't want to come across as needy when he was busy with work.

After a while with no further incidents, she took the pizza out of the oven and bit into a slice, topped up her wine glass and decided to put on a movie for distraction.

Not a horror, though. She couldn't handle anything scary, not tonight.

She was sat on the sofa watching one of her go-to films, *Crazy, Stupid, Love*, and at the scene where Ryan Gosling was showing Emma Stone his pick-up move, when her phone rang. As it was a number she didn't recognise, she left it to go to voicemail.

When she saw the notification that she had a new message, she clicked to listen, chastising herself for not answering when she realised it was the PC who was calling with an update. She fully expected him to say that Gavin had been arrested, so his message had her sitting up straight.

'Ms Reed. It's Police Constable Butterfield. I'm calling with an update on Gavin Brooks. I just wanted you to know that I've spoken to him and he wasn't at your house tonight. He's been with friends all evening and there are witnesses who can verify that.'

He continued talking, but Harper didn't hear the words.

She had been so certain it was Gavin trying to scare her. But if it wasn't him, then who the hell had it been?

And what if they were still out there?

19

There is something delicious about the early stages of courtship, as you go from being strangers to intimate with one another. I enjoy finding out what my housemates like, and more importantly what they don't. And I test out a number of different scenarios to see how they respond.

One of my favourite games is to kill with kindness, giving my chosen lady everything, then, either gradually or abruptly, depending on my mood, snatching it away.

Food, clothing, hope, life. These are all things I have power over and they know it.

The confusion, panic and utter desperation of their reactions is what I live for.

Samantha realises this now and has gone from brave and hostile to compliant and terrified, and that has made our shared living arrangement so much more fun. It all adds to the excitement as she never knows what is coming next.

Now I have put the effort into getting to know her better, I am glad she is living with me. I am getting to try some new ideas on her and she has given me a much-needed distraction, stopping me escalating things too quickly with Harper. I am grateful for that.

Harper is a woman who deserves a slow and steady build-up, and when we are finally together, it needs to be perfect. I can't rush anything with her, which is why I know I must force myself to walk away tonight.

Perhaps I am taking chances, but I couldn't pass up on Halloween. It's the only date in the calendar where no one will look twice if you're hiding your face behind a spooky mask, and it's also the perfect night for a good scare.

Thanks to the camera I had hidden in her lounge, I got to feed on her reaction when I kept ringing the doorbell, which didn't disappoint, as I witnessed her horror when she finally watched the footage of me stood on her doorstep waving at the camera. Knowing she has no idea it was me beneath the mask gave me quite an adrenaline kick.

One more little trick to play as I pull out the spray can, and then I really must go home.

I can't wait until we are together, now, and I can finally reveal my true self to her. There is so much I need to tell her, and I am longing to see her reaction. She has no idea of the bond that connects us or why she is so special to me. And I look forward to showing her.

20

Harper couldn't settle after receiving the voicemail from the police, and even though she put the movie back on, she was barely paying attention to what was happening on the screen; her mind was working overtime trying to figure out who the clown could be.

She had called PC Butterfield back, certain he must be wrong about Gavin. What if his friends had been lying? But the officer had assured her that Gavin's alibi was airtight.

He was still convinced Harper had been targeted by a Halloween prankster looking for kicks and that it had been a one-off incident. But what if he was wrong?

A short while later, her phone pinged with a message from Justin, the teacher she had met on her second date. After an initial flurry of texting, he had fallen quiet, and Harper had wondered if he had perhaps met someone. If so, it wasn't a problem. The idea of friendship he had proposed was a nice one, but perhaps it wasn't meant to be.

The message, although just a brief one, asking how she was,

pleased her and at least gave her a distraction. He seemed in a chatty mood and after they had exchanged a few messages, Harper decided to tell him about her unsettling Halloween evening, surprised when her phone started ringing the moment he had read her text.

'Are you okay?' He sounded genuinely worried and, feeling foolish, she tried to shrug it off.

'I'm fine. Whoever it was has gone. The police officer who came out thinks it was a Halloween prank.'

'But you said he smashed your camera.'

'Yes, but you know what some teenagers are like. He was obviously looking for trouble.'

'Maybe.' He fell quiet for a moment. 'I still don't like it. Look, I'm not doing much. Just marking some papers that can wait until the morning. Do you want me to drive over and keep you company for a couple of hours? Salhouse isn't too far away.'

It was really kind of him and Harper hated being here alone, but she couldn't let him give up his evening. Besides, it would be a bit weird if Luke did show up and Justin was here.

Not that she thought Luke would come over this late.

She told Justin she was appreciative of the offer, but assured him she would be okay.

Perhaps it was her imagination, but he sounded a little bit disappointed. Had he wanted to come over?

He was the one who had said he just wanted to be friends. Had he changed his mind or was she overreacting? Her head was all over the place, so she wasn't really sure about anything right now.

After ending the call, she rang Megan, keen to hear another friendly voice, and told her everything that had happened.

Her friend was noticeably worried, but pleased Harper had called the police, and she stayed on the phone for over an hour with her, trying to persuade Harper to get a train down to London the following morning. Megan and Tom had a guestroom and Harper was welcome to stay for as long as she wanted. It was something to consider.

After saying goodnight and promising Megan she would think about it, Harper made the decision she would stay downstairs on the sofa overnight with Bailey. The earlier incident had scared her witless and at least down here she could keep the TV on for company.

Before she could try to get some sleep, she was going to have to let the dog into the garden to pee, though, and she really didn't want to unlock the door. What if the masked man hadn't left and was lingering outside waiting for her?

That thought had just crossed her mind when the doorbell rang again, the sound echoing through the house and making her bolt upright.

As Bailey danced around her barking, Harper froze, too afraid to move. Was the clown man back? She couldn't even check, because he had broken her camera.

She should call the police again.

The bell rang a second time, this time followed by knocking, and she reached for her phone. She should have done what PC Butterfield had suggested and find somewhere else to stay for the night. Now it was too late.

Another ring of the bell and whatever nerves she had left were in shreds. All she wanted was to go upstairs, crawl under the duvet and make it all go away. But real life didn't work like that. Instead, Bailey continued to bark and Harper's head pounded with tension.

When she saw the letterbox open, she nearly passed out with fright.

'Harper? Are you in there?'

She was so scared, it took a second for her to realise that she recognised the voice.

Luke?

He hadn't messaged to say he was on his way. She had assumed he would have done that as he was leaving the hospital.

Although the tension eased, she was still shaking like a leaf. She tried to steady her breathing, glancing in the hallway mirror to check she didn't look like a nervous wreck.

'Coming,' she told him, attempting to keep her tone light and tremor free.

She hadn't expected him to show up this late. Not that it was a problem. There was still pizza left – albeit cold pizza – and she could really use the company.

Not that she planned to tell him anything about what had happened tonight. She had told Justin, but Luke was different. She didn't want to scare him off with her dramas. If he knew what had happened, he would probably wonder what he was getting himself into. There had already been the nightmare with Gavin. He didn't need to deal with this as well. She still hadn't even told him she was widowed. He knew she had been married and that she was now single, but that was it. They were still getting to know each other and she was picking her moment. She didn't want the shadow of Charlie getting in the way. Or any of the other shit that was going on.

Forcing a smile onto her face, she unlocked the door.

I'm okay. It's all okay.

'Hey,' she managed, not liking how he immediately narrowed his eyes at her.

'Is everything all right?'

'Of course, why wouldn't it be?'

'I rang the bell three times. You had me worried.'

Harper shrugged her shoulders. 'I fell asleep on the sofa,' she lied. 'I wasn't sure you'd be able to make it.'

The smile he gave her, rueful and tugging up one side of his mouth, pulled at her heartstrings. He looked tired. Exhausted even. And it was a reminder that he had been hard at work trying to save lives.

'I'm sorry. It's late. I shouldn't have come. I really wanted to see you, though, and I remembered the wine.' He looked hopeful as he held up the bottle, his lopsided smile rising a little higher, and what was left of her walls slowly crumbled.

'I wanted to see you too,' she admitted, holding the door back so he could step inside.

Bailey was sniffing around him, tail wagging, excited to see him, and looking for Eric.

'Sorry, pal. He's not here,' Luke told him, handing the wine to Harper then dropping down to his knees to make a fuss of him. He glanced up at her. 'Interesting Halloween mural, by the way.'

Harper frowned, and he hooked his thumb back towards the door.

Pushing past him, she looked at the crude red paint, her mouth dropping open.

On the front of her door was a bullseye target. It definitely hadn't been there when PC Butterfield had called round earlier. She was certain it hadn't.

Which meant the clown had either never left or he had come back.

Because it had to be him. The chances of her having two weirdos target her in one night wasn't possible.

'Harper, are you sure you're okay?' Luke was back on his feet and looking at her with concern.

She nodded slowly, trying to process everything, and

deciding that much as she didn't want to confess to what was going on, this needed dealing with once and for all.

Aware this was starting to become a habit, she told him, 'I think we need to call the police.'

21

PC Butterfield wasn't wavering on his theory that Harper had been targeted by Halloween troublemakers, even though he remained patient with her as he sat on the opposite sofa from her and Luke, sipping at the coffee she had made him.

Perhaps he was right, but Harper couldn't shake the feeling that tonight had been personal. Other than Gavin, though, who would want to torment her?

Her mind slid to Adrian, but he didn't have her address.

She mentioned his name to the constable anyway, blushing as she recounted the two previous occasions when she thought she might have had an unwelcome visitor. She had convinced herself she had imagined the night of the missing underwear, and perhaps she had, but her knickers had never shown up, and adding that incident to the night with the knocked over plant pot and patio cap, and then with what had happened this evening, Harper was now reconsidering everything.

It must have all been a bit of an eye-opener for Luke. Though, to his credit, he took everything in his stride.

He already knew she had been registered on the IntoYou

dating site, as he had been with her the night Gavin had attacked her, learning that was how she had met him, but he knew nothing of her other dates. He listened calmly now as she gave PC Butterfield details of them all, including how she had found out that Brad, the man who had stood her up, had turned out to be fake.

At no point did he seem put out that she hadn't told him any of this was going on, and he seemed more concerned that she was okay.

Harper guessed that had a lot to do with his job. She had no idea what he dealt with on a day-to-day basis but suspected there were plenty of surprises along the way.

It was only after learning, in a follow-up question, that she was widowed, that he appeared shocked. She didn't miss his eyes widening, and though he said nothing in the moment, she knew that he had questions.

Ones that he asked as soon as the constable had left.

'Why didn't you tell me?' There was no accusation in his tone. He sounded more surprised than anything.

'You were at work dealing with an emergency. You didn't need to be hearing about my problems.'

'I'm not talking about tonight. Why didn't you tell me your husband is dead?'

Harper bristled a little, tempted to tell him it was none of his business, but that wasn't fair. They were friends; might possibly become more than that. She had let him believe she was divorced, never bothering to correct him, simply because she wasn't ready to have the conversation.

She shrugged, double checking the front door was locked. Luke was here with her, which made her feel safe, and PC Butterfield, who was taking her concerns more seriously now he had the full facts, had promised to look into Adrian. Harper didn't even have Adrian's last name, but she remembered the name of the company he had worked for and knew he lived in Old Catton.

She turned her attention back to Luke and his question about her marital status. 'It's not the easiest subject to broach.'

'I thought you were divorced.'

When she shrugged again but didn't answer, instead going through to the kitchen, he followed.

'How long ago was it?'

Harper unlocked the back door and let Bailey out to pee. Closing it, she turned to face Luke. 'Two years.'

'Can you tell me what happened?'

She was never comfortable talking about it. Apart from that night in the pub with Justin, because he at least understood a little of what she was going through. She had lied to Luke, though. Well, okay, not lied exactly. But she hadn't been entirely honest.

He deserved to know the truth.

'It was a car accident.'

Luke's expression was sympathetic. 'I'm sorry. It must have been a terrible shock happening suddenly like that.'

It had been. The news had completely floored her and she remembered how she had barely been able to breathe at the time.

'What was his name?' Luke asked.

'Charlie. Charlie Bancroft-Reed.'

'Was it local?'

'Yes. Just out past Wroxham.'

Was he wondering if he had been on duty the afternoon of the accident and whether their paths had crossed before? There had only been one vehicle involved – Charlie's perfectly road-worthy car, for some inexplicable reason leaving the road and ending up on its roof. To this day, no one knew exactly what had pre-empted the crash. The tyres had been fine, as had the brakes, and he was a seasoned driver. Alicia had been killed outright, while Charlie was taken to hospital. Soon after, he had succumbed to his injuries.

She remembered the day of the accident as if it had happened yesterday, though most of it had passed in a blur. If Luke had been there, she wouldn't remember.

'You dropped the Bancroft.'

She nodded, not pointing out that she had used the double-barrelled name throughout her marriage, but wanted rid of Charlie's part of it once she learnt about the affair. Luke didn't need to know she had been cheated on. 'Reed's my maiden name and it's what I write under,' she told him by way of explanation. 'It made sense.'

'You don't have any pictures up of him.'

He had noticed that? He had only been in the house a couple of times and never upstairs. The question threw her a little and she took a moment to answer. 'No, it's too painful.'

He had more questions and she answered them patiently, pouring him a glass of wine and topping up her own glass, then taking the pizza box through to the lounge once the dog was back inside. She had long ago lost her appetite, but Luke had been working all day and most of the evening and was going to be hungry.

'So, what about you?' she asked, when she had finally satisfied his curiosity. Before tonight, she had steered clear of asking about his personal life, but he just thoroughly probed hers, so she felt she was justified in asking.

'Am I widowed?' he asked, his tone dry.

'You know what I mean. Have you ever been married? Is there a significant other?'

He gave her a long look. 'Do you think I would be sitting here with you if there was?'

Harper's face heated. He was good at answering questions with more questions, she had noted. Frustrating, and it put the onus straight back onto her.

'I guess it depends what this is,' she challenged, meeting his gaze and raising an eyebrow.

Luke put his wine glass down on the coffee table and turned to face her, dragging one leg up under him on the sofa, the hint of a cheeky smile on his face. 'You don't know? You were the one who invited me over. I assumed you were planning to seduce me.'

His directness had her mouth dropping open in shock, before the smile broke into a grin.

'I'm teasing you, Harper,' he quickly pointed out, perhaps remembering her reaction the last time he had done that, when he had pretended he had stolen Eric. 'This is us getting to know each other. I'm single, you're single. We like each other's company and who knows where it might lead. Does that sound good to you?'

She nodded. 'It sounds good.' Slow and steady and no pressure. She could do this.

He reached across and tugged on the sleeve of her dress. 'You look pretty tonight,' he told her, the compliment full of sincerity, as he let the tips of his fingers trail down her arm and across the back of her hand.

'So do you,' she agreed on a murmur, not meaning to say the words out loud, but earning a good-natured laugh in response.

'Thank you.' The contact was gone, as Luke scrubbed his hands over his face and his fingers through his hair, tipping his head back against the sofa and groaning. 'I don't feel pretty. I'm exhausted. Like I need to sleep for a week.'

'Do you want to go?' Harper tried to hide her disappointment. He must be tired after working such a long shift. 'I understand. We can always do this again another time.'

He sat back up suddenly, surprising her as he caught hold of her hand, squeezing gently. 'No, no. I want to be here. When I said I wanted to see you tonight, I meant it.' He glanced at his watch. 'Unless you want me to go. It's getting late.'

Honestly? After what had happened earlier, Harper was glad of the company. She didn't want him going anywhere. 'No, stay. I don't need to get up early tomorrow.'

'Good. Do you still want to watch a movie?'

'Sure,' she agreed. 'Though I don't think I can do scary. Not now.'

Luke studied her for a moment, then nodded. 'A comedy then.'

That sounded like a good idea and they spent a few minutes deciding what to watch before settling on a recent Jennifer Lawrence release, eating pizza as the film started, then Luke shifting nearer and putting his arm around her, tugging her against him, where she was close enough to feel his heart beating in his chest and breathe in his clean scent. Something citrusy and a little spicy, which told her he had managed to get that shower before heading over.

This was nice and not uncomfortable at all, she realised. He wasn't Charlie and they didn't yet have that intimacy, but it would come in time if things worked out. Right now, she was happy to just enjoy his company.

He only made it halfway through the movie before he crashed and burned, fatigue winning as his head tilted back and he started to snore lightly.

Harper didn't mind, glad he was here, and she finished watching the movie, his arm still wrapped around her. After the credits had rolled, she muted the TV, reluctant for the evening to end. If she woke him, he would probably go home, and she really didn't want him to do that. Instead, she stayed where she was and let her own eyes drop shut.

Without the distraction of the TV or Luke talking to her, it was inevitable that her mind would return to what had happened earlier and she started replaying events in her head.

The camera had been smashed and she didn't feel safe without one. Tomorrow she would sort out a replacement. It was an extra expense she didn't need, but she had to put her safety first.

Gavin was innocent, so now her suspicions had moved to Adrian. He had threatened her and PC Butterfield had taken a screenshot of his message. If Adrian was her tormenter, the police at least had a face and Adrian could be dealt with.

It was the idea that it might be an unknown entity that scared her the most.

If she wasn't sure who was targeting her or what their motive was, how was she supposed to know how to deal with the threat?

No, it had to somehow be connected to the IntoYou site. None of her problems had started until she had joined.

In fact, thinking back, none of her dates had worked out. Adrian had been a cheater, Lee had lied about his age, Brad, or whoever the hell he really was, had catfished her, and Gavin had attacked her after she had turned down his advances.

To be fair, Harper's date with Justin had worked out okay. They might not have been compatible relationship wise, but they had kept in touch as friends. And it had been sweet of him to offer to come over tonight and keep her company.

He had said he wasn't far from Salhouse and she wondered where exactly he lived. She wasn't sure that he had ever told her. In fact, recalling snippets of their conversation in the pub, they

hadn't discussed location at all. With a dreaded jerk of realisation, she remembered they hadn't discussed where she lived. She
had called for a taxi that night, but she had stopped on her way
back from the loo to do so and she didn't think he had heard her
give the company her address.

So how the hell did he know she was in Salhouse?

22

Luke didn't stay asleep for long, his slumber abruptly disturbed when Harper accidentally jabbed him in the ribs.

She had been on edge after realising Justin shouldn't know where she lived, and as her mind went into overdrive, she had managed to convince herself he had been the one terrorising her earlier, even though she had no idea what his motive would be.

Every tiny house noise had been making her flinch, and when a crash came from out front, her elbow had shot out and Luke had woken with a start.

'What the hell?'

'Someone is outside,' she whispered, clutching at his T-shirt, paranoid that if she raised her voice whoever it was might hear her.

'Are you sure?'

No, she wasn't sure. She was skittish and probably not thinking rationally, but there had definitely been a loud noise, and almost as if to back her up, Bailey had moved suddenly towards the door. He wasn't barking or growling, but his ears were back and his tail low, as he whined intermittently.

'Yes. I think so.'

Luke scrubbed a hand over his face, shaking away the remnants of sleep. 'How long was I out for?'

'Most of the movie,' Harper admitted.

'Sorry. You should have woken me.'

'It's okay. You had a long shift.'

Another noise came from outside. It sounded like a shoe crunching against gravel. This time, Luke shot up off the sofa.

'What are you going to do?' Harper asked in panic, her heart beating too fast. 'You can't go outside.'

He gave her a look. 'It's probably just an animal.'

Although he sounded calm, as if he was trying to reassure her, she could tell he was suddenly alert, the energy bouncing off him.

'Wait here, okay?'

She didn't want Luke going outside, and she definitely didn't want to go with him. He could be putting himself, both of them, in danger.

And was Bailey following him as he opened the door?

No, her dog was not to go out there either.

'Stop.'

Neither man nor beast listened to her as she charged after them, Luke catching hold of her hand as she caught him up. 'I said you should stay inside.'

'And I told you the same,' she hissed, annoyed with him, but squeezing his hand for reassurance. The porch light bathed the front of the property in light, showing there was no immediate threat, though it didn't mean someone wasn't lurking in the blackness.

'Bailey!' she yelled, watching the spaniel as he sniffed around, his black coat disguising him as he briefly disappeared into the shadows.

'It's okay. No one's out here, Harper,' Luke reassured her.

She wanted to believe him. Desperate for her home to feel safe again, but she was wound too tightly, her coil about to spring.

'You don't know that,' she told him, frustrated, though she didn't resist as Luke led her back to the house, whistling to the dog, closing and locking the door once all three of them were inside. And Harper could tell from the way he was studying her that he knew how spooked she was.

The clown mask, the target on her door. It was all taking its toll on her and she just wished she could figure out who was tormenting her.

It wasn't Gavin, and the police were checking on Adrian.

Justin knows where you live.

The unwelcome reminder crept into her thoughts again.

No. He had called her from home where he was marking papers, and she had told him about the intruder. He wasn't involved.

Unless he had been lying and he hadn't been at home at all.

She recalled how he had offered to come over, to keep her company. Did he want to feed on her reaction after scaring her silly?

'I need to tell you something,' she blurted now to Luke.

He looked at her, his face carefully blank, gaze sliding to where she was wringing her hands together. 'Okay.'

Although there wasn't anything going on between her and Justin, they had met on a dating site. Technically, nothing had actually happened yet with Luke, and they certainly weren't in a relationship. Still, she felt a little deceitful, knowing that if the situation was reversed, she wouldn't like it.

'My second date from IntoYou, Justin. We're still in touch.'

Harper forced herself to look at Luke. Although he said nothing, waiting for her to continue, she didn't miss the tic in his jaw.

'We're not dating. Nothing like that. We're just friends.'

'Like us.'

Oh God, she was making this sound bad.

'No, nothing like us. I don't fancy him.'

Although Luke continued to watch her, saying nothing, the tiny dimple that appeared at the edge of his mouth, suggested he was fighting a smile.

She had just, in a roundabout way, admitted that she was attracted to him.

Nice one, Harper.

Right now, though, that was the least of her concerns.

'Justin called me tonight and he offered to come over when I freaked out. He knows where I live.' Her voice dropped to a whisper. 'I've never told him my address.'

Luke's eyes narrowed now. 'You think he was the one outside?'

'I don't know. Maybe. Maybe not.' Harper ran agitated fingers through her hair. 'I don't know what to think.' She had looked Justin up on social media and knew he was who he claimed to be, but that didn't automatically make him a good person.

'I can stay here with you tonight,' Luke told her, before quickly adding, 'On the sofa again.'

She opened her mouth to protest, to tell him it wasn't necessary, then closed it again. Tonight's events had scared the crap out of her, and much as she didn't want to be needy, she was relieved he was offering. She wanted him here.

He wouldn't sleep on the sofa, though. This time, she did what she should have done the first time he had stayed, and she offered him the third upstairs bedroom.

She wasn't ready to sleep with him, or even share a bed –

hell, they hadn't even kissed – but she now trusted him enough to let him come upstairs.

After making the bed up for him with fresh sheets and going to her own room, she spent the rest of the night more frustrated than scared.

There were no further disturbances, and as she gradually settled, managing to switch off her thoughts about Justin and Adrian and whether one of them had a vendetta against her, she became very conscious that Luke was sleeping just across the landing.

She had only ever slept with three men, losing her virginity in an awkward encounter with her first boyfriend when she was seventeen. Then there had been Pete, who she had dated for just over a year in her early twenties, followed by a period where she was single, before she had met Charlie. Since his death, she had been celibate.

Until now, the thought of being intimate with another man hadn't interested her, but although the idea was a little scary, this last couple of weeks with Luke had her wondering and wanting. Not that she intended to act on it. At least not yet. He would need to be patient with her.

The following morning was a lot more comfortable than the first time he had stayed over, and she realised as she made him coffee that she liked having him around.

Megan had suggested Harper catch a train to London, but Luke had the day off and he persuaded her to ditch work and spend it with him.

I'm okay, she promised in her WhatsApp message to let Megan know what she had decided. *I really like Luke and I think you will too when you meet him.*

Her friend replied with a thumbs up. *As long as you're safe and happy.*

After ordering a new camera to replace the one on the porch, they took Bailey up to the North Norfolk Coast, parking at Wells-next-the-Sea and walking through the woods to Holkham. It was a cool but dry and bright start to November and as she breathed in the scent of sea air and pine trees, crunching cones underfoot before the ground turned sandy as they approached the dunes, Harper could feel her load lightening.

Bailey loved the time they spent at Holkham, and with the tide out, he charged ahead of Harper and Luke, over the huge expanse of golden beach towards the shoreline in the distance. By the time they started the walk back, he had thoroughly worn himself out.

After stopping for lunch in one of the cafes in Wells, Luke indulged Harper while she explored a few of the craft shops, and she headed back to his car with a painting by a local artist, Xavier Landry, that she planned to hang in the master bedroom, once she had redecorated the room.

The conversation didn't run dry over the hour it took them to drive back to Salhouse, and Harper realised she had barely thought about the events of the previous night, but as the house came into view, tension crept back into her shoulders.

'Do you want to come in?' she asked, as Luke pulled to a halt in the driveway, relieved when he said yes.

'I had a nice time today,' he told her as she put the kettle on to boil, and she could see out of her periphery that he was watching her.

'Me too,' she agreed, meaning it.

He was a breath of fresh air, and the better she got to know him, the more drawn to him she was. It seemed crazy that it had taken so long to get to this point. Had they acted sooner on their spark of attraction, she could have avoided a number of disastrous dates and the seeming repercussions.

He was here now, though, and that mattered she realised, her breathing shallow and heart racing as he stepped closer to her, a dimple in his cheek as his lips curved.

When his mouth touched hers with just the right amount of firmness, she parted her own lips, keen to deepen the kiss. Everything about him felt right and she linked her hands around his neck, holding him close, wanting him to know just how much she liked him.

The little murmur he made in the back of his throat as she mashed against him, her fingers playing with his hair, empowered her. He wanted her and she was aware of the effect she was having on him.

Charlie's death, and his betrayal with one of her closest friends, had knocked her confidence. For the first time in two years, she believed it might be possible to get it back.

After that first kiss, it seemed they couldn't keep their hands off each other, and even as they drank coffee, Luke sat close enough to her on the sofa that Harper could feel the heat of his body, and the tingle of his fingers as he traced circular patterns on her back with his free hand.

'Tell me about him,' he said. Elaborating when she raised her eyebrows, 'Charlie. I want to know what he was like.'

Harper shrugged, unsure where to begin. Was it an unusual thing that he wanted to know about her dead husband? Charlie was gone. Surely Luke should be more interested in finding out new things about her.

But perhaps he was just curious what her type had been. After all, she had loved Charlie enough to marry him, and he had been a significant part of her life.

'What do you want to know?' she asked, keeping her tone light.

Luke moved his hand up her back to gently tug on a strand of her hair. 'How did you meet him?'

That question was easy enough to answer.

'We were at a barbecue thrown by mutual friends.' Harper smiled. 'I actually found him annoying at first. I hadn't dated in a while and I was enjoying being single, just hanging out with my friends. He was determined to talk to me and wouldn't take no for an answer. That was Charlie.' She shrugged. 'He was always very good at getting his own way.'

He was, and she had realised that more and more after he died. He was never controlling as such, but he had been very good at guiding her around to his way of thinking. He wanted to date her, so he had talked her into it, then when he decided they should live together he had just moved his stuff in, ignoring her reservations. And it had been exclusively his idea that they move to Norfolk.

'Did he come from around here?' Luke asked.

'No, we moved up from London. Well, I grew up in Brighton and Charlie in Oxford, but we were both living in London when we met.'

Harper had been a copywriter at the time, still nurturing her dream of becoming an author, while Charlie was already working at the hotel group.

'What about you?' she asked, keen to stop talking about her dead husband and learn more about Luke.

'Am I from Norfolk?'

She heard the teasing in his Irish lilt and nudged him gently in the stomach. 'You know what I mean. What's your story?'

'It's very dull.' He grinned at her, leaning over to peck her on the lips. 'I'd rather talk about you.'

'What part of Ireland are you from?' Harper pushed. He didn't get off that easily. She knew from previous conversations that he had started working at the Norfolk and Norwich University Hospital five years ago, but he had never said anything about his life back home.

'Donegal. A town called Ballyshannon.' He shrugged. 'As I said, nothing exciting.'

'Are your family still there?'

He nodded, but didn't elaborate. 'You know I have another rest day tomorrow, right?' he said instead, changing the subject. 'We can hang out this evening again if you want.'

Trying to shrug off his reluctance to answer her questions, shelving them for another day, she smiled, liking the idea of getting to spend more time with him. 'That would be nice. I probably have enough ingredients in the fridge to throw together a chilli,' she offered, not pointing out that she was a terrible cook. She could just about manage a chilli.

'Or I could take you out,' Luke proposed, surprising her. Adding with a grin, 'On a real date.'

'Really? That would be nice. Where are you thinking of?'

'Leave the planning up to me and I'll surprise you. I want to nip home first and shower, get a change of clothes, but shall I pick you up at just after seven?'

'I can come to you if you like, give you a bit more time. You're just up the road, right?'

'I have time to get back here.'

'But I'd like to see where you live,' Harper said, admitting to her nosiness. She had been curious to the location ever since that night he had followed her back from the pub, racking her brain to think where his house could be. The lane he had turned down was remote and while there were one or two isolated properties, she didn't know of any that had a neighbour. And she knew he had one of those, because he had been looking after her dog.

'Another time. It's nowhere exciting.' He got up from the sofa. 'Be ready for seven, okay?'

Although a little disappointed he was fobbing her off, she nodded, a pleasant fizz of excitement still heating her veins. He was going to take her out on a date. She hadn't been on a proper one in years. This wasn't like meeting for a drink with someone off the internet. It was with someone she already knew and really liked.

Following him to the front door, she gave him a lingering kiss, holding on to Bailey's collar so he didn't follow, and watching as Luke left. Making sure the door was locked, she headed upstairs to the bathroom, turning on the shower, then going into the bedroom to undress and tie her hair back in a knot as the water heated.

As she was about to head back into the bathroom, her mobile phone started ringing, and for a moment she was inclined to ignore it. It could be Luke, though – *please don't let him cancel* – so she paused to answer.

Not Luke, but PC Butterfield and her stomach curdled, knowing it would be about last night.

'Hello?' she asked a little impatiently, needing to know if there were any developments.

She listened as he updated her, conscious she was completely naked, and despite the coolness in the house, sweat was pooling under her armpits.

Adrian wasn't her tormenter. Like Gavin, he had an alibi, his wife able to vouch for his whereabouts.

There was also a further update. On the Sunday when Harper had bumped into him at the beach, Adrian had been attacked. Someone had forced their way into his home and beaten him up. Before leaving, the man had uttered two words to him: Stay away. At the time, despite what had happened with

Harper, Adrian hadn't believed the incidents were connected. He wasn't the most popular man, having been involved in a road rage incident a couple of days prior, plus he had fallen out with one of his neighbours and that had been the direction the police investigation had taken, even though there were strong denials from the accused and no charges were filed.

Now, PC Butterworth was wondering if the attack was linked to Harper.

'I'm afraid I have to ask the question,' he apologised. 'You didn't get anyone to pay Adrian a visit?'

'No,' she quickly protested. 'Of course not. I would never do that.'

Although he said okay and appeared to accept her word, Harper had a nagging feeling that the matter wasn't over, and as she ended the call, heading through to the bathroom, her legs were weak and weight of the accusation forced bile into her throat.

Today had been so nice, spending time with Luke and forgetting about her unwelcome visitor, but now the ugliness was resurfacing.

She thought back to the afternoon at the beach and the encounter with Adrian and his family. Adrian had been the one to threaten her, not the other way around. She didn't even know anyone who would go and beat someone up.

Stay away.

It wasn't possible it was connected. What had happened to Adrian and the recent disturbances at her house were completely separate things.

Weren't they?

23

Growing up as an only child had both its up and its downsides.

I was – and still am – the apple of my mother's eye, and as it was just me, I never had to share, but it also made for a lonely existence. We had moved to Norfolk when I was ten and the large house we lived in was remote, with no other families close by, meaning I was often left to amuse myself.

Born when mum was in her late forties and my father had just turned sixty, I had been an unexpected baby, shaking up their everyday routine. I guess when I look back now, I can see how old-fashioned my parents were in their outlook, but through a child's eyes, their way was normal to me. Dad was the man of the house and Mum waited on him hand and foot, always putting his needs before her own.

He was a strict father and a quiet, serious man, and I learnt from an early age that getting down from the dinner table without permission, questioning him or answering back, and not completing my homework in the set time would be punished. I often felt he tolerated rather than loved me, and I knew he wasn't a fan of children in general, as I was never allowed to have school friends come to visit. My happiest times were when he was locked away in his workshop at the bottom of our sprawling garden. That was when I could relax, and I'm sure Mum did too, though she would never hear a bad word said against him.

'He's a good man,' she told me whenever I sobbed after a beating. 'He only sets the high standards he expects of himself.'

She was right. He had morals, and he was well respected in the local community, friendly with both the vicar and the local councillor, who lived in the nearest village. I often wonder what they would have thought about him, though, if they had known about his dirty little secret.

Everyone has vices and secrets, I understand that now I'm an adult. I have plenty of my own. My pastimes and passions are mine alone to indulge in. But my father? For the first twelve years of my life, I really did believe he was as stuffy and pompous as he tried to make out. Just as I honestly thought he was working on woodwork projects in his shed.

Although I was sometimes sent down there to take him a cup of tea or tell him dinner was ready, I had never been inside. It was his private space, he insisted, somewhere he could get away and clear his head, where he could indulge in his hobbies, and Mum and I were banned from going in there.

It was a humid August afternoon when I got the inkling that something wasn't quite right. Mum had been baking a carrot cake, which was Dad's favourite, and she sent me down to the shed with a large slice for him.

Because of the stuffy weather, the window was ajar, though the curtains were drawn, and I could hear heavy breathing coming from inside, then what I was certain was a scream. Instead of knocking on the door, I stood by the window for a moment, the plate gripped tightly in my hand, and listened.

The screaming came again, followed by moaning, but it was faint, *as though it was coming from a device, the volume turned down. That would make sense as I knew he was alone in the shed.*

Curious, I pressed my face up against the glass, but although there was a faint crack in the curtains, it wasn't enough to see.

What was he doing in there?

I decided the punishment would be worth it to try to find out, and instead of knocking I pushed open the door.

'I've brought—'

The sound of my voice had him looking up abruptly, eyes widening in horror. He was sat at the table, in front of an old laptop, his face sweaty, and although I couldn't see his hand, I was pretty certain it was inside his pants.

As we stared at each other, the screaming came again, this time it sounded agonising, like someone was in pain, and, intrigued, my gaze dropped to the laptop. Was Dad wanking off to horror movies?

The lid of the laptop suddenly snapped shut, bringing my attention back to his face.

'Get out!'

As I flinched, he yelled the words again, his cheeks red with rage.

'But your cake.'

I was playing for time, looking again at the table, spotting a DVD case, but not close enough to see what it said.

'GET THE FUCK OUT!'

He had never sworn at me before and, shocked, the plate slipped out of my hand, smashing on the floor. Before he could react, I turned and ran back to the house.

I thought he might follow, but he didn't. Later, though, hearing his footsteps on the stairs, I knew he was coming up to see me.

The beating I received that night was worse than any other I had experienced, but despite the reminder I was to stay out of his shed, my curiosity was roused. I needed to know what he had been watching.

My opportunity came a couple of days later. Dad was on a fishing trip and Mum had gone to the supermarket. Usually, she insisted I go with her, but the last couple of times she had relented, letting me stay home. After all, I was going to be a teenager in a few weeks.

I knew where my father hid the key – under the loose paving slab at the end of the patio. I had seen him put it there from my bedroom window. As soon as Mum's car left the driveway, I raced down the garden and snatched it up, and as I twisted the key in the lock, entering the forbidden space, my heart somersaulted.

To the back of the room was the woodwork bench, Dad's cordless drill lying on top, and the other various tools he used hung up neatly behind it, but my attention was on the table with the solitary chair, a reminder that the shed was for Dad alone, and the bookcase beside it, where I could see the laptop poking out. On the shelf below were dozens of DVDs, though from the titles, I could see they were all quite boring. Several were about fishing and there were a few classic movies among them. Nothing that sounded like what I had heard.

Dropping to my knees, I rooted through them, in case I had missed one or there were more hidden at the back, bitterly disappointed when my search came up empty.

Perhaps the movie was still in the disc drive. Pulling the laptop from the shelf, I accidentally knocked a couple of the fishing DVDs to the floor, one case opening and the silver disc falling out.

My mouth was dry as I stared at it.

The case said Carp Fishing, but the disc inside didn't match. The title was written in a foreign language and I had no idea what it said, but I suspected it was what I was looking for.

With fumbling fingers, I opened the laptop and switched it on. Sitting down in the chair, I inserted the disc, my eyes widening as the film started playing, showing a basement room and a woman hanging upside down, her wrists bound behind her back. She swung back and forth trying to free herself, muttering words I didn't understand, though I could tell she wasn't happy. As the camera panned in on her, she spat at the lens and I heard a man laughing. Moments later, he grabbed hold of her hair, shocking the life out of me as he forced a plastic bag over her head. She screamed and bucked like a wild animal. The camera close on her face so I could see the plastic moulding to her face as she gasped for air.

I watched in disgust and horror, but mesmerised, unable to tear my eyes from the screen. When the plastic was removed, the woman choked and gulped, her shoulders heaving and her hair and face drenched in sweat. It took a few moments for her to be able to speak, and when she did, she sounded angry, a slew of furious words directed at whoever held the camera.

Was this real or acting? I honestly wasn't sure.

Eager to see what else there was, I opened a second DVD case, and then a third. It was more of the same, though with different faces and positions, and the items of torture varied. Cattle prods and knives, in one a woman was repeatedly dunked in a tub of water, and at some point in each video there were sexual acts. Some looked consensual, which suggested the women being recorded were willing participants, while others were more ambiguous.

My twelve-year-old mind was blown. I simply couldn't equate my straightlaced dad with these videos. Where had he got these films from?

The sound of the shed door opening scared me so much I almost fell off the chair, and looking up, seeing the figure of my father filling the doorway, a look of pure unadulterated rage on his face when he realised what I was watching, I knew I was in deep trouble.

I expected him to drag me up to the house and beat me with his belt, as was his usual style, so he surprised and terrified me when he pulled me off the chair, forcing me face down on his woodwork bench.

'No, please. I'm sorry.' My protests became screams as I heard the sound of the drill, dread coursing through me as I realised he held it in his free hand. What was he going to do to me? 'No, no. Dad. NO.'

For a moment, I was certain he was going to drill into my skull and I was so scared, I lost control of my bladder. As warm piss trickled down my leg, I started to sob. I had seen the videos he liked. I now knew what he was capable of.

My tears seemed to be the thing that finally shook him to his senses, the drill switching off, and after a moment where I lay with my face mashed against the wood, him silent behind me, he caught me off guard, running a tender hand over my hair.

'Go,' he said, his tone emotionless, and as he released his grip, I didn't need to be told twice, racing for the door, my jeans now uncomfortably damp.

I never told my mother what I had found or what had happened in the shed. I also never dared go in there again.

Dad had come home early from his fishing trip with an upset stomach, I had later learned. He didn't say another word about the incident and in the weeks that passed, things gradually returned to normal. Or at least to as normal as they would ever be.

I viewed him through different eyes, though, after that day, and while he disgusted and horrified me, I was fascinated.

I also never forgot about the videos.

24

As December arrived with storms that battered the last of the autumnal leaves from the trees, followed by an unseasonably cold stretch with ice and sleet that seemed like it would never end, Harper settled into her new relationship with Luke.

Because that was what it was now. After he had taken her out to dinner, they had started seeing each other on a frequent basis, Luke staying at hers whenever he wasn't on shift, and he was no longer in the spare room.

Taking things to that next level had been a huge deal to Harper and the first time they had slept together she had been a bag of nerves, but he had been patient and gentle, and she had gradually lost her inhibitions, finding her rhythm and learning to enjoy herself again.

It was a big step forward and helped her to further shake the shadows of her past, and she felt she was finally moving on, even managing to put the events of Halloween behind her.

Despite her initial worries, there had been no further come-back with Adrian, the police seeming to go back to their original theory that the attack had been someone he had upset closer to home.

Her friendship with Justin was no more. Whether he had played a Halloween prank on her or not, it bothered her that he knew where she lived. Luke had suggested she confront him, and had even offered to go with her, but Harper couldn't face the idea of creating a scene, especially when she had no idea if Justin had been responsible. Instead, she took the cowardly approach, telling Justin she was busy when he offered to meet up, and taking ages to reply to his messages. Eventually, he stopped trying to contact her.

And there had been no further disturbances. The broken camera was now replaced, plus a fancy alarm system had been installed, making the house as secure as possible. What had seemed as threatening and frightening at the time had gradually lost its power as the weeks rolled by.

Sometimes, when Luke was on nights, Harper would hear a noise outside and her anxiety levels would creep up, and there had been the odd occasion when she had been out walking Bailey and found herself glancing over her shoulder, sensing someone was behind her, but for the most part she was happier and feeling more capable than she had in years.

And with her manuscript finally delivered to her agent, she was taking those final steps to remove Charlie from her life. The main bedroom had now been redecorated in a calming deep forest green, which worked well against the huge bay window and new white shutters, and she had changed all of the furniture, including the bed. The painting she had bought in Wells hung above it. Now it looked like a different room, and she had reclaimed it as her own.

She kept hold of a few photos and personal knick-knacks, aware that no matter what Charlie had done, he was still a part of her history, but they were now packed away in a drawer, where she didn't have to look at them.

All that was left to tackle was his home office.

The house had enough reception rooms that they had each been able to have a personal space, and as she was the one working from home, Harper had taken the original dining room with its French doors leading into the garden. The kitchen was big enough to include a table, so they didn't need a separate area for eating in, and it gave her a larger space to work in, leaving the smaller purpose-designed study free.

Charlie had been on the road a lot with his job, but he still had items that required storing and it was useful for him to have a desk and computer set up for the odd occasion he was working from home. It was a room that Harper had seldom had reason to enter and she knew he had always liked to keep it private, but she had studiously avoided it following his death, keeping the door shut and trying to forget it was a part of the house. As she opened it early in December, wanting to get the task over and done with before she decorated for Christmas, a waft of cool, stale air expelled from inside.

The last time she had been in here, she remembered she had been a wreck. She had needed important documents, things like his passport and birth certificate, and she recalled how she had broken down while sitting in his office chair, as a wave of shocked grief hit her that he would never walk in this room again.

Two years down the line, she was ready to do what needed to be done, and she had a box and a bin liner with her – one for the things she would keep, the other for everything she planned to get rid of.

It was a painstaking process, taking longer than when she had cleared the bedroom. There were documents to go through and she couldn't risk throwing away anything important that might be needed further down the line.

Anything work related, she slung. Charlie's bosses hadn't asked for any documents in the two years since he had died, and her dealings with the firm regarding his pension was all sorted. His contract of employment, business cards and work assessments all went in the bin liner, along with the jokey desk calendar, the stress ball he had often been squeezing whenever she had poked her head in the room, and various bits of stationery she had no need or want for.

A folder containing documents for the house came next, and although it appeared to be mostly out-of-date utility bills, she went through each piece of paper carefully.

One particular document at the back caught her eye and she blinked in surprise as she read it. It was the deed of transfer to a property in Waxham, which Harper knew was a village on the Norfolk coast. But why did Charlie have it?

And, more importantly, why was his name on it?

At first, Harper wondered if this was something his grandfather had left to him. Though, if so, why had he never mentioned the place to her? But studying it more thoroughly, she could see it was a place he had purchased after his grandfather's death. In fact, not long after they had moved to Norfolk.

Why would he have done that without telling her? They were married.

She could see he hadn't paid much for it. Still, he must have hidden some of the money away that he received from the will, as she would have noticed such a large amount disappearing from their joint bank account.

Either that or there had to be some kind of mistake.

What kind of mistake, though, she couldn't imagine.

She picked up her phone and searched for the address, surprised by the remote cottage that came up on Google Maps.

A nasty thought crept into her head. Had this been a place for him and Alicia? A love nest.

Even the idea of it stung hard, making her catch her breath, and for now she set the document to one side, knowing it would require further investigation. She needed to tidy up this mess she had created first.

The next shock came with Charlie's work diaries. Cumbersome leatherbound A4 books that were all stacked up in the larger bottom drawer. As she went to sling them, something fell out of one, and snatching the small square piece of paper up from the floor, her stomach curdled.

Not a piece of paper. It was a polaroid photo, she realised as she flipped it over, of a woman on her knees in the centre of a bed. She wore a sexy baby doll nightie, her cleavage on show, and her cherry red lips pouting seductively. Not Alicia, and Harper had no idea who she was, but it suggested the girl was intimate with whoever was behind the camera. And as the picture had been found in Charlie's diary, the photographer had to be him.

So, Alicia hadn't been a one-off? There had been other women?

She was healing. She was supposed to be getting past this. Instead, Harper felt like someone, something, had just reached down her throat and ripped her heart out.

How could Charlie have done this to her? Did their marriage vows mean nothing to him? Had there ever been a point when she alone was enough for him?

The polaroid camera she found tucked further back in the drawer suggested her suspicions were right.

Wishing she hadn't seen the photo, but knowing that now

she had it was going to eat away at her unless she tried to find out who the woman was, Harper pulled the diaries back out of the bin liner.

There was a secret cottage and a photo of a scantily clad woman. Exactly what other secrets had her husband hidden from her?

Thoughts of emptying the room were put on hold as she pored over the pages, looking for some kind of clue. At first, it appeared there was nothing. The diaries were all filled with work-related commitments. They detailed his schedule and where he was supposed to be; the names of the hotels he regularly visited were written in his almost too neat handwriting. There were no unusual appointments or hints of anything out of the ordinary.

It was the date of their last wedding anniversary that eventually proved she might be on to something. It had been three months before Charlie had been killed and Harper remembered it clearly. The fight they'd had in the lead-up was still vivid in her mind.

She had booked a fancy restaurant as a surprise, knowing he always kept their anniversary free to spend with her, but when she had told him a few days before, he had told her he wouldn't be able to make it, as he had an important meeting in Nottingham. One that couldn't be changed.

At the time, Harper had been furious. It seemed he was spending more and more time travelling and putting his job before their marriage. Usually, she was understanding, but this was their anniversary.

Charlie had insisted on going anyway, sacrificing their relationship for work. After calling her selfish and ungrateful, he had promised to make it up to her – though, that had never happened.

She stared now at the date in the diary. Why, when he recorded everything else, was it blank? There was no mention of the important Nottingham visit. And given all that had come to light following his death, she couldn't help but question if he had made it up. Had he spent their anniversary on some kind of romantic date with Alicia?

Or had it been with the woman in the picture?

Flicking back over the pages, she looked for clues, wishing Charlie's firm hadn't taken back his company laptop after he had died.

There was nothing obvious, but the Y she stumbled across had her pausing. It had been written eight days before their anniversary. Just that one letter, capitalised, right at the top of the page.

What the hell was that supposed to mean?

Was there anything else in the diary to give a clue?

She searched back, this time keeping a closer eye, realising that there were more random letters she had missed the first time. Making a note each time she came across one.

After she had exhausted the diaries, she went back over her own calendar, and the text and WhatsApp messages she had exchanged with Charlie, comparing dates and plotting a timeline of what they had been doing at the time.

It wasn't productive, she knew that, but she was compelled. And she also knew she wouldn't rest easy until she found out the truth.

Gradually, a pattern emerged. She was able to piece together other times when she had believed he was away on work trips, but there was nothing scheduled in the diary.

So where had he been?

At this secret cottage fucking other women?

By the time Luke arrived later that evening, Harper was an

inconsolable mess, still sat on the office floor surrounded by paperwork.

The week before, she had given him a key. Yes, perhaps it was too early, but it felt right. They had only been together for six weeks and every expert out there would probably tell Harper she was rushing things, but she no longer cared. Screw the self-help guides and the rulebooks, she had decided to go with her own instinct, ignoring the tiny niggle that there was still so much she didn't know about him.

'Harper?' The study door opened and Bailey, who had managed to fish Charlie's stress ball out of the bin liner and sat there with it in his mouth, got up to greet him, his tail wagging madly.

Luke paused to make a fuss of the dog, but his focus was on Harper and he quickly dropped to the floor beside her.

'What's wrong?'

She couldn't tell him, struggling to even breathe for the first few minutes, the desperate sobs that wracked through her getting worse when he pulled her into his arms and cradled her.

'It's okay, I've got you,' he soothed as her tears soaked the scrubs he hadn't yet changed out of.

She had never told him about Charlie's affair with Alicia. It just hadn't felt relevant to what was happening between them and, truthfully, she was embarrassed. Why would she want to tell the man she was attracted to, who she was starting to develop real feelings for, that she been cheated on? It wasn't good for her self-esteem.

But now things were different. It hadn't just been Alicia. All of the times Charlie had been away with work, when Harper had trusted him, he had been having the time of his life, sticking his dick in anything that moved, it would seem. This was more than she had realised, and given the shock she was in, she couldn't keep it hidden.

'He was cheating on me,' she managed, finally saying the words out loud. Humiliation and despair tearing her apart.

It took time for Luke to get the full story out of her. When Harper had eventually stopped crying, she started to clam up, but he kneaded away, somehow managing the right amount of coaxing and flattery to break through her defences. Making her feel she was enough as she gradually told him about her shock finds.

He was good, and perhaps he had missed his vocation in life, she would wonder later. He should have been a therapist, the way he focused on her, making her feel safe and important as she revealed the secrets Charlie had kept.

'I need to go there,' she told him, after revealing that her husband had bought a cottage he had kept secret from her.

'Of course. Do you fancy some company? It will be easier if you don't have to do it alone.'

Harper managed a watery smile. 'Yes, please.'

It was something she was dreading doing, but given she had inherited everything else from Charlie, she assumed the cottage was her responsibility now too, and she knew she couldn't put off dealing with it.

It was time to find out the real truth about her husband.

25

Luke had sat quietly in the passenger seat of Harper's car; a calm and steadying presence, stopping her from freaking out as they neared Waxham, while Bailey rode in the back, his nose to the open crack of the window.

As they passed through the village of Sea Palling, Harper's stomach tightened with fresh nerves, knowing they were almost there, her knuckles whitening as she gripped on the steering wheel.

Luke had offered to drive, but she had needed this. The car was the only thing she felt in control of right now, and as the houses became few and far between, flat open fields now on either side of the coast road, the sea visible in the distance over the ones to her left, her heart threatened to thump out of her chest.

'Are you okay?' he asked, as the satnav instructed them to take a turn onto a narrow dirt track lane before advising they had reached their destination.

No, she wanted to scream, seeing the cottage come into sight.

She would never be okay about any of this, but she was also realising that it wasn't productive to say so.

Last night, she had cried a river, repeatedly questioning why Charlie would have done this to her. Luke had been patient as he'd listened, but Harper was aware that everyone had their limits. Besides, she had nothing new to add and she couldn't keep repeating herself. She wanted to move on, desperately so, and over the last few weeks, she had been happy for the first time in a long while. She somehow needed to find a way to deal with what felt like a whole new level of betrayal, while holding on to what was now important to her.

Her stomach turned over as she pulled the car to a halt in the driveway of the cottage, and her legs were like lead as she climbed out of the warm car, the bite of chilly winter sea air almost taking her breath away. Feeling the warmth of Luke's hand as he took hold of hers helped stabilise her. She could do this, she told herself as they approached the cottage door and she reached in her pocket for the key that she hoped would fit.

It had taken considerable effort to find the key and Harper had spent hours searching every possible place she thought it could be before remembering the one she had found in Charlie's socks, that she had put in her jeans pocket.

Would it unlock the door? She didn't intend to leave without seeing inside the cottage, so would break a window if she had to.

The key missed the lock on her first attempt, her hand trembling and making her fumble, but it slid in the second time she tried, making a satisfying click as the lock released. As the door swung open, Bailey pushed past her legs, eager to explore.

Harper went next, drawing in a steadying breath, trying to ready herself for whatever she was about to find, and Luke followed last, watching her closely as she glanced around the compact living area.

Was this her husband's own personal whore house? It didn't look like he had done much with it. Harper had expected a romantic cosy getaway, but the walls were in desperate need of plastering and there was a dirty threadbare carpet on the floor. And there were only a couple of bits of furniture in the room: a tired-looking fabric sofa and a chipped, cheap-looking coffee table.

In the kitchen, which had seen better days, stood an old-fashioned refrigerator humming away in the corner of the room.

That meant the place had electricity. How had he been paying for that? She had never seen anything to alert her about this place. But then she supposed he had found a way to pull the wool over her eyes about everything else.

Turning on the sink tap, she realised there was running water too.

She opened the fridge door in trepidation, scrunching up her nose, unsure what horrors she might find. The cottage would have been sitting empty since Charlie's last visit, and although the fridge was on, she dreaded to think what state any food would be in. Luckily, the only items it contained was a sealed pack of bottled water and a couple of cans of lager.

A wet nose found its way into her free hand as she closed the door again. Bailey never missed the sound of the fridge opening. Harper stroked his soft head, comforted that they had brought him with them. He was a little bit of canine therapy as she learnt just how great a sham her marriage had been.

'Check this out.'

She turned to see Luke had the wall unit open. It was stacked high with tins. Baked beans, macaroni, ravioli, pineapple rings, pears and mandarins in fruit juice.

Not all for human consumption, she realised. Among the

cheap meals were cans of dog food. There was also a large plastic feeding dish.

But why? Harper and Charlie had never owned a dog together.

'Did your husband really eat this stuff?'

'No. Never.' Charlie had always been particular about what he put into his body. He had been a bit of a health freak, obsessed with keeping himself in shape and avoiding any kind of processed foods. 'We didn't have a dog either.'

As Luke glanced at Bailey, eyebrows raised, she elaborated.

'I only adopted him a few months ago.'

Had someone else been staying here? Squatters, perhaps. The cottage had stood empty for a long time. Though there was no sign of forced entry.

Briskly, she pushed forward into the inner hallway, finding a shower room and a bedroom, opening the door to the latter, disappointment cutting deep when she spotted the double bed. It was made up neatly with a plumped pillow, sheets and a duvet, and there was one side table with a lamp on it.

So, he had slept here.

Who had he been with?

'This isn't the room,' Luke murmured from behind her.

'What?'

She had been so caught up in her own little world that for a moment she had forgotten he was with her.

'This isn't the room in the photo.'

He was referring to the polaroid of the woman kneeling on the bed.

Harper looked at the plain grey duvet cover. Charlie could have changed it.

Except, no, Luke was right. Now she was paying closer attention, the wall behind the woman in the photo had been a stark white. In this bedroom, ugly striped wallpaper was peeling off the walls. Perhaps it should appease her that this place didn't appear to be a love nest, but instead it only unsettled her. Where else had he met these women?

'I need to get rid of everything,' she announced, keeping her tone neutral. She would not break down again. Charlie did not deserve any more of her tears. 'I want all of this stuff gone.'

'We can come back,' Luke suggested.

'No, I want to do it now.'

There wasn't much, and once the cottage was empty, she hopefully would never have to come here again.

She had spotted there were several heavy-duty bin liners in the kitchen under the sink, and leaving Luke in the living room to break apart the furniture, she focused her efforts on the bedroom.

The bedding went into the bin liner first. Even touching it made her feel icky, unsure who had slept on the sheets or even who her husband had truly been at this point.

Once the mattress was stripped, she focused on the one solitary bedside unit, relieved when she found the top drawer practically empty. There was a packet of the mints Charlie favoured, along with a set of earplugs. He had always needed absolute silence to sleep.

The bottom drawer contained underwear and socks.

As she emptied both, Bailey, who had been dividing his time between Harper and Luke, curious to what they were both doing, wandered through, poking his nose in the bin bag.

Harper distracted him with a treat she had in her coat pocket, before turning her attention to the wardrobe. It was a built-in one and expecting to find more of his things hanging in there, her mouth dropped open in shock when she pulled back the door.

It was packed with clothes, but none of them had been her husband's. Looking through the garments, she could see they were women's clothes. Mostly dresses, in an array of colours, sizes and styles, from glamorous evening gowns to fishnet and rubber outfits that left little to the imagination.

Her throat tightened. So he had definitely brought women here.

How many?

She would never know.

Realising that if she stopped to think about it she would come undone again, she tore off a new bin liner and started pulling the dresses out and piling them into the bag.

There were shoes in the bottom of the wardrobe and they went into a third liner, along with a large bag of women's under-wear, which she couldn't bring herself to go through. She could already see that the contents were a mix of sexy and slutty; black lace and red silk. Nothing like she had ever worn. She'd had no idea Charlie even liked this stuff.

In the bathroom, the mirrored cabinet contained more unwelcome items. A make-up bag filled with cosmetics – red lipsticks, smoky eyeshadows and black mascara – was further proof that another woman had been here, while on the upper shelf was a large packet of condoms.

Charlie. Why?

How could she have not known about any of this? Were there signs that she had missed? It wasn't like they hadn't had a good sex life and she had always shown willing whenever he wanted to try anything new.

He must have thought she was such a fool. She had been so trusting.

'How are you getting on?'

Jumping at Luke's voice, she instinctively closed the cabinet door and swung around. 'Okay, okay. You?' She forced her voice to sound normal, though wasn't sure how good a job she had done as he hesitated, looking like he was about to push her on that, before seeming to change his mind.

'Yeah, all good. I'm finished in the living room. Do you want me to take the bed apart?'

'Please.' Harper had knotted the bin liners so he wouldn't see what was inside them.

Even though he knew Charlie had been cheating on her, what she had discovered here today brought with it fresh humiliation. She didn't want Luke thinking she was an idiot for not knowing what had been going on.

He nodded, eyes lingering on her for a moment, before disappearing, Bailey following after him, and Harper quickly opened the bathroom cabinet again, emptying the offending items into the rubbish bag.

Going through to the kitchen, she removed the contents from the fridge and then took all of the tins out of the cupboard. There were very few other items. She had already made good use of the bin liners, and the only other contents were a bottle of washing-up liquid, a ratty-looking tea towel and in one of the drawers was a can opener and a dessert spoon.

Considering some of the items she had found today, it surprised her there weren't any creature comforts in the cottage. She would have expected a kettle and perhaps a few cooking utensils, but there was nothing. Not even any other cutlery.

Nothing seemed to add up. The cheap tinned food and the stuff for the non-existent dog, the dresses and lingerie in the wardrobe, and the make-up in the bathroom cabinet. Harper couldn't make head nor tail of it.

* * *

She was quiet on the ride back to Salhouse.

They had filled the boot up with as many of the bin bags and bits of broken-up furniture as they could fit, and they stopped off at the rubbish tip en route to dump it all.

There were still a few things left at the cottage and Luke suggested they head back to get them when he next had a day off.

'How do you feel about today?' he asked, as they arrived back home.

Harper shrugged. 'Okay, I guess. I think it helped going.' It wasn't completely a lie, even if it had thrown up some nasty truths. And she needed time to come to terms with those. It seemed the deeper she delved, the less she knew Charlie. The affair with Alicia was bad enough, but there had been other women. And he obviously had another bank account somewhere that she knew nothing about.

Would the secrets he had kept and the lies he had told ever stop?

It had helped having Luke with her today, but also she felt exposed and more than a little vulnerable. She was aware she had been relying on him a lot lately. They hadn't known each other long and already she was using him as a crutch. Perhaps she should dial things back a bit. Take it a little slower. She hadn't even told Megan yet about the cottage.

'Look, I'm pretty tired and I think I'm just going to have a bath, then get into bed,' she said. 'Do you mind if we call it a night?'

'If that's what you want.'

If he was offended that she was trying to get rid of him, he didn't say. Still, she felt shitty. He had just given up his day to help her clear the cottage.

Making an effort, she moved into him, linking her arms around his waist and breathing him in. It may have only been a matter of weeks, but already he was becoming familiar to her, and while she needed a little time to herself, she didn't want to push him away.

She hugged him tightly. 'Thank you for coming with me today. I'm not sure I could have done it by myself.'

'Any time, though you don't have to thank me. I'm here for you, Harper.' He drew back, steady blue eyes locking on to hers. 'I mean that.'

For a moment, the air between them heated, sizzled even, and Harper reconsidered asking him to leave. Then the loud squeak of Bailey's rubber chicken toy cut through the tension, and they both stared down to where he had plonked himself beside them, dark brown eyes wide and hopeful as he looked between them, the toy stuffed in his mouth, and tail thumping against the floor.

'Do you want me to take him around the block before I go?' Luke offered.

'No, it's okay, thanks. He's had plenty of exercise today. I'll let him out in the garden later.'

He nodded. 'I'm back on shift tomorrow, so I guess I'll speak to you at some point.' He rubbed his hand up and down her arm. 'Call me if you need me.'

Harper followed him to the door, waiting until he was in his Audi and pulling out of the driveway before she closed and locked it again, and she tried to quash down her guilt. He had really been there for her today, but it was important that she slow things down a little.

Looking back, she had rushed her relationship with Charlie

and it had been full on from the beginning. At the time, Harper had been so caught up, she had barely noticed, but the time frame from that first meeting at the barbecue to Charlie moving himself in, then deciding they should get married, had been less than a year.

And yes, their marriage had lasted, but if she was honest with herself, there had been as many downs as ups, increasingly so, and there were times she had felt Charlie closing her out. She had accepted it, telling herself that every relationship had bumps. But never had she suspected that everything was built on a lie.

She couldn't afford to make that mistake again.

Luke said all of the right things, but she was still getting to know him, and when she really thought about it, other than meeting a few of his friends and what information he had told her, she actually knew very little about him. He worked at the hospital. His friends could vouch for that, and she had no reason to doubt that all of his family was back in Ireland. Still, though, she had never met them.

Not that it should make that big a difference, she supposed. She had known Charlie's parents and they hadn't given her a better understanding of their son.

It did bother her that she still hadn't seen where Luke lived. Especially as it was just down the road.

Admittedly, the subject hadn't really come up again. He seemed keen to spend time at Harper's and she hadn't tried to stop him. Just like with Charlie, she had fallen into the easiness of the situation.

When they were next together, she was going to ask again to see his home, and this time wouldn't let him sidetrack her.

Either that or she could pay him a surprise visit.

She knew the road he lived on. Surely it wouldn't be too difficult to find his place.

Mulling the idea over, she fixed Bailey's dinner. Ignoring her own rumbling stomach and leaving the dog to eat, she went back through into Charlie's office.

It was time to try to find out exactly what her late husband had been up to.

26

Everything happens for a reason. I am a firm believer in that.

I was meant to discover my father's dirty little secret, just as he was supposed to fall down the stairs and break his neck after discovering I had stolen some of his precious DVDs, wanting my own collection, obsessed with what I had seen. He had found them in my bedroom and was incandescent with rage as he chased after me. Knowing I was going to get a beating, I had fled down the stairs, and as he followed, he had lost his footing.

Without him there ruling the household with his iron fist, I was able to flourish and have the space to explore who I really was. Mum was no bother and never questioned my behaviour, always turning a blind eye. It was as if the mantle had been passed from Dad to me, and I was now the man of the house, to be respected. It was fate, I realise now. Everything falling into order and how it should be. In return, I have always made sure she is taken care of.

It is also fate that brought Harper back into my life. There she was, again and again. It was as if someone was poking me in the shoulder, urging me to take the gift I was being presented with.

As for Samantha, at first I had believed she was a mistake, but it turns out, even she has had a reason for coming into my life. She has been the perfect dry run.

Having her here with me has provided a distraction from my growing obsession with Harper, and she has taught me patience and control.

Before she moved in, the longest any of my housemates had lasted was seventeen days. Samantha has been here for almost eight weeks. That is a staggering record for me, especially given how disinterested I was in her at the start, and it proves that I am now ready.

She has shown me that I finally have the restraint I need before Harper moves in, and it has taken our relationship to a whole new level. I have experienced new highs I didn't realise existed, and I know I will also always have Samantha to thank for that. She has changed me, and she has shown me I can be stronger. That I can be better.

I am almost sad that tonight it needs to end, but Harper has changed things by finding out about the cottage. I have often wondered if I should go back there. Maybe even set fire to it. In the end, I decided to leave well alone. I have been careful and I'm as certain as I can be that nothing there will link back to me.

Still, knowing she has been there is making my skin itchy. Just how much does she know?

It's safer all round if she comes to live here sooner rather than later, which is why Samantha can no longer stay.

I think she understands that as we eat a final dinner together. I have cooked her favourite and she seems suspicious of my motives, huge eyes looking up at me as she chews on a mouthful.

Her features have become more pronounced over the time she has been here and she has lost weight. She was skinny when I first met her, but now she is skeletal, and the dress I have asked her to wear hangs on her like an unflattering sack.

It's because she mostly has one meal a day and depending on what I choose to feed her, there is not always a lot of it.

I do my bit, though, by ensuring she finishes every last mouthful, even when it is a punishment meal. At first, she had protested with those, pushing the dish away, insisting she would rather starve herself than eat the food, then retching when I force fed her. In recent weeks, I haven't needed to go to such extreme measures. She is always hungry enough that she gratefully falls on whatever she is served.

'You're going to kill me, aren't you?' There's a tremor in her voice, as she speaks the words quietly, and I can see the fear in her eyes.

Samantha has a fighting nature and she wants to live, regardless of everything that has happened, and in spite of all I have done to her.

Death scares her. She has admitted that to me when we have talked late at night, and it has fascinated me that she would rather live in pain than have her suffering end. She doesn't know it, but each time I think about that revelation, the blood heats in my veins. All of the control I have shown in keeping her alive for so long has meant the need building inside of me is burning away and ready to unleash.

I will ensure her last night here is spectacular. It's what she deserves.

'Yes,' I tell her, my voice void of emotion, watching her as tears spill out of her eyes.

I have told her all about Harper and how this room will be needed.

Samantha knows she can't stay. Just as she knows I will never let her walk out of here alive.

It has been a memorable eight weeks, though. I have enjoyed having her as a housemate and she has helped me learn a lot about myself. I am going to miss her.

When I remember back to when I met her, I can see how far we have both come.

The first time I had gone to Harper's house and watched her through the windows, I had left with an urgency building inside of me and steam that I needed to blow off.

I wanted Harper, but I knew it was too soon. Knowing I would have to find something else to distract me, I had gone for a drive.

It had been to my good fortune that I had encountered Samantha while cruising the back roads of West Norfolk. Later, I would learn she had been in the pub with friends. The bravado of alcohol convincing her that she would be safe walking the mile and a half home, and slowing her reactions when I caught her off guard.

Seeing her stumbling as she moved to one side to let me pass, I knew she would be easy pickings, and even though this wasn't my usual method and I knew nothing about her, I found myself pulling over into the entrance of a field, and awaiting her approach.

There were a few houses dotted along the lane, but the spot I had picked wasn't overlooked by any of them. The struggle when I grabbed hold of her from behind, locking my arm around her neck in a choke-hold, was over quickly, and once I felt her go limp, I lifted her into the boot of the car, using the rope I kept handy for all manner of emergencies, car related or not, to bind her wrists and ankles. She was already coming to before I had finished tying her up, but by then it was too late.

Back home, I introduced her to her new accommodation, ignoring the niggle of doubt that I had fucked up. I knew nothing about her and she wasn't my usual type.

Why had I brought her here?

I had asked myself that question several times over the course of the first week, uninterested in even playing with her. Perhaps I should just kill her and be done with it.

But then, after days of being sulky, rude and aggressive, I had seen the one emotion I longed for. Fear.

That night, I had played. I had set up my lighting and cameras and dressed her up like the whore she was, before testing her limits, eager to learn more about this stranger I had brought to live with me. It had been worth every second.

'Finish your dinner,' I instruct her now, realising she is playing for time.

I watch as she takes another mouthful, struggling to swallow it. When she suddenly bursts into tears and starts pleading with me to let her live, I reach for the remote control beside me. Her eyes go wide in horror and she frantically shakes her head.

'No, please.'

'Stop crying and finish eating your dinner,' I repeat.

Trying to calm herself down, she attempts another mouthful of food.

She understands her place here now, though I know her well enough that I am certain there will be a lot more begging to come as the evening progresses.

Tonight is going to be a lot of fun.

27

This time, Harper left nothing to chance, emptying both the box and bin liner of items from Charlie's office and going through every single one again in painstaking detail.

With his laptop gone, her only chance of finding out what he had been up to would be within these documents, and she had known it wouldn't be a quick or an easy job. As midnight eventually came and went, she was still poring over everything, desperately seeking a clue.

A notepad sat beside her that she was slowly filling up with information. Anything she thought might lead to something, even though she wasn't sure what.

She had the list of dates she had already made, when Charlie had claimed to be working but she now knew he wasn't, and she cross-checked them against every new document she read through, but everything led to a blank.

Bailey had eventually wandered through to find her, bringing with him a rubber ball, and whining in frustration, wanting attention.

Harper paused to stroke a hand over his soft ears, taking the soggy ball and rolling it out of the office and down the hallway, hearing the scuffle of toenails against wood as the dog charged after it.

As she rubbed her palms over her tired eyes, he came back, tail wagging and ball dropping in her lap.

Although she made more fuss of him, she pushed the ball onto the floor, ignoring his whimper of protest at the short-lived game.

'Not now,' she told him. 'I need to do this. I'll play with you tomorrow, I promise.'

She should really quit and go to bed. There wasn't much left to go through, but she still needed to look at it with fresh eyes. Just another ten minutes and she would stop.

Barking distracted her – Bailey, bored, had settled himself down beside her and had managed to lose his ball under the desk.

At first, Harper ignored him, but he was getting agitated. Huffing out a sigh, she reached beneath the unit, her fingers coming away empty. It must have rolled to the back.

'Okay,' she told the dog, resigned as she climbed to her feet, every muscle aching and reminding her she had been sat in a cramped position for far too long. She would find the ball and call it a night. Start over again tomorrow.

Pulling the desk away from the wall, she leant down behind it and scooped the ball up, throwing it to Bailey. As she went to move everything back, she noticed that the cover on the old decorative vent grille in the wall was loose.

When she reached down to clip it back into place, it fell off completely.

Swearing under her breath, Harper pulled the desk further out and dropped to her knees. It was then she realised the small space had something in it. A small drawstring black bag that was soft and velvety to the touch, she realised as she tugged it out.

Why had Charlie hidden it in the wall? Because she had to assume it was Charlie. There were vent grilles in all of the rooms and Harper remembered cleaning them all out before they had decorated. No one else had been in Charlie's office, she was certain of that.

Pulling the bag open, she let the contents fall out.

Two items. A mobile phone and a key.

So Charlie had another phone. He had always used just the one for both personal and business. The fact that this one was hidden in the wall told her he hadn't wanted her to know about it. As for the key, she already had the one for the cottage. Besides, this one looked too small for a door. What was it for? And why was it hidden away?

Her head was spinning trying to figure out what had been going on.

Aware of how late it was, but knowing she wouldn't sleep until she had answers, she got up, switching off the light to the office, pocketing the key and taking the phone with her through to the lounge.

She knew it would need charging before she could use it. It was an older-style Galaxy and that could be a problem as Harper only had cables for her iPhone. But then she remembered her Kindle charger, and going upstairs to fetch it, she was relieved to see it fit.

After letting Bailey out for a late-night wee, she went back to the charging phone and switched it on, a little dismayed, though unsurprised, when it asked her for a pin number.

She tried a few different options, memorable dates that she knew Charlie had used for various things in the past, but none of them worked.

Having never owned a Galaxy, she was reluctant to have too many wrong attempts in case the phone locked her out completely. Deciding to leave it for now, she let Bailey back in the house and headed up to bed.

Despite a restless night, unable to switch her mind off, the following morning she was up early and, still in her pyjamas, she decided to finish going through the paperwork in Charlie's office, hopeful that he had written the pin number down somewhere, but it was to no avail.

Bailey was slumped outside the office door and he looked up eagerly when eventually she hauled the bin liner outside.

'We'll go out in a minute,' Harper promised him, guiltily, aware she had kept him waiting, and going upstairs to dress after throwing the bin bag in the wheelie bin.

She had reached the point where she wanted to bang her head against a wall. Nothing was adding up, and she had no idea what to try next. Maybe the fresh air would do her good.

It was on her way back from the walk that her phone started vibrating in her pocket. Pulling it out and spotting Megan's name on the screen, Harper quickly answered. She had been so preoccupied with going through everything in Charlie's study again, she still hadn't got around to updating her friend, who still knew nothing about the cottage or her late husband's many lovers.

'Hey, how are you?'

'I'm good,' came Megan's reply. 'What about you? Can you talk?'

'Yes, I'm just out with the dog. Is everything okay?'

Harper wanted to tell Megan everything, but it was only fair to let her friend go first.

She listened as Megan talked about Tom and how he had recently been offered a promotion. 'The timing couldn't be better,' she said after a pause. 'We could do with the extra cash.'

'I thought everything was okay moneywise?' Harper pushed, concerned that she had selfishly missed some sign of trouble. It seemed whenever they spoke these days, she hogged the conversation. Megan hadn't mentioned before that they were having problems and both her and Tom had good jobs.

Megan fell silent for a moment, before she spoke. 'I was going to wait until I'd had my first ultrasound before I said anything, but it's only a couple of weeks away and Harper, I wanted you to be the first friend I told. I'm pregnant.' There was the hint of apprehension in Megan's tone and Harper realised she had been nervous about telling her. It knocked it home how one-sided their friendship had become.

Yes, she was a little taken back. She hadn't even realised Megan and Tom had been trying for a baby, and her friend was now about to embark on a new chapter of her life, one Harper had hoped for herself, but that didn't stop her being excited.

'Megan. That's fantastic news. I'm so happy for you.'

'You are?'

'Of course I am. Why wouldn't I be?'

'It's just I know you and Charlie—'

'There is no me and Charlie, any more,' Harper insisted, glad she hadn't hijacked the conversation to tell Megan about his myriad affairs. She decided her news could wait until a later date. Today was all about Megan and, from now on, she resolved to be a better friend.

'How are things going with Luke?'

'Really well.'

'I'm happy for you, Harper. You deserve this. I'm glad you're finally moving on.'

'I am, and so are you. A baby. This is so exciting. We need to all get together and celebrate. Maybe after Christmas, I can bring Luke to London to meet you and we can have a proper catch-up.'

Harper made an effort to keep the conversation focused on Megan for the rest of the walk home, purposely keeping her tone cheerful and only giving in to a pang of regret after they had ended the call.

She had wanted a baby with Charlie, but he had continually put her off, saying the timing wasn't right. Now she understood that a child would have probably interfered with his extracurricular activities. With hindsight, it was for the best that she had never fallen pregnant, but it didn't stop her craving what could have been if her husband hadn't turned out to be a cheat.

Opening Facebook, she clicked onto Charlie's profile.

It was still live, though the last update had been more than a month before his death. She looked now at the smiling face of the man she had loved and who she had made vows to, and she wondered yet again why she hadn't been enough for him.

Caught up in a mix of nostalgia and self-pity, she started scrolling through his photos. Holidays they had taken and parties they had been to. There were pictures of their home – this home – taken not long after they had moved in, as they knocked the place about, trying to remould it into their dream house. Harper with her blonde hair tied back and a paintbrush in her hand as Charlie snapped her frowning at him. She remembered how she had been annoyed in that moment, as she struggled to keep him focused on work.

The next picture he had taken was a selfie as he lampooned for the camera, blobs of paint on his T-shirt. It was one of his favourite tops, and she had warned him not to wear it, knowing it would likely get ruined.

Staring at the T-shirt now, the name of his favourite band, The 1975, written across the front, her eyes narrowed. 1975 was four digits. Was it possible he might have used the band name as the code for his secret phone?

She was all out of ideas, so it was worth a try.

Fetching the phone, she typed the code in, double blinking at the home screen as the phone unlocked. It had been a long shot and she hadn't really expected it to work. Now she was in, nerves fluttered in her stomach and she was a little anxious as to what she might find. The polaroid picture she had discovered in Charlie's study had devastated her and the clothes and make-up she had found at the cottage had kept her awake for most of the night. Was she ready for this?

Knowing she had to find out the truth, she opened his contact list.

What was left of her heart was ripped into pieces as she scrolled through the list of names. All of them females.

Christina, Claire, Louise, Michelle, Jennifer, Yasmin.

How many women had he been seeing behind her back?

His job had taken him on the road a lot and he usually overnighted somewhere at least twice a week. Harper had trusted him, and learning that their marriage vows had meant nothing to him was a stab in the chest.

Interestingly, she noted, Alicia's number wasn't there. Was that because they had only just started seeing each other when the accident had happened?

Charlie hadn't set up WhatsApp, but there were several text message exchanges.

Harper opened a couple of them, but glancing over the flirty banter, she knew she would need a stiff drink before she could read them in depth.

In the image gallery, a quick scroll through showed her it was mostly pictures of women. The ones he was messaging, she presumed. Many of them were shots taken at a distance, but, in others, the women were smiling at him, some laughing or seeming annoyed that he was taking their photo. Much the same as the decorating day when he kept pointing his phone camera at Harper. Although she had been working and struggling to get him to focus, part of her had liked that he'd wanted to keep taking her photo. Now, though, the intimacy of that moment was ruined.

She didn't need to pause scrolling to note that the women were pretty. They all seemed to be a particular type: dark-haired and voluptuous with brown eyes. If that was his preference, why had he married blonde-haired, green-eyed Harper? She couldn't be more different.

Unable to face going through any more photos, she logged out of the gallery and looked to see what other apps were on the phone.

There were only a few. One was for a bank, which she assumed would be how he had paid for the utility bills at the cottage. A quick glance at that showed her it wasn't going to be easy to log in to and she would probably have to get her solicitor involved to help gain access to the account. There was also an app for a dating site. Not a paid one like IntoYou. Instead, it was a freebie site, Hooked, which Harper knew had a reputation for being a bit of a meat market. To be fair, IntoYou hadn't been much better.

Was that where Charlie had met these women? Had he actively gone out looking to find them? Was he really that unhappy with their marriage?

She tried to log in to the site, hoping the password was stored. When she realised it wasn't going to be that easy, she checked Charlie's email, pleased that she could at least get straight into that.

Going back to Hooked, she requested a new password be sent so she could log in.

While she waited for it to pop up, she scrolled through the

Gmail emails, realising Charlie had an Amazon account which was registered to the cottage address.

Looking at the order confirmations of his purchases, she realised that this was where he had bought many of the dresses, shoes and underwear she had seen in the wardrobe. The make-up too.

Why would Charlie have bought these women their make-up?

He had never got anything like that for Harper and she wouldn't have wanted him to, preferring to make her own choices when it came to cosmetics. Her clothes too, though that didn't seem quite as odd as the make-up.

Her own phone vibrated beside her, making her jump and providing a momentary distraction. Glancing down, she saw Luke's name had flashed up on the screen. She picked it up, reading his message offering to bring over takeaway when his shift had finished.

Harper was already learning that dating a doctor meant his hours often ran over, so he was making a bold assumption that he would be finished in time for them to eat together. Besides, her head was full of all this Charlie stuff and she didn't think she would be the best company right now.

She typed a reply, hoping she didn't seem too off with him.

> Thanks, but I have a really bad headache. Do you mind if we skip tonight? I'm going to head up to bed early. Xx

As soon as she pressed send, she started to feel bad. Would he buy her excuse or had she overegged it? Luke was great and, if she was honest, she was starting to really fall for him, but until she laid these Charlie demons to rest, she didn't feel she could fully move on.

She just needed a few days to come to terms with everything.

Perhaps she should have told him that. He already knew Charlie had cheated on her, but Harper was embarrassed that he had made such a fool of her. It was humiliating and she didn't want Luke to start thinking she was so stupid that he could pull the wool over her eyes too.

She was thinking the worst of him, she realised that, and although she knew it wasn't fair, right now she was vulnerable.

When his reply came, she inwardly cringed a little as she read it.

Fine. I could do with an early night myself. x

Was she being paranoid? His message seemed a little cool, as if he knew she was lying and trying to brush him off.

Stop it.

She was overthinking things. Besides, text messages were so easy to misinterpret.

Charlie's betrayal was making her doubt everything and she was feeling guilty for lying to Luke. She would make it up to him, she promised.

Looking at the secret phone again, she saw the temporary password to access Hooked had come through on Charlie's Gmail messages, and all thoughts of Luke vanished from her mind.

Drawing in a deep breath and trying to mentally prepare herself for whatever she might find, she clicked on the link to take her into the site.

28

The first thing Harper spotted was that the profile picture wasn't of her husband. The second thing was his bio sounded nothing like Charlie at all. He claimed to like football and cars – Charlie had been into neither. And apparently he was a big animal lover. Another lie. It wasn't the only one he had told. His occupation was listed as photographer and his age was shown as twenty-eight. He had shaved eight years off.

The man staring back at her on the screen was very attrac-tive, with dark eyes and a Mediterranean tan, suggesting Spanish or Italian descent. Again, nothing like fair-haired Charlie.

She furrowed her brow in confusion. Maybe she had all of this wrong and it wasn't Charlie's phone.

The thought had her briefly clinging to hope before she remembered that the Amazon account had been in his name and the delivery address was for the cottage. It had to be Charlie's account. So what was this? Was he catfishing like 'Brad'?

Unlike IntoYou, where users were required to give their Christian name, Hooked offered its members anonymity by allowing them to hide behind a username, and Charlie's was Dream-Chaser.

His 'about me' section was brief but hit her hard.

My perfect girl is out there. I just haven't met her yet.

Everything about the profile might be a lie, but that one line caught Harper in the gut, tears blurring her vision. She swiped at them angrily. How dare he?

His inbox was full, no doubt thanks to the hot guy he had used in his picture, and reading through a few of the exchanges she soon realised he had given a fake name too.

Carlos. The Spanish version of Charles.

The irony of it was like some kind of sick joke and she could almost imagine him rationalising to himself that he wasn't being that deceitful by using a variation of his real name.

The email exchanges turned her stomach, but Harper read them all, regardless, recognising names as introductions were made. Yasmin, Christina, Jennifer, Michelle. These were all of the women stored on the fake phone, and further down the chats, she could see where he had offered the number, flattering each one by telling them he could feel a connection, complimenting their pictures and saying how they had the perfect bone structure or smile and he would like to photograph them.

It was actually scary how easily they bought into his bullshit, but then they hadn't known it was a lie. Thinking back to 'Brad', Harper had been just as gullible. He had catfished her, just as Charlie appeared to have catfished these women.

On a whim, she opened the text messages, going into the most recent one – Jennifer. Their last exchange had been arranging to meet a month before Charlie's accident, which suggested he hadn't been seeing Alicia for long.

Either that or he had been cheating on her too. At this point, Harper wouldn't have put anything past him.

Charlie had arranged to meet Jennifer in a countryside pub out near Dereham in the west of the county, and Jennifer had typed *Can't wait to meet you tonight.*

After that, there were no more messages.

What had happened when they had met and Jennifer realised Carlos was Charlie and looked nothing like his profile photo? Her ex-husband could be persuasive, but few women would forgive that kind of deceit.

The next contact had been with Christina two months prior to Jennifer. Reading through their messages, Harper saw that they too had planned to meet on the day of their last exchange. Christina must have cottoned on, though, as her final message called him a time-waster and a dickhead and told him never to contact her again.

It looked like he hadn't shown up to meet Yasmin, the third girl in his messages. Her repeated texts asking where he was and if he was okay reminded Harper again of her encounter with Brad.

In fact, the more she thought about it, they were uncannily similar.

Luckily, she was of sound mind, otherwise she might have started questioning if she had been catfished by her dead husband. It was already spooking the hell out of her that all of this had been going on. How had she known so little about the man she was married to?

The deeper she was digging, the more upsetting this was becoming, but she couldn't stop. As stupid as it probably sounded, learning just how little respect he'd had for her was helping to loosen his grip. If she had done this two years ago, and discovered that Charlie had betrayed her with multiple women, maybe she wouldn't have wasted two years of her life grieving him and trying to work out what Alicia had that she didn't.

Alicia hadn't been special. She had just been another notch on Charlie's bedpost.

Harper continued to read through the messages as day turned into night, going over every exchange on the Hooked app and those sent via text message. And when she was done, she then went through Charlie's Amazon shopping history, scrutinising every purchase he had made from his secret account.

Apart from the clothing and make-up, she could see he had bought the dog food she had found in the cupboard at the cottage. It still flummoxed her why he needed it, unless he'd had secret canine friends as well as lovers. Unlikely, though, as Charlie hadn't particularly liked dogs.

There were other mundane items too. Tools and gardening equipment, plus cleaning products, that suggested he had intended to do some work to the cottage at some point, although he had clearly not got round to even starting on it.

The ring of the doorbell pulled her from her thoughts, making her jump, and guiltily, though she had no idea why she should feel that way, she dropped the phone. Picking it up, Harper put it down on the coffee table next to her own and went to the door.

Unsure who was on the other side, she hesitated before sliding the chain across. Seeing Luke standing there gave her mixed emotions.

She had asked him not to come over and irritation bristled that he had ignored her, though another part of her was pleased he had. Guilt also crept in that she had lied to him, pretending she'd had a headache.

Removing the chain, she opened the door fully. 'What are you doing here?'

Nice one, Harper. She hadn't meant to sound so accusatory.

He didn't seem to notice her tone. Instead, he asked, 'Can I come in?'

It dawned on her that he hadn't used the key she had given him. Instead he had respected her boundaries, ringing the doorbell, instead of just letting himself into her house.

She nodded, thawing by the second, 'Okay,' and stepped back to let him pass.

For the first time, she noticed his serious expression.

'What's going on? Is something wrong?' she asked.

He turned to face her. Still no smile. Was he about to break up with her?

'There's something I need to tell you.'

Oh God. That sounded bad. Had he met someone else?

'What?' Harper demanded, her tone impatient.

'Why don't we sit down?'

'I don't want to sit down. Luke! What's going on?'

'Okay. There was a woman brought into A&E tonight. Suspected heart attack.'

Why was he telling her this? 'Do I know her?'

She couldn't imagine who she would know. Her social circle was tiny, and inside of Norfolk, practically non-existent. Well, present company excluded.

'It ended up being anxiety,' he pushed on, ignoring her question. 'A panic attack.'

'Okay. I'm glad it wasn't more serious, but what does this have to do with me?'

'She collapsed after the police informed her they had found her son's body,' Luke said, sounding a little annoyed that Harper wouldn't let him finish. 'And I shouldn't be telling you this at all.'

'So why are you?' she pushed, desperate to know where this was leading.

'Because her son was Gavin Brooks, Harper. The Gavin who attacked you and who we are supposed to be testifying against. He's dead.'

There was a huge pause in conversation as she took all of that in.

Gavin was dead?

'How?' she demanded, as numbness crept over her.

'I don't know the full details as it's an ongoing investigation,' Luke told her. 'But Heather... Mrs Brooks told me the police suspect foul play.'

'You mean he was murdered?' Harper's eyes went wide.

'Possibly.' He shrugged. 'Probably. I thought you should know. I assume the police will be contacting you at some point.'

Panic clawed its way into Harper's throat. 'Why? Because they think I'm responsible?'

'No, of course not. But they'll need to let you know there won't be a trial.'

'Oh, yes. I guess so.'

The news had completely thrown her, and she fell quiet, trying to process it all. Someone had killed Gavin. Murdered him. Had it been a random attack or was he targeted? Perhaps it had been the ex-girlfriend, Angie.

Her mind crept back to Adrian. He had been beaten up in a random attack. Now Gavin was dead. That was two men Harper had been on dates with.

No, it was stupid to even try to link the two. She was not a common denominator. It was coincidence. She was just shocked, was all, and jumping to erratic conclusions.

Besides, Luke was fine. No one had tried to hurt him.

He was looking a little tired, dark smudges under his eyes and the curls of his hair unruly, and he was still in his work scrubs, though handsome as hell as he stood before her waiting for her to react. He had come straight here from his shift to tell her about Gavin so the news didn't come as a shock to her, and knowing that made her heart squeeze.

'I was going to make some dinner. Are you hungry?' she offered, not wanting him to leave.

He hesitated. 'How's your head?'

Harper reddened. 'I'm actually feeling a bit better. And I would like you to stay. If you want to, that is.'

Finally, that serious expression he was wearing softened into a smile. 'I'd like that too. I can nip down to Rackheath and pick up fish and chips if you want.'

'No, you're tired,' she told him, giving into the urge to hug him and pleased when he reciprocated, the scent of him and the feel of his hands gently rubbing circles on her back now so familiar. 'I don't mind cooking.'

'We could order in,' he suggested, warm mouth close to her ear.

'It's fine. There's stuff in the fridge.'

'Okay, I'll help.'

Harper drew back, narrowing her eyes as she studied his face. 'Do you not trust me in the kitchen?'

'Well... I'm not saying you're a bad cook, but—'

'Luke!' She thumped at his shoulder playfully, unable to hide her smile. 'I'm not that bad.'

His eyes crinkled at the corners. 'Define bad.'

That earned him another thump, even though she was now laughing, knowing he had already experienced a couple of her disaster meals, and for a moment she was distracted enough to forget about Gavin, even about Charlie.

It didn't take long for her thoughts to return to her husband, though, as Luke's gaze honed in on the coffee table and Charlie's mobile sitting there beside her own.

'New phone?' The smile had dropped from his face, though he kept his tone light.

'Um, it's just one of my old ones. I found it in the cupboard when I went to get out the Christmas decorations and I thought I'd check one of those mobile sites, see if it is worth anything.'

He stared at her for a moment, blue eyes cool and questioning, and Harper's cheeks heated at the lie. Why had she told him that?

Over the last couple of days, she had opened up to him, leaned on him too, and he had been her ally and her rock as she dealt with the cottage, but these new revelations about Charlie, they were just so personal. She wasn't ready to share everything yet, not when her and Luke were still getting to know each other.

'And is it?'

'Sorry?'

'The phone. Is it worth anything?'

'Oh, um, I haven't checked yet.' She snatched up the handset, keen to put it somewhere safe, out of the way.

'Do you want me to help you decorate?'

'What?' Harper stared at him.

'You said you got the Christmas decorations out. I can help if you like.' She noticed he made a point of glancing around the room. 'Where are they?'

'They're still in the cupboard. I was distracted by the phone.'

It was intentional. He knew she was lying and he was trying to catch her out. Annoyance smothered her embarrassment. Luke wasn't perfect. He had secrets of his own.

'Why won't you let me see where you live?' she blurted, aiming for a subject change and going on the defensive instead.

Her question had his eyes widening and for a moment he looked confused.

'Sorry?'

'We've been seeing each other for what, six, seven weeks? But you're always here. You've never invited me over to your place.'

Luke's jaw tightened. 'I thought you wanted me here. You were the one who insisted on giving me a key.'

'I do want you here, but I'd like to see where you live too.'

'Why? It's nothing special.'

'It doesn't matter. It's still a part of you.'

'I didn't realise it was such a big deal.' He shrugged. 'If you wanted to see my house so badly, then maybe you should've asked.'

'I've dropped enough hints!'

'Have you?' He stared at her before arching a brow and adding dryly, 'I'm a man. You should know we're not very good with those.'

He was going for humour now, trying to lighten the moment, but Harper wasn't going to let him off that easy.

'So, when?'

'When what?'

'When can I come over?'

'I don't know. Whenever you like.' He sounded exasperated.

'How about now?'

'Harper, we're here now and I've just finished a long shift. I'm knackered.'

'When then?'

He was getting wound up, she could tell. His cheeks flushed and he was running agitated fingers through his hair. Just what was he hiding from her?

The revelations about Charlie had knocked her for six. She couldn't cope with another man who had secrets.

'When, Luke? If not tonight, then tomorrow.'

'I'll be at the hospital all day. I don't know what time I'll be off.'

Harper glared at him and he backed down, holding his hands up in a gesture of peace.

'Friday. I'm not working, so come over. It'll give me a chance to tidy up and I can cook dinner.'

Friday was still three days away, but at least, she supposed, he had given her a date.

'Okay,' she told him grudgingly.

They both eyed each other warily, neither speaking, the invisible lines of the battlefield still drawn. Their first fight, and both easing away from it, seeing how the other would react.

Luke was the first to break the silence. 'Can we please eat now? I'm starving.'

Harper nodded. She was still a little bit irritated, but the edges of her temper softened when she remembered the reason he was here. That he had come to break the news to her about Gavin.

'We can get a curry delivered if you want,' she told him, caving.

'I'd like that.'

As the atmosphere between them gradually thawed, they slipped back into an easy banter and eventually Harper's annoyance completely evaporated.

Luke ended up staying over, telling her he would nip back home in the morning for a change of clothes before heading into work, and as Harper lay beside him, she wondered if she was overreacting. It was only natural that the things she had discovered about Charlie were making her paranoid.

Still, it didn't stop her following Luke when he left the next day, throwing on a jumper and a pair of old joggers and leaving the house without brushing her hair or her teeth, so she didn't lose sight of his car.

Friday was too far off and she couldn't wait until then. Besides, he might come up with an excuse to cancel by then.

She didn't intend to stop or get out of the car. All she wanted to do was see his house, then she would drive straight back home.

He had several seconds' head start on her and she didn't see him until she turned into the lane where he lived. Catching sight of his Audi in the distance, she was careful not to get too close. If he found out she was following him, she would be mortified, and she had no idea how he would react.

At first, she didn't think he was going to stop, and knowing that the lane would eventually reach a T junction leading onto a main road, she began to wonder if he had lied to her about where he lived. But then, without indicating, he pulled into the driveway of a large detached property, and Harper slowed her own car to a crawl, not wanting to approach too quickly and risk him seeing her.

By the time she cruised by, he was parked next to a spanking new Range Rover and out of his car, presumably already in the house. Deciding to find a turning point, she drove on, her head full of questions.

The house looked nice, though it was much larger than she had expected. Although she had no idea what the salary of an accident and emergency doctor was, she was surprised that Luke was able to afford it. And was the Range Rover his too? She remembered him saying he lived alone, but why would he need two cars?

Pulling into the entrance of a field, she turned the car around, perplexed as to why he wouldn't want her to know where he lived.

As she approached the house again, she eased her foot off the accelerator, slowing to a crawl and glancing towards the front door, surprised to see it was open and a fair-headed woman had stepped out. She was smartly but warmly dressed, and accompanied by Eric, who was tugging at his lead. The terrier was supposed to belong to Luke's neighbour, so why was the woman in his house? Besides, there were no other properties close by.

Apprehension crept in. Had he lied to Harper? Was he living with this woman? In which case that meant Eric had been his dog all along. As though to confirm her suspicions, Luke stepped out behind the woman and she turned to him, reaching out to touch his face affectionately.

Not wanting them to see her, Harper floored the accelerator, biting down on the sting of shock and hurt as she drove away from the house. A numbness crept over her as she tried to make sense of what she had just seen.

This woman had to be the reason why he didn't want Harper to see where he lived.

By the time she arrived home, she had worked herself into a melancholy mood. She had known Luke had secrets, but still she had trusted him, letting herself fall for him. The woman she had seen had to be his wife or his girlfriend. How could she be so stupid to fall for another man's bullshit?

And he knew Charlie had cheated on her with multiple women. Hell, he had even comforted her when she had discovered the truth. What a fool she was.

Bailey's tail was wagging as she stepped back into the house. She had left so hurriedly, not wanting to lose sight of Luke, the dog must have wondered where the hell she was going. Pleased to have her back, he tried to lead her into the kitchen, turning around to check she was following, as if wanting to remind her he hadn't had any breakfast.

Harper made a fuss of him, trying to ignore the leaden feeling in her stomach as she cleaned and filled his bowls. Part of her was tempted to call Megan. It might help to talk through what she had just seen. Her friend was pregnant, though, and happy. She had her own things going on. It wasn't fair of Harper to keep turning to her for help every time something went wrong, which was far too often these days.

Luke had told her he wasn't on Facebook or Instagram, but she picked up her phone, checking anyway, wishing she knew who the woman was, so she could try to stalk her too.

What the hell was she supposed to say to him when he contacted her later in the day? She couldn't tell him she knew he lived with a woman, because he would realise she had been following him. But, equally, she didn't want to ever see him again.

So much for the fresh start she had hoped for.

Drawing a social media blank – at least he had been truthful about that, she supposed – Harper showered and redressed, this time in jeans and a warm hoodie, before putting on her thick winter coat and trainers, then grabbing Bailey's lead.

As she took him for a long walk, the sharp cold air of the winter's day stinging her face, she debated what to do. Perhaps she shouldn't tell Luke what she had seen. She could just say things weren't working out for her, then walk away with a shred of dignity.

Yes, that was what she would do, she decided matter-of-factly as she returned home, trying to ignore the pain and sense of yearning for what she had just lost.

She had felt a real connection with him. It was something she had feared she would not find again with another man and it stung that she had been contemplating a future together with him.

Determined to push him from her mind, she pulled out the box of Christmas decorations. Although she didn't feel remotely festive, she would put them up anyway. She hadn't bothered the last two years after losing Charlie. But before then, she had loved Christmas. It was something else that had been stolen from her and she determined to get it back, even if it did look like she would now be eating alone on Christmas Day.

Luke was working night shifts over the festive period, so wouldn't be returning home to Ireland, and they had talked about spending the day together. Thank God, she had only bought him just a couple of token gifts and not wasted unnecessary money.

By the time she had put up the tree, bands of silver and blue, with tiny fairy lights twinkling, it was gone midday. As she fixed herself some lunch, Harper's attention was drawn back to the key she had found alongside Charlie's secret mobile phone in the vent in the wall.

She still hadn't figured out what it was for, and if she was honest, until now, she had forgotten about it. Now, in a bid to keep her mind off Luke, she focused again on where it might fit. It didn't belong anywhere in the house, and given that the phone seemed to be tied to Charlie's secret life at the cottage, it occurred to her that perhaps it had come from there.

There were still some bits in the cottage that needed taking to the rubbish tip. Next time she went up there, she would take the key with her.

She settled back at her desk after eating, replying to an email from her agent, who told her he was enjoying the new book, then opening up her ideas file, knowing she needed to start thinking about her next story.

The bare bones of a plot were starting to come together when Luke messaged, telling her his shift was turning out to be a busy one and he wasn't sure what time he would finish.

Relief that she might be able to delay telling him she was

ending things mingled with anxiety that she wouldn't have closure until she got her key back.

She replied with a non-committal *No worries*, then tried to get back to work, but she couldn't shake him from her thoughts.

Although she supposed they had still been in that honey-moon phase of their relationship, things were already relaxed and familiar with him. He was so good with Bailey, who was going to miss him terribly – of course, Harper now knew that Luke had experience with dogs, since he had one of his own – but there were other things too. She would no longer hear him singing loudly and badly in the shower, and if she got up in the night to pee, he wouldn't be waiting to snuggle up against her when she got back into bed. And, God, she was going to miss that slightly goofy, lopsided smile of his.

He was the only person who seemed to find her funny these days, perhaps because they both shared the same dry sense of humour. Knowing she was going to lose that cut her deep.

Frustrated, she shoved her fingers back into her hair, real-ising the words weren't going to come. *Damn you, Luke.*

Deciding she needed a longer break, she made an on-the-spot decision that she would head back up to the cottage now. It would hopefully stop her thinking about Luke, and she might finally find out what the key was for. And if not, at least she could get the place cleared out so it could go on the market.

On a whim, she grabbed Charlie's secret phone, then whis-tled to Bailey. Perhaps once she was done at the cottage, they could go for a walk on the beach.

But first, time to go and face whatever demons Charlie had left behind and rid herself of them once and for all.

29

The mystery key was too small to fit a door, so instead, Harper checked the windows and the kitchen units, before again opening the wardrobe, just in case something had been missed the first time around.

With the remaining furniture broken up in a pile on the living-room floor, it took only a couple of minutes to establish that there was nothing else inside the cottage that had a lock.

Frustrated, she stared out of the grime-smeared bedroom window that was in desperate need of a clean, wondering what the hell else the key could be for. The back garden was extensive, enclosed by high brick walls and mostly laid to a lawn that was now far too overgrown, though wide borders around the edges contained evergreen plants that looked to be getting out of control, the tips of their branches covered in frost.

Had Charlie planted those? She didn't recall her husband being much of a gardener.

Well, that she knew of. She no longer recognised the man she had been married to.

As her gaze travelled over the plants she realised with a jolt of surprise that a shed stood at the rear of the garden, visible through the tall blades of grass. Old and dilapidated with a cracked window and broken strips of wood holding it together. Was it possible the key fitted the shed door or something inside it?

With Bailey hot on her trail, Harper let herself out of the cottage and followed the pathway down to the lawn. Immediately, the scent of what smelt like eucalyptus overpowered the cold, salty sea air. Possibly from the plants in the borders?

Charlie hadn't been particularly adventurous with his gardening, as he had chosen just the one hardy shrub, planting several of them along the length of the border. Harper wasn't particularly green-fingered, but she thought it might be rosemary.

The wet grass brushed against her jeans as she trampled her way across the lawn, heading down to the shed, and as Bailey charged ahead, his tail was wagging furiously, excited by all the new smells.

Before she could sell the cottage, she would have to get in a gardener to take care of this mess. Someone to clean up inside too. It had to go. She couldn't possibly keep it knowing what her husband had used this place for.

The shed door was held shut by a rusty bolt, but it wasn't secured by any kind of lock, and it was stiff as Harper pulled it open. Inside the shadowy, dank space, an odour of dampness, dirt and neglect hit her. Cobwebs covered the two windows and various gardening tools lined the back wall. A rusty old lawn-mower, bags of topsoil and a large wheelbarrow occupied the floor space. All regular items you might find in a shed and none of them requiring a key of any sorts. Still, she checked each one carefully, just to be sure, before concluding that she was wasting her time.

Despondent, she headed back to the cottage, whistling to Bailey, who seemed to be attracted by the rosemary shrubs. She had no idea if the plant was okay for dogs and wasn't going to take any risks.

The chill coming in from the sea made her glad she had wrapped up warm, and now she knew there was nothing here, she couldn't wait to get back in her car so she could get the heater blasting.

In the living room, she glanced again at the remaining rubbish she and Luke hadn't been able to fit in the car on their previous visit. There wasn't much left. Although Harper was reluctant to prolong her stay, if she took care of it now, she wouldn't have to come back.

Leaving Bailey to sniff around, she focused on the task, as she did repeat trips back and forth to her car, her arms filled with the last remaining bits of Charlie's secret love den.

Finally done, she did one last walk through to ensure she hadn't missed anything. All that remained, apart from the items in the shed, which she would leave for whoever she eventually got in to take care of the garden, was a tatty old rug that covered the wooden floor in the inner hallway. Almost as an afterthought, she snatched it up. No point leaving it and it might as well go to the tip with the rest of the stuff.

Spotting the trapdoor underneath it had her double blinking.

The cottage had a cellar?

Part of her was tempted to just go. She had no interest in going inside a dirty old cellar, especially as there was maybe only a couple of hours of daylight left and the only torch she had was on her phone. The trapdoor didn't appear to be locked though, so she supposed it wouldn't take more than a second or two just to peek inside.

Putting down the mat, she dropped to her knees and pulled

back the heavy wooden door. The creak it gave sounded ominously loud against the silence.

Turning her phone light on, Harper shone it inside the dark hole.

Wooden steps led down and she could see that just inside the door was a piece of cord. Giving it a tentative tug, warm light filled the space below and she could see the bottom of a shelf unit, filled with tins. Was that paint?

Curiosity was now getting the better of her, though still she was reluctant to venture down into the cellar while she was here all alone.

It was Bailey who took that decision from her, appearing suddenly beside her, then before she could reach for his collar to pull him back, charging down the wooden stairs.

Damn it.

Harper whistled and called to the spaniel, but he had turned conveniently deaf and the hairs stood up on the back of her neck when he started to growl.

'Bailey! Come here.'

Something down there was bothering him as he completely ignored her, and when the growling became agitated whining and she heard him scraping at either the wall or floor, she knew she had no choice but to go down and get him.

Reluctantly, she started to descend the steps.

As she got lower, Harper had a better view of the space. A large table took up the bulk of it and various bits of wood lined up against one wall suggested it had been used for carpentry.

Charlie had always claimed to be useless at anything DIY related, using his lack of skill as a way of getting out of doing maintenance around the house. According to the range of tools that hung from the shelves, he had been lying about that too.

She was learning so much about her late husband, so

shouldn't really be surprised by any of these new discoveries, but still each one stung with fresh betrayal.

There was also a washing machine in the corner of the room, with a supermarket own brand detergent sat on top, while the shelf unit she had seen sat beside it.

The tins of paint were all the same plain white, but nowhere in the cottage had been painted. They had been used somewhere though, as dried drips of emulsion stained the sides.

What had Charlie used them for?

The other items on the shelves weren't really of interest. Rolls of plastic and dust sheets, a few more rolls of bin liners. A jar of paintbrushes, bottles of white spirit and a pot containing screws and bolts. A box on another shelf was filled with hammers, screwdrivers and spanners. Nothing out of the ordinary, except the paint and the fact her dead husband had a secret woodwork cellar.

Harper whistled to her dog, ready to go. She wouldn't clear this room out. As much as she would like everything over and done with, it would be dark soon. Bailey wasn't paying attention, though. Instead, he was scraping at the floor by a shelf unit.

As Harper went to get him, her attention was drawn to the plug sockets between the washing machine and the shelves. There were four in total and all were being used. One was for the washing machine, but the leads for the other three plugs were neatly clipped to the lower part of the wall and led behind the shelves, though quite why they were wasn't clear, and Harper couldn't imagine what they were for.

Keen to know where they went, she pushed the unit away from the wall, her heart rate accelerating when she spotted the outline of a door behind where it had stood. Had Charlie positioned the shelves there intentionally?

She could see the cables now. They ran along between the

wall and the door. Into what? A secret room? Her gaze dropped to the padlock that had been fitted just above the handle, and she struggled to swallow, her mouth dry.

Even before she pulled the key from her pocket, Harper knew it was going to fit.

As it clicked undone, she pushed down on the handle, easing the door open, terrified for what she might find. Nowhere in her imagination could she come up with a reason for Charlie to need a locked room in a cellar.

The room was dark with shadows and she fumbled for a light switch cord, eventually finding one. When the light came on, the harsh beam made her squint, and it took a second for her eyes to adjust. As they did, she could see what the white paint was for. Every wall, as well as the floor and ceiling had been painted in it, giving the room a cold and clinical look. Her attention, though, was drawn to the bed. It was dressed in black, with handcuffs hanging from either corner of the headboard.

This was where the polaroid picture of the girl had been shot. And now, taking in the other features of the room, she could see two huge floor lamps positioned at the foot of the bed, facing it. In between them stood a tripod with a video camera.

So, he hadn't just taken polaroid pictures of the women, he had recorded them too. Nausea churned in her stomach.

Why down here, though? Why behind a locked door?

She glanced around at the rest of the room. To her immediate left was a desk and chair and behind them stood a large metal cabinet. A computer sat on the desk and on the floor beside it was a console box and a couple of machines that looked as though they were to do with film editing.

Had Charlie been making some kind of kinky movie? Harper knew he'd had a few fetishes, but this all seemed rather extreme.

There was also a gurney, like ones she had seen in hospital

corridors, and beyond the bed was an area closed off by a curtain that was pulled around it, again not dissimilar to a hospital cubicle, though this one was draped in plastic sheeting.

Crossing the room, she peered inside, expecting to see another bed and was surprised to find a large metal table.

The first sliver of fear crept down her spine. What had her husband been up to?

Knowing she couldn't leave until she knew the truth, she went to the cabinet.

Same as the door had been, it was padlocked, but she found the key after hunting through the desk drawers.

Opening the cabinet doors, her stomach dropped. Everything inside was neatly organised, from the arrangement of knives that were set out like a display to the shelf of heavy-duty tools, which included an expensive-looking drill with numerous attachments and what Harper thought was a blowtorch. Sets of manacles hung inside the door, while other shelves were packed with needles and bottles, vicious-looking hooks and scalpels, and more plastic sheeting and reels of tape, which another glance at the homemade cubicle told her was used to hold the plastic together.

Charlie, please, no.

She didn't want to think the worst of her husband, but nothing about this set-up painted him in a good light.

Thinking back to the women he had been exchanging messages with, had he lured them here? He had used a fake profile on Hooked and Harper had wondered how they reacted when they learnt he wasn't who he claimed to be. Had he kept them here against their will?

The bolt on the door and the cuffs indicated that he had. As for the other items in front of her, she really didn't want to consider their purpose.

Something nudged into her and she yelped in fright, her heart hammering and half expecting to find Charlie standing behind her, even though that wasn't in any way possible.

Her sob of relief when she realised it was Bailey made her realise just how shaken she was.

Her dog was growling again, his tail low. This room was unsettling him too. But they couldn't go yet. Harper glanced at the computer, knowing she had to try and get into it.

Although she would rather take it home with her, the set-up was cumbersome and it would take a lot of effort to get everything upstairs and into her car. She could see it was already plugged in, and as scared as she was, she needed to know the truth about Charlie.

Reluctantly, she sat at the desk and switched the machine on, sick with nerves when the screen lit up, asking for a password.

Deciding to go with the same one that had unlocked the phone, she typed 1975, the muscles in her shoulders tightening when it was accepted and the desktop started to load.

Was she finally going to learn the truth about her husband?

The screen background gave nothing away, it was just a generic one, and there was only one folder icon on the home screen, which wasn't even titled. Charlie's email account opened automatically, but it was the same one that Harper had accessed through his second phone. Nothing new to see there.

Instead, she opened the folder, finding several video files. Drawing in a steadying breath, she clicked on the first one, recognising the plastic sheeted area.

A woman was strapped down on the metal table, and Harper could see she was dressed in one of the slutty outfits that had been hanging in the wardrobe, a black rubber dress that left little to the imagination, her face crudely painted with exaggerated black eyeliner that had run down her cheeks, while her bright red lipstick had been sloppily applied. Her eyes were wide with fear as a figure approached, and she started pleading, her struggles intensifying as she tried to free herself.

'Someone has been a bad girl and needs to be punished,' her captor said, sounding amused, and Harper recognised the voice, even before he turned to face the camera.

A sob escaped her as Charlie grinned into the lens, and to her own horror and that of the woman in the video, he held up a large, vicious-looking pair of scissors, snipping them in torment. 'Now where shall we start?'

No.

Every one of Harper's worst fears came true and she struggled to register what was happening on the screen. This was her husband. A man she had loved and then grieved. How had she never seen this side of him?

She couldn't watch this, dread filling her, understanding what was about to happen, but before her trembling fingers could stop the video, she realised the camera was moving. Round to the side of the table and zooming in close to catch the woman's terrified expression as her begging turned to screams.

It wasn't on a tripod. Someone was holding it.

The fresh shock reverberated through Harper as she acknowledged what that meant.

Charlie hadn't been doing this alone.

He had an accomplice.

_____

30

When she first went to the cottage, I worried it might be a problem, and I knew I needed to step up my plan for us to be together. The fact she has gone back there again today tells me I need to move now.

What has she found? Does she know about the cellar? The door to our special room is padlocked shut and hidden behind the shelf unit, and even though I have tried to remove every trace that I was ever there, my fingerprints wiped clean, the videos that my face appeared in deleted, everything set up to suggest that Charlie worked alone, I now worry that I might have missed something.

I felt physically sick when the tag I placed in Harper's car alerted me she was heading back to Waxham, and now I need an excuse to get out of work and deal with this.

I'm not ready for her yet. Samantha has only just gone and I have things I need to put in place. There is a sequence I like to follow, one that helps keep my secrets safe, and Harper's nosiness has just messed it up. Now I am going to have to improvise in order to pull things back under my control and that means getting to her before she causes me further trouble.

She will have to be punished for this.

Everything is escalating, but despite my panic, the fizz of excitement is heating my veins. Months of waiting, of being patient, are about to pay off early. Yes, I am going to have to deviate from my usual pattern, but once this problem is taken care of, my fun can begin.

31

Harper watched Bailey charge across the vast stretch of sand, close to the shoreline, so distracted that she couldn't enjoy the pretty surroundings of Waxham beach. She was just glad that the few people who were there all kept their distance, giving her time alone with her thoughts. It was bitterly cold, but she appreciated the icy chill coming off the water, as it helped cut through the numbness that had taken hold.

The sky was starting to get dusky and people were beginning to head back to the coastal path. In a few minutes, she would follow, and then she would have to call the police, knowing she couldn't put it off any longer. She should have done it already, instead of walking down to the beach, but she needed a short while to herself, to deal with the shock of who – no, what – Charlie was and that he had an accomplice, before her world unravelled.

Because it would. Once word got out that she had been married to a monster, everything was going to change.

The women were dead, Charlie was dead. He would no longer have to answer to his crimes. Would the public turn on her instead? Would they believe the truth, that she had known nothing about what was going on? What if the police thought that she had been his accomplice, the one holding the video camera?

The panic that she could be found guilty had her considering if she should walk away. Just leave the cellar room, never go to the cottage again. If she hadn't started poking around, she would have been none the wiser.

No, she couldn't do that.

Although she had only watched a brief segment of the video, the terror of the woman on the table and her petrified screams was going to haunt her for a long time. Just the thought of what she might have endured before she died had made Harper physically sick, and she had barely made it upstairs to the bathroom before puking in the toilet.

These poor women, their families, they needed justice for the awful things that had been done to them. This was where she could help.

Had their bodies ever been found or were they still presumed missing? She had to give the victims and the people who cared for them closure. And the police had to find out who had been in the cellar with Charlie.

Charlie might not be able to pay, but his accomplice could if they caught him...

Or her.

The thought stopped her short.

Charlie had been in the car with Alicia.

Harper had assumed they were having an affair, but did they have a more sinister relationship?

No, Alicia wasn't a killer. She had been a vegan, for Christ's sake, and was all about every creature having the right to live.

Unless it was a front. An act to disguise her true nature.

Damn it. Harper's head was spinning even considering the possibility, as names such as Rose West and Myra Hindley crept into her mind.

She whistled to Bailey as the cloak of darkness moved in, knowing she could no longer delay the inevitable. As he bounded back towards her, her pocket vibrated signalling a new message.

Eager for the extra stalled moment, she clipped on Bailey's lead, then unzipped her pocket, digging out her phone. Her heart sank when Luke's name appeared on her screen.

> Change of plan. I've managed to get away from work early. Are you home? xx

Shit. She had forgotten about her other problem. The most recent revelation of her late husband's extramarital activities had made Luke's betrayal pale in significance. He still needed dealing with, but later. She had to go to the police first. Once the truth came out about Charlie, chances were Luke wouldn't want anything to do with her anyway. The situation might take care of itself.

A nasty little doubt crept into her head as she thought back to the cellar. The gurney looked like one found in a hospital and so did some of the torturous instruments she had seen in the cabinet.

Luke was a doctor...

No. Her imagination was getting carried away with her. She hadn't met him until recently. There was no way he could have known Charlie. It was far too much of a coincidence.

Unless, his meeting Harper was planned.

Thinking back, she had met him at the beach when he had stepped in to help her. Then, after that, she had continued to bump into him.

And that night when Gavin had followed her home, Luke had conveniently been there to play the hero.

It wasn't possible. Was it?

Had he played her, worked his way into her life and heart because of who she was?

He had insisted on accompanying her to the cottage the first time. Had that been because he didn't want her to discover the cellar?

Stop it, Harper.

She was paranoid and jumping to conclusions.

Luke had been shocked when he had discovered she was widowed.

Of course, that could have been an act. He had lied about his home life quite convincingly.

And he had been very interested in Charlie, she remembered now. Keen to talk about him and asking Harper what he had been like. At the time, she hadn't read anything into it, but now she was analysing every little detail.

Which was ridiculous. She was creating her own narrative based on the things she had found in the cellar and the way she had met him. There was absolutely nothing tangible to connect him to Charlie or to suggest he had been an accomplice to murder.

That didn't let him off the hook with his earlier deception, though, and deciding to ignore him for now, she slipped her phone back in her pocket.

Lost in her thoughts as she and Bailey headed back onto the wooded track that led to the road, she almost didn't see the man approaching. It wasn't until he spoke her name, sounding surprised, that she looked up, startled to recognise Justin.

Although they had stayed in touch for a while, it was the first time she had seen him since their date, and, in all honesty, she hadn't expected to see him again, so his sudden appearance threw her.

'What are you doing here?'

Her question was blunt and her tone perhaps sounded a little bit rude and hostile, as his eyes widened in surprise, but it seemed a relevant one to ask. She knew he didn't live around here.

He indicated the camera around his neck. 'I've been taking pictures.'

Now he said it, Harper remembered he was a keen photographer.

'How have you been?' he asked, seeming pleased to see her, bending to make a fuss of Bailey, whose tail was wagging like crazy.

Remembering how she had cut Justin off, she was wracked with guilt. Only for a moment, though, as she remembered why.

He had known where she lived, yet she had never told him. And now he was here, at dusk, on this cold and deserted beach.

Jesus, Harper. Stop it.

First she was suspecting Alicia, then Luke and now Justin.

He enjoyed photography, and she knew he often used the beach as a location. Besides, he had been as surprised to see her as she was him.

Though, why, if he had just been taking pictures – he had said it in past tense – was he walking to the beach instead of away from it?

Perhaps she should call him out on it, but right now they were the only two on the track and she was pretty certain she had been the last on the beach to leave. Those who had left before her were probably already back at their cars. That meant there was no one around to help if she needed it.

Was he really a danger? He hadn't attacked her. He was just

asking how she was, and instead of answering, she was completely overreacting.

Had he followed her?

The thought crept into her head. It seemed ridiculous, but right now she was paranoid and skittish, and bumping into him here felt like more than coincidence.

And if he had followed her, had he been at the cottage? The person behind the camera? Had he known Charlie? Did he know that she had been in the cellar?

No. She needed to stop. Her overactive imagination was getting carried away. What she needed to do was call the police and let them deal with everything.

He had straightened, standing back up to face her. Much taller and an obstacle in her way. 'Harper? Are you okay?' His voice dripped with concern, but was it fake?

Innocent or not. She couldn't be here with him.

'I'm sorry. I can't be here. I have to go.'

She pushed past him, the action seeming to catch him off guard as he stumbled backwards. Not stopping to check he was okay, she picked up pace, hurrying back along the trail, part of her terrified that at any moment she would feel his hand on her arm as he pulled her to a halt.

'Harper, wait?'

His voice came from behind her, but she pressed on, glad Bailey seemed to think this was a game, charging ahead of her, almost pulling her along.

By the time she reached the road, the sky was almost dark and there were probably only a few minutes of light left. Although her stomach ached and she was out of breath, she didn't stop running until she made it back to the cottage.

Her plan had changed. She wouldn't go back inside. The idea of being in there, knowing what was in the cellar, gave her the creeps. And if Justin was following her, she didn't want to be there alone.

Instead, she headed straight for her car, letting Bailey jump in ahead of her, not stopping to attach his harness, before climbing into the driver's seat and locking the doors.

Once she was a safe distance away, she would pull over and call the police.

Key fob.

She patted her coat, remembering it was in the opposite pocket to her phone. Unzipping it, she pulled the fob out with shaking fingers and went to start the engine. But nothing happened.

Why wasn't it working?

She tried again, her heart hammering when she realised the engine was completely dead.

This couldn't be happening. Not now.

Calling the police moved to number one on her priority list, as she glanced in the rearview mirror for any sign of Justin, relieved when she didn't see him.

That didn't mean she was safe, though.

What were the chances of her car breaking down after everything that had happened? Yes, it was an older model, but she had only recently had it serviced.

Call the police and then perhaps she would call Megan while she waited. Her friend would stay on the phone with her until they arrived.

Except where was her phone? The pocket it had been in was empty.

That wasn't possible. She'd had the phone on the beach, remembering seeing Luke's message. Frantically, she searched the other pockets in her coat, even though she knew exactly which one it had been in.

On the passenger seat beside her, Bailey whined but Harper was too worked up to react to him.

What the hell was she supposed to do now?

She must have dropped her phone on the trail back from the beach. Thinking back, she couldn't recall zipping her pocket again after reading Luke's message. At the time, she had been distracted.

Stupid, Harper.

Okay, think. She needed to stop panicking and come up with a plan.

Going back to the trail wasn't an option. For starters, by the time she got there it would be too dark under the cover of the trees to probably see her phone. Plus, there was a chance of bumping into Justin.

He could be innocent, but was she willing to take that risk?

What if he had tampered with her engine?

Oh God. That made her a sitting duck.

She should go back into the cottage. Although there was no phone, she could message the police from Charlie's computer.

But if Justin broke in...

Besides, she wasn't sure she could face going back down into the cellar.

The only other option was to walk into Waxham itself. Harper was pretty certain there was a cafe there. Would it still be open?

Or there might be a house on her route. The cottage stood isolated, but there had to be other properties dotted along the road.

Of course she ran the risk of meeting Justin again, but it was one she would have to take. She had no other choice.

Letting a frustrated Bailey out of the car again, she went to the boot, fishing out the tyre wrench. Although she wasn't sure how much use it would be if she was attacked, the weight of it felt good and at least she had something she could use as a weapon.

Her pace somewhere between a fast run and a jog, she headed back up to the main coast road, Bailey keeping up beside her. As they approached the junction, taking the turn towards Waxham, the sound of a vehicle rumbled in the distance.

Harper's first thought was to flag it down, but then she worried, what if it was Justin? Had he lain in wait, knowing she would have to go for help when she realised her car wasn't working? She was too far from the woods to find a hiding place, with only open fields around her. There was nowhere to hide.

As the sound of the engine approached, she heard it slowing. *Fuck.*

Clenching the wrench, she focused ahead, refusing to drop her pace, and as the car pulled up alongside her, the driver's window was down.

'Harper?'

Pausing, realising it wasn't Justin, she looked at the driver, relief easing some of the tension out of her as she stared at the smiling face.

She was so grateful it was someone she knew that she didn't even pause to consider the coincidence of them being here.

'Harper?'

Another voice was calling her name now. It came from further away, and glancing up, her eyes widened as she spotted Justin heading towards them.

'What's wrong?' the driver asked, door now open and stepping out into the road. He hadn't spotted Justin. His focus solely on Harper. 'You're shaking. Has something happened?'

'We have to go.'

'What?'

'Please. I'll tell you once we're in the car. But we have to go, now.'

The driver nodded, and, grateful, Harper rushed round to the passenger side, quickly urging Bailey into the back seat, then getting in the front.

'Go!' she urged, aware that Justin was still approaching, and glad that the driver didn't need to be asked a second time. As he pulled away, she glanced in the side mirror and saw Justin hold his hands up in what looked like frustration, but then he was a speck in the distance.

Letting out a shaky breath, Harper slid her seat belt into the lock, then tried to relax back against the headrest, aware of the tension still thrumming through her.

'Thank God you showed up when you did,' she managed, relieved to be out of harm's way.

The driver turned to her and smiled again. 'Don't worry. I'll keep you safe.'

PART III

Give them pleasure.

The same pleasure they have when they wake up from a nightmare.

— ALFRED HITCHCOCK

32

When I look back, I suppose the darkness was always inside of me.

Although it was never spoken about, I knew the move to Norfolk had been because of me. That at a school friend's birthday party when I was just nine years old, I had found a box of matches and set fire to the summerhouse at the foot of the garden.

No one had died, but two of the kids had been taken to hospital, and as everyone viewed my actions with horror, my mortified parents had made the decision to start over and move to Norfolk, where no one would know what I had done.

Matches and lighters were banned and I never got to see friends out of school. They weren't welcome in our home, and I was no longer trusted to go for playdates at other people's houses.

Left to amuse myself, I played with the fish in the pond. My favourite pastime was catching them in a net, then watching them flip about on the grass as they struggled to breathe. Of course, I always put them back. Until one day I decided to take things further, using a stick I had been sharpening.

After that day, there were only dead fish in the pond, and my fun was over. I earned a clip around the ear when my crime was discov-

ered, and Dad became stricter, keeping me on a tighter leash, while Mum tried to smother me with kindness, convinced that love would cure my badness.

It never went away, though they managed to control it until that day in Dad's shed.

At first, the feelings confused me. After viewing the DVDs, I couldn't stop thinking about them, but I was also old enough by then to understand right from wrong.

It actually scared me for a while, this need I had to cause pain, and for a long while I suppressed my urges by mutilating my mother's old dolls that I found in the attic. Then, after Dad died, I obsessively watched his DVDs, wishing it was me in the room, that I was the one holding the cattle prod or the knife.

I was a weird kid, I knew that, but the luck of good genes meant I attracted attention from girls. Years of beatings from my father also meant I knew how to behave and be unfailingly polite. It was like slipping on a disguise.

So, I dated, but something kept me back from ever becoming intimate. I would always end things before that happened, for fear that if I got too horny, I wouldn't be able to stop myself for fulfilling my dark desires.

But then I met Charlie Bancroft-Reed, and everything changed.

Our paths first crossed in the bar of the Swan Inn at Coltishall, one of the hotels he managed, and although there was nothing obvious about him, the odd little comments and knowing glances he sometimes gave me suggested he could see inside my head and knew there was a depraved monster living there.

Initially, that made me self-conscious, like I had been caught out, but the better I got to know him, I started to notice things, and I began to suspect that he was recognising one of his kind.

Charlie fascinated me. For starters, he was older and I knew he was married. Was it possible he was able to keep up the facade of a happy family life, yet have dark cravings? And did he control them like me?

I wanted to ask him, but how the fuck do you bring up something like that in conversation? *Have you ever killed anyone? Does the idea of slicing a woman's throat from ear-to-ear fuel your wildest fantasies?*

Unsure what to do, I started following him. I watched his house, saw him with his wife – Harper, her name was, and she was a looker. Honey-blonde hair that fell in waves around her shoulders, and clear sea-green eyes. And she had a proper peachy arse on her. She ticked every one of my boxes.

But apparently not Charlie's.

When I eventually followed him to the cottage, curiosity got the better of me. He was inside for ages, but when I peeked through the windows, I couldn't see him in any of the rooms. When he finally left, I broke in, eventually finding the cellar and the special room he had hidden behind the bookcase.

The brunette strapped down on the metal table was Mediter-ranean in appearance. Brown eyes and olive skin. Maybe Spanish or Italian origins, and although she wasn't my type, my dick was rock hard.

She was begging me to help her, sobbing with relief that I had found her.

'We need to get out of here before he comes back.'

Ignoring her, I stared at the cuts and bruises covering her body before my attention was drawn to the trolley of items that had obvi-ously been used to inflict the wounds. They were laid out so neatly, it was like an operating theatre, and the blood staining them heated up everything inside of me.

I knew she was expecting me to cut her loose, and it would be the right thing to do, but the need was too strong. She was tied down and helpless, all of the toys there ready for me to play with. It was like she *was being offered to me as a gift, and after years of battling my urges, I couldn't stop myself, finally giving into them.*

The moment she understood my intention was when I picked a metal dental face gag, forcing it into her mouth. The unintelligible sounds she made as she fought to get it out, her eyes going wide in horror, only spurred me on, and I took out my phone, making my own little recording for later pleasures, before picking up a scalpel.

Of course, I didn't mean to kill her. I just wanted a taste. I planned to play and then leave, but then I made the mistake of climbing on the table and sticking my dick inside her, my hands almost possessed as they went to her throat.

That was the moment Charlie arrived back, realising what I had done.

He tried to kill me that day.

I had broken his plaything, and he was livid with rage as he came after me with a hammer. Luckily, I was bigger and stronger, and I had the table full of weapons. Things got messy, but I managed to escape, fleeing home as adrenaline buzzed through my veins.

This wasn't over. I understood that. I now knew his secret and he would need to deal with me. Realising I needed a bargaining chip, I messaged him with a tiny non-incriminating portion of the video I had made.

> It gets worse, but I don't want to show this to anyone. Can we meet?

His reply came almost instantly. Just one word.

> Where?

I picked a pub beer garden on a Sunday afternoon. One I knew had tables spaced out so no one would hear our conversation but that also had plenty of people about.

The look he gave me as he arrived with his pint, sitting down across from me, made it clear he still wanted to kill me, but that wasn't going to happen.

'The video is somewhere safe,' I told him. 'You won't find it. I've made sure of that. And it won't get opened unless I am dead. Then everyone will know what you are.'

It was ballsy, what I did. Yes, I had hidden the video, but although its contents were X rated, it didn't necessarily incriminate him, but he didn't know that I was calling his bluff.

As I suspected, he couldn't afford to risk finding out if I was.

'What do you want?' he asked eventually. 'I can get my hands on some cash immediately, but most of it is tied up in bonds.'

He thought I wanted money. The idea brought a smile to my face.

'This isn't fucking funny,' he snarled, trying to keep his tone low as he glanced around at the other drinkers.

'I know it isn't.'

'Then what the hell are you laughing for?'

I sat back and smirked at him, knowing he was the answer to everything I had been looking for. 'I don't want your money, Charlie.'

'Then what do you want?' he demanded.

Time to lay out my stall. 'I will keep your secret, but I want to be a part of this.'

'What?' Despite his question, he wasn't stupid. He knew what I had done in the cellar. I was just like him.

'I want to watch.'

'No.'

The answer was immediate, but we both knew he didn't really have a choice.

'Yes.' I told him. 'I want to watch, but I also want to play.'

I knew he didn't like my proposition from the tightening lines around his mouth. He continued to argue with me, but the outcome was a foregone conclusion.

Our alliance was never evenly balanced and for much of it there was resentment. At first from Charlie, who wanted to work alone and didn't appreciate having a pupil, as he thought of it. But then also from me. Initially, I was happy to tag along. His victims, him taking the lead. Sometimes he would make me watch. Other times he would let me get involved. It was always over too quickly, though. I preferred the idea of having someone to return to, to prolong the experience, and I had new ideas I wanted to bring to our arrangement. Some he embraced, agreeing to go from polaroid photos to video, but others he scorned. He wouldn't deviate from his type and let me choose a victim, and sometimes he got to have all of the fun, while I felt just like a bystander.

As my confidence grew, I toyed with teaching him a lesson. Maybe I should get to know that wife of his better. I suggested it one day, tongue in cheek to see how he reacted, and he went off the deep end.

'She is off limits,' he raged. 'You don't go near her.'

So, he did love her, even if blondes weren't his type.

Something to store away for the future.

After that conversation, he did relax a little, letting me have more input and involvement and we developed a slightly begrudging but more evenly matched respect for one another. He even started to trust me towards the end, and if our time together hadn't been cut short, I believe we could have eventually had a great partnership.

But he is gone now, and while I learnt a lot from him, perhaps it was time for me to develop on my own. I had a lot of ideas I wanted to try, and without him there, I was able to thrive and grow, become comfortable in my own skin.

Perhaps I should have gone after Harper sooner, but there was always this barrier between us. She had been Charlie's wife, and much as I wanted her, she felt untouchable. As if she was someone who could be coveted, but never a target.

Until she walked back into my life.

She had only ever met me a couple of times and both occasions had been fleeting enough that she didn't remember me. I had never forgotten her, though.

Initially, I ignored my craving, out of respect for Charlie, I suppose, but then the second time I saw her, I wondered why I was considering him at all. He had always believed he was better than me, and if the video hadn't been hanging over him, the threat of being exposed, he would have killed me in an instant. He had no loyalty to me, so why did I revere him so much? I was better than him, and certainly more creative.

Charlie had believed he was king, but the mantle had passed, and taking his wife was the ultimate way to say fuck you.

33

The thumping in her head was the first thing Harper was aware of and for a moment she couldn't focus on anything else. It was making her nauseous and she rolled onto her side, trying to find a more comfortable position.

As she gradually crept closer to consciousness, she struggled to swallow. Her throat was tight and sore, as if something had been, or was, crushing against her windpipe, and her lips and mouth were dry too.

Desperately thirsty, she reached for the glass of water she kept on her bedside table, her fingers instead hitting brick. In her foggy state, it took several seconds for her brain to register that something was wrong.

Forcing her eyes open, she blinked to clear her blurry vision. At first, it didn't work, but gradually the room swam into focus.

Exposed brick walls, dark wooden beams and the only light coming from the bare bulb hanging from the ceiling. The air was damp, its scent musty, but mingled with body odour and urine, and something else – a pungent, foul smell she couldn't quite decipher, that only added to the growling sickness in her gut.

This wasn't her bedroom and the lack of light and windows added claustrophobia to her increasing alarm. Where the hell was she?

Sitting up too fast, her head thumped harder, the room almost spinning off its axis.

Harper winced and waited a moment for the dizziness to pass, though she was desperate to figure out what the hell was going on, and why she was in this place she didn't recognise.

Her memories were so hazy and she struggled just to think.

Oh God. She had been at the cottage.

The cellar.

She glanced frantically around now, aware this place seemed like some kind of basement room, but it was different. There was no clinical white starkness here. It looked like your typical cellar, a place used for storage or perhaps a washing machine and dryer, and although she had been sleeping, it wasn't in a proper bed, she understood now, realising the mattress she sat on was on the floor. A stripey one that had no bedding. There was no duvet or pillow, or sheets to dress it, and she could see now as she studied it that it was covered in stains.

Was that blood?

The realisation had her leaping to her feet. Too fast, as fresh nausea hit, and for a second, she had to steady herself against the cold brick wall, scared her legs were going to give way under her.

Justin. She had bumped into Justin. They were on the beach and she had been frightened of him. Scared he might be Charlie's accomplice. She had been walking Bailey, but where was he?

Oh shit. Luke.

She suddenly remembered him.

The gurney and the medical instruments she had found.

Oh God.

He had left work early.

Her phone. Where was her phone?

She needed to find her phone so she could call someone to help her, and she needed to find her dog.

As she looked for both things, her gaze passed over a tatty old sofa and a hardback wooden chair, both positioned in front of a wall-mounted TV, and her eyes widened, spotting what looked like a medieval torture rack bench at the far end of the room. Hanging blades and other vicious-looking implements above it had her stomach dropping and dread creeping in.

She needed to get the hell out of this room.

Spotting the closed door, she stumbled towards it, shocked when pressure against her throat stopped her, jerking her sharply back. Stumbling and choking as she lost her balance, her bum took the brunt of the fall and she grasped frantically at her neck, horrified when found something tied around it.

A collar, she realised, her fingers feeling the cool metal, and there was a chain coming out of it that she could now see was attached to the wall. It allowed her to move only a few feet from the bed.

Harper's heart was almost beating out of her chest, panic clogging her throat and making it difficult to breathe. Why was she here? What was going to happen to her?

Another memory. The video she had watched of her husband torturing the brunette.

But Charlie was dead.

He hadn't worked alone, though. There had been two of them.

Everything came crashing back now, the last of the cobwebs clearing as she fully regained her memory, and fresh panic at who had done this to her sent shockwaves trembling through her body. If she hadn't tried to move on, and if Megan hadn't encouraged her to sign up to that blasted dating site, their paths wouldn't have crossed.

But they had and she had trusted him enough to get in the car.

She remembered now the relief at believing she was safe when he had pulled over, then the prick of a needle.

Recalling what she had seen on the video, the torture, pain and humiliation the woman had been subjected to, Harper understood why she was here.

That was when she started to scream.

34

The last time Adrian Fox had been in the Black Dog, he had met up with Harper.

A waste of bloody time that had been. The silly cow had caused him no end of problems and he hadn't even got to fuck her.

He still held her responsible for the collapse of his marriage and she was going to pay for that. His stupid wife, Jenny, had initially forgiven him for the sake of their kids and because she felt sorry for him after he had been beaten up, but his indiscretion had played on her mind. For the last two weeks, she had been staying with her parents, and she had taken the kids with her. She had made it clear he had until this weekend to find somewhere to go and she wanted all of his things moved out before she returned.

Luckily, he had held on to his late parents' place. It was a run-down semi out in the sticks. Two bedrooms, one bathroom, living room, old-fashioned kitchen and a decent-sized cellar. He had used it as his man pad, whenever he needed a break from Jenny and the kids, but the idea of living there permanently didn't fill him with joy, even if he did have a new toy to go home to tonight.

'What can I get you?'

The bartender broke through Adrian's thoughts, addressing him directly with cool eyes, even though he was in a group of five. All of them were friends from childhood and they were out tonight to wet the head of Jimmy's new baby. Somehow, his friends had managed to stand slightly back, meaning Adrian was left to buy the first round.

Wankers.

Grudgingly, he looked at the group, not missing their smirks. He knew he had a reputation for being tight with his money. They had probably set it up so he would be first at the bar.

'Pints or shots?' he asked half-heartedly.

The unanimous vote was to start with beer. Adrian had driven to the pub, not planning on a late night, but that seemed to be out of the window now.

Watching the bartender pour the drinks, he realised it was the same kid who had served him when he was here before.

Well, not really a kid. The guy was probably in his twenties.

That age felt a lifetime ago, something that irked Adrian beyond belief. He had loved being young, and hated that his fortieth birthday was only just over a year away. His hair was greying and he had to dye it to maintain the colour, and don't get him started on the lines starting to crease his face, or his aching back.

Of course, a lot of that pain could be attributed to the attack he had suffered. Most of his injuries had healed, now, but he had landed on his coccyx and, shit, that had been painful. It had never been right since.

'Twenty-four seventy,' the bartender told him, his tone blunt and his face unsmiling as he stared across the counter.

He had a bit of an attitude, this kid.

Reluctantly taking his card from his wallet, Adrian tapped the reader.

'Did that hurt, Adrian?' Kurt, the joker of their group, sniggered, prompting laughter from the rest of them.

If he'd have had his way, they wouldn't have come here and would instead be in the centre of Norwich, in a Wetherspoons or somewhere else cheaper, but Jimmy had chosen the place and as it was his night, his kid, his decision was final.

They were here now, and as he had been collared into buying the first round, he would definitely stay to get his money's worth. He didn't want to get too drunk, though. Tonight was his first time with his new toy and he couldn't wait to get home and play.

Isaac Collins watched the group of men getting steadily more inebriated as he wiped down the bar. They were on their fourth round and sounding louder by the second. It was irritating and making his head hurt.

'They look like they're having fun,' Karen, the landlady, commented, patting his shoulder as she moved past him to get to the fridge.

'Yeah,' he muttered in agreement, quashing down what he really thought of them.

He wasn't a drinker. Hated the stuff. Ironic really, given that he worked in a pub. He did like it here, though. He had started out in corporate, tending the bar in a hotel, and this was better, more relaxed. Karen was a good boss and she was understanding of his family situation. That his mother was suffering with dementia and he sometimes had to adjust his shifts to take care of her.

This bad mood he was in was irritating him and he needed to shake it off. It was almost Christmas, the atmosphere in the pub, with its lit fire and giant twinkling tree, was festive and jovial, despite the fact he had to listen to the same Christmas songs day and night, and life was treating him well. He shouldn't let himself get wound up by a group of drunks.

Not just any group of drunks. He had recognised Adrian, who bought the first round, remembering serving him when he had been in the pub with Harper.

This had been her dating venue until things had gone wrong for her, and Isaac had enjoyed watching her negotiate each new meeting. Adrian had been the first.

That was the thing with bartending, you got to know the regulars and you got to people-watch. He and Karen, and the rest of the staff, had affectionate little nicknames for most of them, then there were those who they knew by name.

He remembered how he had made the mocktail for Harper after she had been stood up. Her next date had been with Gavin Brooks and Isaac had been forced to intervene after Brooks turned violent. The police had visited the pub the following day, telling them about the attack at Harper's home. She hadn't been back to the Black Dog since, and Karen and Isaac had both given witness statements. Had Brooks not turned up dead, the story all over the local news, they would have gone to court to testify.

That night when he had attacked Harper seemed so long ago, even though it was only in October. So much had happened since then, and now they were rapidly approaching the end of the year. It would be Christmas next week.

This was the only place that felt festive to him, though. Isaac hadn't bothered to decorate at home, knowing his mother, who had once loved Christmas, no longer had any idea what time of year it was. He hadn't bothered with presents either, but now he was wondering if that was a mistake, especially as they had company staying. It was also his first Christmas not working in five years. He really should stop being a grinch.

Deciding that instead of ignoring the holiday season, he would fully embrace it, he spent the rest of his shift planning gifts and decorations, and a Christmas lunch extravaganza, while trying his best to ignore the idiots getting drunk in front of him.

They were knocking back shots by the time last orders were called and making noisy plans to head into the city, one of them on the phone trying to get hold of a taxi.

Isaac could have told them they would struggle to get one, with most cabs already booked up for the night or busy with Christmas revellers.

'We'll need a minibus too,' the one he had heard them call Kurt shouted. 'There's five of us,' he announced after drunkenly counting heads.

'We can't get a regular bloody taxi, let alone a minibus,' the one whose baby they had been toasting said, realisation dawning after fifteen minutes of calls. 'We'll have to walk.'

There were moans at that, even though it would only take them twenty minutes tops.

'I'm actually going home,' Adrian slurred, earning himself jeers and comments about being a lightweight.

Isaac rolled his eyes. These were grown men, probably in their late thirties, yet they were behaving like children.

'You're coming with us,' Kurt insisted.

'No, I can't. I need to get home.'

'Why? You got a woman there waiting for you?' one of the others bellowed, making the others hoot with laughter.

Adrian went to tap his nose, as if it was a secret, and missed, stabbing his finger into his eye.

'You bloody idiot,' the baby friend laughed. 'You might as

well come with us. You're not gonna get a cab. You can't walk back.'

'S'okay,' Adrian managed, producing a key fob and waving it in the air. 'I have my car.'

'Mate, you can't drive home. You're pissed.'

'It'll be fine.'

Karen's razor-sharp hearing, even though she was the other end of the bar, had already picked up the exchange, and she glanced over at Isaac to make sure he was there to back her up as she approached the group.

'I'm going to need you to surrender your keys, please. We can't let you drive home. You're over the limit.'

As expected, Adrian protested he was fine, getting a little bolshy, but luckily the group backed Karen up.

'Where does he live?' she asked, trying to ascertain if it was in walking distance.

'Old Catton,' one of them piped up.

'No, he's at his parents' house, remember?' baby man corrected. 'Freethorpe.'

This wasn't Karen's problem to sort. Adrian shouldn't have let himself get in this ridiculous state in the first place. She should kick him out and let his friends figure out what to do with him. His boss was too soft, though, and Isaac knew she wouldn't.

Freethorpe wasn't too far from where he lived in Cantley. He supposed he could drop the man off. Much as he hated the idea of having the alcohol fumes in his car, it would earn him another golden star with Karen. Isaac tried his best to be a model employee, knowing it made his boss more receptive to doing him favours and letting him have time off, especially when it came to hospital appointments with his mum.

'I can drop him off home,' he offered.

Karen's look of relief told him he'd made the right call. 'Are you sure you don't mind, love?'

'It's only slightly out of my way. It's fine.'

Adrian's friends seemed glad to be rid of the problem too, quickly piling out of the door before Isaac could change his mind, Kurt slapping him on the back and saying he owed him a pint.

'You're a good lad,' Karen told him, insisting she would finish closing the bar so Isaac could be on his way, calling her teenage son, Archie, down to help Isaac get Adrian to the car.

The man could barely walk or string a sentence together, vomiting in the bushes before they got him strapped into the Toyota.

If he barfed again while he was in the car, Isaac would kill him.

Managing to get the address out of him, Isaac thanked Archie for his help and, wondering if he had made a big mistake trying to help, pulled out of the car park.

* * *

The exchange with Harper had left Justin Seaton feeling unsettled, and he really didn't know quite what to make of her.

When they had first met for their date, he had felt there was a connection, but it became apparent throughout the evening that it wasn't there for her. Justin had always been good at reading people and he knew Harper wasn't attracted to him from her mannerisms and the shifts in conversation. They did get along, though, and unable to face having his ego crushed, he had jumped in before she could reject him, suggesting they be friends. It was a starting point he could build on and perhaps once she got to know him better, she might develop deeper feelings towards him.

At the time, she had agreed, but then, as they headed into winter, she had cooled towards him.

He didn't understand why.

At least he didn't until he saw her with another man.

He already knew plenty about Harper, having googled her after their date. He knew she was a romance author and her name wasn't an overly common one. It had been easy to find out about her and there were plenty of interviews which revealed snippets of her life, telling him she lived in the countryside, one revealing she was in Salhouse. And a couple of the photos she shared on social media were recognisable as Salhouse Broad, with its small beach and jetty looking out over the wide expanse of water.

That was where he saw them.

He had taken photos down at the broad before, so it wasn't unusual for him to be down there. At least that's what he had convinced himself, making his third trip there in a matter of weeks.

Perhaps part of him had hoped to bump into Harper, but he didn't expect to see her with someone else. They were walking the dog she had told him about, a bouncy black spaniel, and it was clear from the way her companion's hand grazed down Harper's back and over her arse in a casual, yet intimate gesture, that they were involved.

Harper hadn't seen Justin, and he was grateful for that, because he didn't know that he would be able to disguise his disappointment. Instead, he had slipped away back onto the wooded trail that led back to his car, and over the weeks that followed he had tried to push her from his thoughts.

That's why this afternoon on the beach had started off as such a surprise.

The private school he worked for had already broken up for Christmas and not a huge fan of the festive season since his wife had passed, he had decided to head to the beach, hoping to get in some good wintery shots. The seals on the water's edge were just begging to be photographed and knowing he would need a longer lens, not wanting to get too close to the creatures, he had headed back to his car to fetch it. It had been while returning along the trail, hoping he hadn't left it too late and that there was still enough light to get his pictures, he had run into Harper, but by all accounts, she hadn't seemed happy to see him.

He hadn't dreamt he would bump into her again and certainly not in Waxham. Although it was a beach he often frequented, he had never seen Harper here before. But she had shocked him, acting like a spooked animal. It was almost as if she was frightened of him. Why, though?

After she had fled with her dog, so keen to get away from him, Justin had been tempted to pursue her, but he didn't want to upset her further, so he had continued with his plan to revisit the beach, managing to snap just a handful of photos before resigning himself to the fact it was now getting too dark to do them justice.

It was as he was heading back along the trail that he had heard a vibration and saw a flash of light on the ground ahead.

A phone. Harper's phone, he'd realised, scooping it up. The screen picture was of her dog.

Justin had slipped it in his pocket and headed back to his car. She was probably long gone by now, but he would figure out a way to contact her, so he could return it.

Maybe then he could find out why she had been acting weird.

What he hadn't expected, as he headed back to where his car was parked along the side of the road, was to see her and the dog walking towards him. He had been about to call to her, when the car had pulled up alongside her.

Was she about to accept a lift from a stranger?

Justin shouted her name, wanting to stop her, but as she glanced in his direction, the driver's door opened. She knew him. It was all okay.

Still, he had her phone and needed to let her know, pulling it from his pocket and waving it in the air to show her.

It was too late, though, as she was already in the car, and gone.

* * *

The first time Luke O'Mara had laid eyes on Harper Reed, he had felt a connection.

Still, it was something he tried to ignore. Right person, wrong time, and all that.

There had been another woman in his life at that point, though it hadn't been working out. As that bond severed, sliding to its inevitable conclusion, he hadn't been able to get Harper out of his head.

The second time he had bumped into her he had made her cry.

Stupid, Luke.

Her vulnerability added another layer to an already intriguing woman. One he knew he needed to get to know better.

Then, at the end of their third encounter, he had wanted to kiss her, sensing that she wanted that too.

But there was a problem. He wasn't ready.

Still, she consumed most of his waking thoughts, and eventually he gave into the urge to be with her, to get to know her better, all the while knowing he needed to get his shit together and put plans in place, before he could bring her to his home.

One thing he was learning about Harper, though, was that when she wanted to know something, she was bloody stubborn, and she wouldn't let things drop. She kept pushing and digging deeper, until he realised he couldn't hold off any longer. She had left him with no other choice.

Perhaps he was overreacting, but it all came down to self-preservation. She wanted to know the real him and so he was finally going to show her.

Everyone had secrets and Harper was going to discover his.

It would be interesting to see how she reacted.

Heading round to the back of the house, he pulled his keys from his pocket and unlocked the door, flipping on the light switch and stepping down into the basement.

35

The thing about us serial killers is we all have a preferred style.

Not that I had any idea about that or what mine was when I first hooked up with Charlie. Until I killed the woman on his table, I didn't even know I had it in me to take another human being's life.

I knew I had violent tendencies. I had been fascinated and then obsessed with Dad's videos, and I yearned to do more than just watch, and when I was younger, I had mutilated my mother's precious fish, but if I hadn't encountered Charlie Bancroft-Reed, would I have followed this path or would it have stayed in my head, a fantasy to jerk off to?

If that man gave me anything, it was belief that I could follow my dream and the confidence that I would get away with it.

Anyway, I digress.

Charlie had a style and he was very by the book, rarely deviating. The only real change I ever persuaded him to make was to introduce video play, but other than that it was all his way.

Initially I was intrigued by his routine and quirks, I suppose I will call them.

As I mentioned before, he had a type, one very different to his wife, and watching him certainly taught me a few things – such as it's not all about the kill. Inflict the injuries right and you can have yourself days of fun. Foreplay, I like to think of it as.

He also had a full visual thing going on, liking to dress them up revealing their inner slut, and forcing them to pose for the camera. To anyone viewing his first round of polaroids, before their wounds became too noticeable, it would look like a cheap and whorish photo shoot.

I have introduced some of this into my own routine, taking a few of my favourite outfits from the cottage, but mostly that was Charlie's kink.

The one habit of his I have copied, because it works so damn well, is the bargaining tools.

Things can be earnt and they can also be taken away. In my special place, I am God and my housemates soon find out that their lives can be made better or infinitely worse. Behave and they will have real food. Okay, by real food, I mean tins of pasta and fruit. However, piss me off and they get dog meat. The best bit is when they get to the point of desperate hunger. Then they gladly eat it.

And no cutlery. Every meal – good or bad – is eaten straight out of a bowl on the floor. Like an animal. It adds that extra layer of humiliation, reminding my housemates that I now control everything.

When it comes to our methods of inflicting pain, I am more adventurous than Charlie ever was.

He had all the tools, but he rarely veered away from his knives. He was a big fan of cutting, and while I love to cut too – there is nothing so sweet as drawing your blade across unblemished clammy skin, the scent of blood and terror oozing out – I have a far bigger imagination. There are so many ways to hurt someone, and I find switching things up keeps my housemates living in a constant state of fear. Not knowing what our next session might involve keeps them on their toes and stops things from becoming boring for me.

And don't get me started on those stupid rosemary plants. I never got the point of those, one planted above each victim's body in Charlie's garden of death, but I suppose it was his thing. Very ritualistic, and not me at all.

Once they're dead, they're gone. Dismember the body, black refuse sacks, then drive out to the woods and bury everything deep.

That is what I was doing late last night with Samantha.

I had grown fond of her during our time together, and I was actually a little sad things had come to an end, but I was eager to move Harper in. It's lucky Samantha is taken care of, because Harper's meddling means I had to take her early.

Normally I clean and prepare the room between housemates, giving them the home comfort of freshly laundered bed linen when they first arrive. It's something I can take away when they misbehave. But things have moved so quickly, and the sheets aren't ready. They are still drenched in Samantha's sweat and some of her blood. I have to soak them in cold water overnight, then use hydrogen peroxide to help shift stubborn stains, before I can wash them. Harper will have to make do with the mattress. But, perhaps that's what she deserves. After all, she's caused me considerable trouble.

Still, knowing that she is mine now, safe and secure, and waiting for me in my special room, both calms and excites me. We have so many adventures ahead of us, and a whole host of new things to try. I can't wait to get started.

36

The plan had been to have two drinks and leave, and Adrian was inwardly cursing himself for fucking things up.

After he had barfed, his world had briefly stopped spinning, and he realised he was in the bartender's car. Vaguely recalling giving his address, he knew the kid – Isaac, that was his name, wasn't it? – was driving him home. Something he didn't want or need.

Why had he allowed himself to get in this state? All he had wanted was to go back to his parents' house in Freethorpe and play, but that was unlikely to happen now. Instead, he tried to focus on not throwing up again, glad the radio was on so he didn't have to make conversation as he slipped in and out of drunken consciousness.

All he had to do was get to his front door, then send the kid on his way. Whatever happened, he didn't want him coming inside the house.

He wasn't even aware they had arrived home until he felt a tapping on his cheek.

'We're here. Where are your keys? I'll help you get inside.'

'No!' Adrian managed to snap, realising Isaac was out of the car and leaning in from the passenger side. He didn't want him coming in.

He didn't miss Isaac's eye roll or the heaving sigh of frustration. 'Where are your keys?' he repeated. 'I promised Karen I would make sure you got inside.'

Who was Karen? Was she the barmaid?

Silly bitch. It was all her fault he had to leave his car at the pub. Now he was going to have to get a cab back there tomorrow to get it.

He fished for his house key in his pocket, attempting to get out of the car without undoing the seat belt, then fumbling for it, annoyed when Isaac reached across to help.

'I've got it,' he snapped, Isaac reaching for the keys as Adrian stumbled from the car.

He made it to the front door, stabbing the key at the lock, unable to get it in.

'Here, let me do it,' Isaac said impatiently, snatching the key.

Next thing Adrian knew, the front door was open, the light switch flipping on, and he was being ushered inside.

'You can go now,' he said, rudely.

Ignoring him, Isaac went through to the kitchen. 'I'll get you a glass of water,' he shouted through, and Adrian heard the tap running as he slumped down on the sofa.

From the position where he was sat, he could see the cellar door leading off the inner hallway. It was ajar and the light on. He must have been distracted when he was down there earlier.

He watched Isaac bring the water to him, needing to get the kid out now, keen to get to his new toy.

'Can you just fuck off home now?' he snapped, refusing to take the glass.

Unperturbed, Isaac set it down on the coffee table. As he

straightened, he frowned, staring at the cellar door, before going over to it. 'Let me sort that.'

'Just leave it.'

Ignoring him, Isaac instead pulled it open, staring down at the steps. 'You don't want to fall down those while you're drunk,' he commented.

Adrian was up off the sofa, stumbling towards the kid. 'I told you to bloody leave it. Get the fuck out of my house.' As he reached for him, intending to pull him back, he wobbled forwards, losing his balance.

A warm hand touched his back and for a horrifying moment he thought it was going to push him, but then he realised it had hold of his jumper, and was tugging him back.

'Point proven,' Isaac muttered dryly, as Adrian let out a sigh of relief.

* * *

Perhaps Isaac should have given Adrian a hard shove, instead of stopping him falling. The man was obnoxious and rude, and deserved to break his neck. Instead, he exercised restraint, turning off the light and bolting the cellar door, ignoring the insults.

Adrian was no longer his problem.

Satisfied he had done his bit, he went to let himself out of the front door, spotting the brand-new PlayStation sat in front of the TV. The box had been opened and the controller was already out on the floor.

Glancing back at Adrian, whose eyes had fallen shut as he slumped back on the sofa, Isaac smiled to himself, before stepping on the controller and hearing a satisfying crunch beneath his boot.

Nothing to prove he had done it. Adrian was a drunken mess and still had his shoes on too.

It was petty but satisfying, knowing he had broken the man's new toy and it added to Isaac's good mood as he drove home to Cantley.

The house he had moved to with his parents when he was ten was now in his name, though his mother still lived with him. He tried to take care of her as best as he could, reluctant to have her put in a home, and downplaying how severe her dementia was getting.

Letting himself inside, he went straight through to the kitchen and boiled the kettle, making a cup of tea. Then he took it upstairs, unlocking his mother's bedroom door, relieved to find her sat in her chair in the corner of the room. The door was only ever locked when he went out. It was for her safety, as were the bars on the windows, and he had been careful to remove any objects she might be able to hurt herself with. The house was toasty warm to ensure she didn't catch a chill.

As was his usual routine, he sat with her, chatting about his day, as he helped her sip the drink, and listening as she told him about hers. Some days she was more coherent than others, and other times she didn't even recognise him. Luckily, this wasn't one of those occasions, though she was still delusional as she rattled on about how she had gone to lunch with his dad, telling Isaac that next time he should bring his girlfriend and join them.

He indulged her, not having the heart to point out that his father was dead and that there was no girlfriend.

'Time for bed, Mum,' he told her gently, taking the cup from her before helping her getting undressed and tucking her in.

How the roles had reversed over the years.

After kissing her tenderly on the forehead, he took the cup downstairs, taking time to wash it up, while staring out over the back garden which held so many childhood memories. The old shed glowed in the darkness, now lit up by a string of fairy lights.

The cup dried and placed back in the cupboard, Isaac glanced around, satisfying himself that the kitchen was spotless. He didn't like clutter and everything had to be clean and neat.

Well, apart from one room. The place where he could be himself.

Pulling the key he kept with him at all times from his pocket, he went into the hallway and opened the cellar door. A blast of cool air hit him, recharging his senses.

As he descended the steps, he thought again of Adrian Fox and how easily he could have pushed him. The fact that he didn't was testament to just how far he had come. Every action was now carefully thought out and he was no longer impetuous, as he had been when he had gone to Adrian's home in Old Catton and given the man a beating for upsetting Harper.

No one was allowed to hurt her. Well, no one else.

That's why he had taken care of Gavin Brooks too. How dare he touch Isaac's property?

Still, he had to exercise a certain amount of caution and couldn't go after everyone in Harper's life. It would look too suspicious. Especially when she disappeared.

Isaac knew he had to appear as normal as possible to the outside world, which is why he saved all of his dark cravings for this sacred space.

He had disguised the room as his man cave. A huge TV screen took up one wall with a leather sofa facing it, and a cooler hummed away, filled with bottles of Coke. The side walls were covered in framed movie posters he had little interest in. It was all for illusion.

The back wall, behind the sofa, was his masterpiece. Floor-to-ceiling shelves he had built himself covered the entire wall.

They were filled with DVDs he never watched and books he never read. Removing the *Game of Thrones* boxset, he released the catch behind it, pulling the section of shelf away from the wall. Sliding the bolt back from the second heavier door he had fitted behind it, he stepped inside.

Harper was already on her feet, having heard his approach, and after closing the door again, he turned to face her, drinking her in. Slender and blonde, and wearing far too many clothes for his liking. Normally, he would have taken care of that at the start, but he had to get back to work, so this had been a rush job. He would soon find her something more suitable to wear. Red, he remembered. He wanted her in red.

She was scared of him, he could see that, and he knew she would also be confused – they always were at first – but there was also fury in her eyes and determination in the tilt of her chin. She was everything he wanted in a housemate, and he was going to enjoy breaking her.

'Let me go.'

Her words were demanding, but Isaac didn't miss the tiny tremor of panic in her voice.

'I don't want to do that. You've only just arrived,' he told her, slipping off his coat and enjoying that she took a quick step back as he approached. 'We have so much fun ahead of us.'

'Why are you doing this?'

The tremor was more evident this time. Her confidence was already ebbing.

Disappointing. He had wanted her to fight harder.

Still, fear was intoxicating. He would get high on that instead.

Needing to smell hers, he took a step closer, not realising until it was too late that she was holding something behind her back. As it smashed into his face, pain exploded, and he stumbled backwards. His face was on fire, the taste of blood in his mouth.

Harper went to hit him again, but the chain on the collar meant she couldn't quite reach him this time. Moving quickly to the sofa, Isaac snatched up his remote control, jamming his thumb hard against the button, and watching as electricity surged through the collar, shocking her into dropping her weapon. As she cried out in pain, her hands going to her neck as her eyes rolled back, she fell to her knees.

He rubbed at his sore nose, glancing at the boot on the floor, realising for the first time she only had socks on her feet.

Resourceful, he grudgingly admired, rubbing at his bleeding nose. He was always careful to keep any potential weapons out of his housemates' reach. Kicking it to one side, he glanced around for the other boot, guessing she had hidden it, giving her a second shock when she looked like she was about to get up.

He found the other one tucked down by the side of the mattress. Making sure both were out of her reach, he let her have a moment to recover, wanting to be sure he had her attention.

'This is what happens when you don't behave,' he said, showing her the remote. 'There's enough electricity in that collar to fry your brain. Of course, I don't want to do that. It wouldn't be much fun. But I will if I have to.'

'Why are you doing this?' Harper managed, still clutching at the collar and sounding a lot less sure of herself now.

Had she really believed he was that stupid he would allow her to escape after hitting him with her boot? The collar wasn't coming off apart from the times that he released it, and when that happened, she would be suitably restrained in other ways.

The design was his own and he had gone to great lengths to ensure it gave a painful enough shock that his housemates were forced to obey him. He had lied when he said it was powerful enough to kill her, but it certainly had enough juice to subdue her, causing her to vomit and lose control of her bladder and bowels if she didn't behave.

It was the perfect humiliation tool and exactly what he needed it to be, the same as everything else in this room.

He was good with his hands, both with wood and metalwork – skills learnt from his father – and he was proud to have built most of the apparatus he used. He was going to enjoy introducing Harper to his work.

It was the second time she had asked him why he was doing this, and he supposed he should tell her. Dropping down to her level, he placed his free hand under her chin, forcing her head up so she had to look at him.

'I'm doing this because I want to,' he told her bluntly. 'The same way your husband liked to.'

He watched for her reaction, still unsure if she knew the truth about Charlie. Had she been in the cellar at the cottage?

Her eyes filled with tears, but her voice was hateful when she spoke. 'You were with him. It was you holding the camera.'

So she did know. And she had seen the videos.

A prelude of what was in store for her.

'Correct.' Isaac smiled cruelly. 'And you'll be pleased to hear he taught me everything I know.'

This was perfect, and he decided he would make her watch some more of those videos before he touched her.

It would build the anticipation for them both. Harper would get to see what he was capable of and how depraved his mind could be, while he could feed on her reactions, and work out what terrified her the most.

When it was time for their first play session, he wanted it to be spectacular.

—————

37

When Luke had first moved to Norfolk, he had come over from Ireland to be with his then girlfriend, Rachel, who he had met when she was visiting friends in Ballyshannon. She had a terrace in Norwich that they shared for the first year he was here.

Sadly, living together exposed the flaws in their relationship, and after they split up, he needed to find somewhere else to live. Returning to Ireland wasn't something he wanted to do. Although he was close with his parents and siblings and travelled home to visit them several times a year, he had a growing friendship circle in Norwich and was happy with his job. Needing somewhere immediate, he had found the house in Salhouse.

It was only ever supposed to be a temporary arrangement, until he could find time to buy a property of his own, but he liked the area; he could paddleboard at Salhouse Broad, and the location was convenient for biking out to the coast, and he got on well with Penny, his landlady, helping out with DIY jobs around the house.

For a while, that relationship had spilled over into something more, though, over time they realised they both wanted different things. Things had already been fizzling out when he had first met Harper, and they had ended shortly after.

He knew he needed to get his life in order. He was a thirty-five-year-old man living in the basement room of his ex-girlfriend's house. It was ridiculous. And after he started dating Harper, he had ignored all of her hints to see where he lived, embarrassed by the truth. He didn't want her to know he was still living like a student. And the idea of bringing her over when she was bound to bump into Penny was even worse.

He was still on good terms with his ex, who had no problems with him being there, and he had looked after Eric, Penny's dog, for her when she was away, but still, he wasn't sure how Harper would react, knowing they had dated. Especially as he had already told her Eric's owner was simply his neighbour. And it didn't help that Penny was openly affectionate and confident. She was such a tactile person and big on hugs. The opposite to Harper, who had been wound as tight as a coil when Luke had first met her.

He knew Harper had struggled after losing her husband and suspected it was worse than she liked to let on. And learning that she had been cheated on too, he understood why.

Another reason why he had to come clean with her. Charlie had kept secrets from her. Luke promised himself he would not do the same.

He had been looking for somewhere else to live, telling Penny it was time he moved on, so that at least when he told Harper where he lived, she knew he was actively doing something about it. But rental prices had rocketed and he didn't want to plunder the savings he had for when he did buy.

He glanced around the space now, wondering if he was over-reacting. He had his own entrance and the room was en suite. It was just really the kitchen in the main house that he needed access to.

Harper knew he worked long and unpredictable hours. Maybe she would understand.

He had hoped to find out tonight, because the plan had been to finally show her. No point in waiting for Friday. He might as well get it over with.

At least he would have done if she had replied to his damn WhatsApp message.

He knew she had read it, yet for whatever reason, she was taking her sweet time in responding. It was out of character for her, and it was unlike him to be fazed. He had never been the kind of person to get hung up waiting for a message. But then, things were different with Harper, he realised.

He really liked her. And now he had made his mind up that she deserved to know the truth there was an urgency to tell her. But he was determined not to harass her, knowing she would get back to him when she could, and he had tried to keep himself distracted all evening, eventually heading out for a run.

The cold December air had almost taken his breath away as his feet pounded the quiet country lanes, lit only by his head torch. As he made his way into the main village of Salhouse, several of the houses were decked out for Christmas with icicle fairy lights hanging from rooftops and Christmas trees twinkling in the windows of the few properties that hadn't drawn their curtains.

This Christmas would be his first with Harper and although he had pulled the late shift at work, he had hoped to make Christmas Day with her as special as possible. She had dealt with so much since Charlie had died and he knew the recent discoveries she had made about their marriage had knocked her for six. She deserved better.

He just wished she wouldn't keep looking to her past. Yes, she had to face it, but it was also a rabbit hole that she was going to fall down if she wasn't careful. Luke was trying to be there for support, but it was difficult watching the woman he was falling in love with break a little further as each new revelation pummelled her.

First there was the photo she had found in the office, then the discovery that Charlie had a secret cottage. And there was the phone lying on her coffee table last night.

Harper had tried to pretend it was hers, but Luke suspected it had belonged to Charlie. If she kept obsessing over the past, trying to find answers that were no longer available, it would destroy her. He really didn't want to watch that happen and he was torn between trying to edge his way closer in an attempt to break down her defences or giving her extra space.

Having already unsuccessfully tried the first option, he was now giving the second one a go. Which was why, after showering, he went to bed, determined not to give in to the temptation to call her.

She would come to him when she was ready.

38

It seemed that Isaac Collins liked the sound of his own voice. And right now, Harper was hoping he kept talking, terrified that if he stopped, then the real torture would begin. She could only imagine what some of the apparatus in this room was used for and knowing that unless she could find a way out of this hellhole she was going to find out for real had every inch of her trembling.

The collar wasn't coming off. She had already wasted precious energy trying to remove it and yanking at the chain attaching it to the wall, before Isaac had stepped into the room. Learning that he had rigged it to shock her if she disobeyed him only depleted her further.

For a while when she had first realised she was wearing it, the collar had felt like it was slowly choking her and the fear of what was going to happen had her screaming herself hoarse, desperately trying to get help. Eventually exhausted, she had collapsed on the mattress and sobbed until she had no energy left for tears.

The stillness and the silence that followed could have worked against her, but instead it had fuelled a new determination, one which ignited anger.

How dare he kidnap her and lock her up like this?

She was finally, after all of this time, finding hope and a way forward. And she had reasons now to get up every morning, a purpose for existing. She wanted to live.

'Where's my dog?'

That had been the first question she had asked him after he confirmed he was Charlie's accomplice.

She could see it had surprised him. He had expected more questions about Charlie, and yes, she had plenty of those, but Bailey came first. He was more important.

To a sick psychopath like Isaac, she supposed he couldn't relate or feel empathy for the welfare of another living creature.

'He's not your concern any more,' he had eventually answered, and Harper had balled her fists together wanting to throttle him, biting down on her anger in case he had hurt Bailey.

'Where's my dog?' she repeated, forcing her tone to remain calm.

It took fifteen minutes of stubborn silence as he tried to goad her, before he finally told her. She knew he wanted to talk about this cellar and all of the sick things he had done and he wanted her participation, her fear. Something she refused to show him until she had what she wanted.

And she could sense his building frustration, watched him getting antsy with the remote, trying to ready herself for another shock, before he put it down, instead picking up a vicious-looking knife. He played with it menacingly for a few minutes, even running the blade along his finger and letting blood drip to the floor – Harper supposed to demonstrate how sharp it was, and she tried her best to block him out, even as sweat pooled in her armpits and at the nape of her neck, despite the freezing temperature in the room.

Eventually, he caved.

'I let him out of the car,' he said, bored. 'As I said, he's no longer your concern.'

Harper gave him a challenging look, unsure whether to believe him. She had read about serial killers and animals. If he had hurt Bailey...

'Relax.' Isaac rolled his eyes, getting up from the sofa suddenly, causing her to flinch. He smiled, looking pleased at her reaction. 'I'm not interested in wasting my time with a stupid dog. I have far more interesting things to play with.' He waggled his eyebrows suggestively and she almost vomited. 'This is your new home,' he continued. 'And we don't need any interruptions. Now, are you going to get undressed for me or do I have to help you?' He held out the knife, letting the tip touch the collar of her coat.

What?

Harper's heart thumped. She wasn't taking her clothes off.

'How did you meet Charlie?' she blurted.

He had wanted to talk, so she would indulge him. Anything to stay dressed. The idea of taking her clothes off, of being vulnerable in front of him, was unthinkable. Plus, it was bloody freezing down here.

'So now you want to talk about your husband?' Isaac sounded amused. 'I will tell you about him later. We have plenty of time. Clothes off, please.'

'What about Alicia?' Harper asked, taking her time as she slowly undid the top button on her coat. 'Was she part of your sick little group too?'

It was a question she was desperate to find out the answer to. All this time, she had assumed her former friend had been having an affair with Charlie, but the discovery of the torture room in the cottage had her wondering if their connection had been more sinister. Isaac had been Charlie's accomplice, but did he have more than one?

Was Alicia a part of this or had Harper's initial assumption been correct and she had been a lover, unaware of his extracurricular activities?

'Alicia?' Isaac paused for a moment, as if recalling her. 'Yes, of course. Alicia. Your husband's big downfall. She was your friend, wasn't she?'

'What do you mean, downfall?'

Harper stared at him, fingers stilling on the second button.

'Keep going, please.'

He sounded so bloody polite, the way he was asking her, which made the act of what she was being forced to do all the more surreal.

She started undoing the second button, relieved when he returned to the sofa, sitting down and studying the knife, as he chuckled to himself. She wasn't sure what was supposed to be so amusing, but at least for now he seemed distracted.

'Charlie had a pattern. He went for a specific look in his women, which, ironically, was nothing like you. I assumed you were just a cover for him at first. A way for him to portray normality. The perfect little wife. But then I pushed his buttons one day and told him you were my type. He went crazy and told me you were off limits. I think in his sick and twisted way he did actually love you.'

There was a point when knowing that would have given Harper comfort, but not any more. Her husband had been a monster. A tear escaped, rolling down her cheek, but she didn't attempt to brush it away, not wanting Isaac to notice the movement.

Not that he was paying her any attention right now, studying the knife as he warmed up to his subject. 'He used to find his victims on the internet,' he continued. 'And he had fake profiles on different dating sites, though Hooked was where he was most successful. It's amazing how many of you silly bitches fall for a picture of a generic good-looking guy. All we have to do is read about what you like, then pretend we're into the same shit. You all lap it up, don't you, Harper?'

He was talking as though she was one of these gullible women and it took a moment before she remembered the date where she had been catfished.

'You were Brad,' she said quietly.

Now Isaac looked smug. 'I wanted you to come to the pub, to get talking to you.' He had made her a mocktail that night, lamenting with her that she had been stood up. 'Brad was a little test to see how easily you could be manipulated. Plus, I wanted to be sure you were the one.'

'The one what?' Harper asked, and immediately wished she hadn't.

'This. Here. I didn't just bring you down here on a whim, Harper. You're special. I've been planning this for a while.'

He had? Her stomach knotted tighter as fresh fear trembled through her.

'Why?'

'Because you were his. You were always untouchable. For a long time after he died, I continued to respect that rule, but then you showed up in my bar for your date with Adrian Fox and I realised Charlie is no longer here. I can do what I want. I don't have to answer to him any longer.'

'You recognised me?'

Harper recalled that first date night. He had been staring at her when she had walked into the pub. At the time, she had put it down to her own paranoia.

'I never forgot you. I always had a soft spot for you, Harper.' The way his voice dropped an octave as he finished his sentence made her skin crawl.

'I don't remember ever meeting you.'

'You wouldn't.' His tone turned bitter. 'You never noticed me. Though, you're going to now, I promise you that.'

Harper shuddered.

'Do you remember The Swan Inn at Coltishall? It was one of the hotels Charlie looked after. I used to work behind the bar there.'

She did; memories of going to the hotel a couple of times with Charlie for corporate dinners surfaced. She didn't recall seeing Isaac there, though he was younger than her by what, twelve, fifteen years? He would have been about eighteen at the time.

Had he been murdering women when he was in his teens? Had Charlie taken him under his wing like some kind of protégé? The thought made her stomach churn.

'I followed Charlie one day. Discovered his little secret at the cottage. He thought I was going to blackmail him, that I wanted money.' Isaac laughed. 'All I wanted to do was join in, and learn. And I did, though your husband was bloody selfish at times. It was always about what *he* wanted. It was actually a blessing when Alicia killed him.'

'What?' Harper's intake of breath was sharp and for a moment she forgot she was supposed to be making a show of unbuttoning her coat.

'Get that off quicker, please,' Isaac instructed, pointing at the garment with his knife. 'Or I will help you.'

'Charlie and Alicia died in a car accident,' she reminded him, reluctantly undoing the final button and letting the coat fall open.

'Yes, the one she caused.'

'How do you know that?'

Isaac's mouth twisted into a smirk. 'Because I was there.'

39

Frustration gnawed at Luke's gut when he didn't hear from Harper the following morning and, by then, a sliver of worry had started to creep in.

Giving her space was one thing, but she had dealt with a lot of stuff over the last few days. Not just the revelations about Charlie, but there was the news about Gavin Brooks too. What if she wasn't coping?

Deciding to stop by her place on his way to work, needing to reassure himself that she was okay, he was surprised to find her car wasn't in the driveway. It was possible she had left it somewhere, though Luke knew it was unlikely, and glancing up at the bedroom window he could see the curtains weren't drawn. Was she up already?

Although he had a key, he wouldn't let himself in. Not if she was home and in bed. He didn't want to spook her. Instead, he rang the doorbell and waited, anxiety gnawing at his gut when he didn't hear Bailey bark.

There was nowhere he could think they would be at this time of the day.

Taking his phone from his pocket, he pulled up her number and hit call.

* * *

Justin still had Harper's phone and was aware that he had to return it. He had tried to get the lock off, hoping to access her phonebook so he could call some of her contacts who might be able to alert her, but it was one of those fancy iPhones which required facial recognition.

No, he would have to hand it in to the police. Something he intended to do later that morning. For now, it sat on the kitchen table beside his own handset, while he made himself some breakfast.

He had just buttered his toast when Harper's phone started vibrating, lighting up as it bounced around on the table, alerting him that a call was coming through. The name 'Luke' was showing on the screen.

Justin picked it up, hesitating only briefly, before he realised there was an option to answer.

'Hello?'

The voice that answered him was instantly suspicious. 'Who is this?'

'My name's Justin. You're Luke—'

'Where's Harper?'

Luke didn't sound at all happy and Justin drew in a calming breath before answering.

'She dropped her phone and I found it. I was going to hand it in to the police this morning.'

There was a pause as Luke took that information in.

'Where?'

'Sorry?'

'Where did you find it?' He hesitated before apologising. 'I'm sorry. I didn't mean to snap. But I don't know where she is. I'm getting worried about her.'

Now he had spoken more than a few words, Justin realised that he had an Irish accent. Was this Harper's boyfriend? The man with the dark curly hair he had seen her with? The twinge of jealousy he felt was quickly outweighed by the revelation that Harper might be missing.

'I bumped into her on the trail at Waxham beach,' he said now.

'You know her?'

'Yes.' It was too complicated to go into now, so Justin didn't. 'I was taking photos and she had been walking her dog.'

'This was when, yesterday?'

'Yes, late afternoon. It was just getting dark.'

'So she was up at the cottage,' Luke mused.

'She has a cottage up there?' Harper had never mentioned it, but then, Justin realised, apart from their one meeting, they had only messaged and called a handful of times.

Luke ignored his question. 'I should go up there, check she's okay. Are you in Norwich? She's going to need her phone.'

Justin reeled off his address, guessing it made sense for Luke to stop by and pick it up, even if he didn't relish the idea of meeting Harper's boyfriend.

'I don't know if she's still at the coast, though,' he said, as Luke was about to end the call.

'Why not?'

'A car stopped as she was walking back and she and the dog both got in.'

'What car?'

'A Toyota Corolla, I think,' Justin told him, furrowing his brow. 'I might be wrong. Maybe this friend is staying with her.'

'What friend? You knew them?' Luke's voice sounded tight with annoyance that Justin was only just telling him this.

'I don't know him personally, but I recognised him from when I've been in the Black Dog Inn. He works behind the bar.'

The room was freezing cold and pitch black, and Harper couldn't stop her teeth chattering together, huddled on the mattress, desperately trying to stay warm.

The bastard had taken her clothes.

After telling her the truth about Alicia and what had happened in the lead-up to the accident – the revelation leaving her reeling – he had decided to help her undress. She had fought him every step of the way, but he was bigger and stronger, and he had a knife and the shock collar. It was a battle she was never going to win.

To her relief, he hadn't raped her – yet. Instead, he had made her put on a clingy red dress that barely covered her thighs and left little to the imagination, and presented her with a bag of make-up, forcing her to apply mascara, heavy eyeshadow, thick black eyeliner and red lipstick. She only saw her reflection briefly before he snatched the mirror back from her, and she barely recognised herself.

The make-up had mostly smeared off now and the mascara was running down her cheeks. She knew that because she had tried to swipe her tears away before he had finally left her alone down here and her hand had come away black.

There was only one saving grace with the make-up and that was the eyeshadow brush, which she had been able to sneak down the side of the mattress when he wasn't looking.

How it was going to help her, she didn't know, but the end point was sharp, so it might come in use somehow.

'You look just like the perfect slut,' he had told her, not even trying to hide his bulging hard-on. 'My soulmate. You wanted another one of those, didn't you, Harper?'

At the time, she hadn't registered what he was talking about, but then he had revealed that he had read her journal.

So it *had* been him in the house that night. She hadn't imagined it. He had stolen her underwear and he had read her innermost thoughts.

It didn't seem possible she could feel any more violated, but she did.

'You worried if Charlie was it for you or if there was someone else out there. Well, here I am,' Isaac had taunted, running his finger along the blade of the knife he still held. 'I understand all about love and pain. They are closer than you realise. We are going to be perfect together.'

She had been convinced he was going to use the knife on her now he finally had her dressed how he wanted, but it seemed the weapon was there only to scare her.

At least for now.

Instead, he had tormented her by tying her to the wooden chair in front of the TV and forcing her to watch home videos with him, pausing the screen each time she looked away or squeezed her eyes shut, horrified at what he had subjected these poor women to.

It was psychological, she knew that. He was messing with her head and wanted her to know what fate awaited her.

He had forced her to use a bucket to pee in before he'd left the room, watching her the whole time, her humiliation now complete, and Harper had begged him for a blanket when he'd ordered her back onto the soiled mattress. She was so cold.

Ignoring her, he had turned out the light as he'd left, plunging the room into darkness and wishing her sweet dreams before the door bolted shut.

She had barely slept, unable to shut out the horrors of what she had just seen, wondering where her poor dog was, and if Luke, Megan, or anyone else had realised she was missing.

And, of course, she thought about Alicia.

For the last two years, she had demonised the woman, hating her for the supposed affair with Charlie.

If only she had known the truth.

* * *

'Your friend became a problem when she saw Charlie with Ashley Knowles,' Isaac had told her as he'd hurried Harper to lose her coat.

She remembered the name. Ashley was a local girl who had been in the news around the time of Charlie's accident, her disappearance out of character. The story had been on the radio Harper played to try to drown out the silence in the house. Eventually, the lack of fresh leads and incoming bigger stories had pushed her name from the headlines, and then people had stopped talking about her completely.

'He had a pattern. Lure a potential victim to a bar using one of his fake profiles, wait for them to leave when they realised they had been stood up, then follow them home. Because he travelled, he could use that ruse all over the country.'

Isaac's words had made Harper shudder. He spoke about it as if it was so normal.

'Ashley was different and he broke his own code. She had been out running one evening in the country lanes around where you live, when she slipped over, twisting her ankle and smashing her phone. Good old Charlie had seen her, coming straight to her rescue and, knowing you were out, he had taken her back to your house with the promise she could use his phone. Alicia had been driving by and saw them together, his arm around her as he helped Ashley into his car.'

Harper had cast her mind back, remembering how a few days before Charlie's accident he had messaged her while she was at the gym. The duty manager had walked out of one of his Norfolk hotels, he had said, and he needed to step in and sort the mess out. He had promised he would be back as soon as possible, and, true to his word, he had returned in the middle of the night. Was that when he had taken Ashley Knowles to the cottage?

'Did Charlie know he had been seen?'

Isaac had shaken his head. 'No. He wouldn't have known, but Alicia told him. Accused him of cheating on you. He swore it was innocent, but knew she didn't believe him. We had already spoken about the problem, unsure if Alicia would recognise Ashley. We didn't know how clearly she had seen her. At the time, she hadn't been reported missing. She lived alone and worked from home a couple of days a week, and she wasn't close with her family. But then the news broke and Alicia contacted Charlie. She wanted to talk to him urgently. It was about the woman she had seen him with. He was out on the road at the time and knew he needed to resolve the Alicia situation before it became a real problem. That's when he called me. He didn't have his key for the cellar on him and we needed to take care of her.'

Harper had swallowed. 'You mean kill her,' she'd managed, her voice not much more than a whisper.

'If you want to be dramatic about it, yes.' Isaac had shrugged. 'She was turning into a problem.'

All of this time she had believed Alicia had gone behind her back. How wrong she had been.

'As it turned out, Alicia hadn't seen the news about Ashley. She still thought Charlie was having an affair and wanted to tell you. It was still a problem, though, and one that needed dealing with. He managed to persuade her to drive up to the coast with him, insisting he had been planning a surprise for you and he would show her, to prove to her that she was wrong. They picked me up along the way and as soon as I got in the car, I got the impression Alicia was nervous. It was as though she was sensing something was off. As we neared Waxham, she had her phone out and started typing a message. I couldn't have that, so I intervened, and she started begging Charlie to stop the car. When he didn't, she grabbed the wheel. The next thing I knew, we had careened off the road and the car had flipped onto its roof. I was the only one who got out unscathed and I didn't stick around. Alicia was already dead and Charlie was in a bad way. I needed to get the hell out of there before the police arrived and started asking awkward questions.' He had shrugged again, as if it was no big deal and they were talking about something mundane. 'So now you know the truth. Does it make you feel any better?'

No, it didn't. And as she recalled their conversation now, guilt crept in.

Alicia had been loyal until the end and Harper had believed the worst of her. If there was any saving grace, it was that her friend had died before she'd reached the cottage.

Unlike her, Alicia had been spared this hell.

'I found a necklace with a red heart pendant,' Harper had murmured, almost to herself. 'I thought Charlie had bought it to give to Alicia. I thought they were having an affair.'

Isaac's lips had twisted into a smile. 'It was Ashley's. Charlie took it as a souvenir. We like the memories.'

Harper didn't bother pointing out that he had his sick videos. Photos too. She suspected they would never be enough for him.

Her eyes had adjusted to the darkness now and she could make out the shape of the sofa and some of the other furniture in the room, but really she had no idea what time it was.

With the absence of her phone and daylight, it was impossible to tell how long she had been trapped down here. And even if Luke had alerted the police, they were never going to find this place.

Her stomach was raw with hunger, though she didn't think she could eat anything even if it was offered, and she was desperately thirsty.

Somehow she needed to find a way to either break free or raise the alarm, so someone knew she was trapped down here.

If she didn't, Harper knew she wouldn't be leaving this room alive.

41

Luke hated the idea of calling in sick and this was the first time he had done since moving to Norfolk. He couldn't go to work, though. Not until he knew Harper was okay.

Instead, he'd met up with Justin to collect her phone, grilling the man again about his encounter with Harper and Bailey the previous afternoon.

Was he certain it had been the barman from the Black Dog?

What direction had the car been heading?

Had Harper mentioned why she was at the cottage?

How had she seemed?

At first, Justin had been reticent and Luke remembered Harper's concerns that he had known where she lived. Was he somehow involved in her disappearance?

No, he had said, she was with the barman from the Black Dog. He had no reason to say that if it wasn't true.

'Please let me know when you find her,' Justin had asked as Luke left, and Luke hoped he was right and the man was telling him the truth.

Harper had last been seen in Waxham, so that was where he

headed next. Perhaps she was still at the cottage, though that made no sense. Why would she want to be in the place where her husband had cheated on her?

That led his mind to darker paths. What if Harper had suffered an accident, or, God forbid, she had tried to hurt herself? Urgency to find her had him stepping on the accelerator, and when he eventually arrived at the cottage, spotting her car parked out front, he almost fell out of his Audi, desperate to know she was safe.

'Harper?' He called her name, even as he knocked on the front door.

There was no answer and he moved to the window, peering inside, but seeing no sign of her.

Where the hell was she?

That was when he heard barking, realising it came from behind the cottage.

Bailey?

Would he find Harper and the dog round back?

As he went to check, he collided with the spaniel, who came bounding round the corner. Bailey, delighted to see him, wagged his tail frantically as he attempted to cover him with licks.

'Hey, mate.' Luke made a fuss of the dog, as some of his unease lifted. Harper had to be here. 'Shall we go find your mum? Harper?' He called her name as Bailey followed him, surprised when she wasn't there.

She wouldn't leave her dog. He knew she wouldn't. But there was no denying Bailey was agitated. Despite being pleased to see Luke, he wouldn't settle and kept barking and whining.

'Where is she, boy?'

He tried the back door that led into the kitchen, finding it locked, his frustration growing. Although he didn't like the idea of breaking into the cottage, he couldn't leave here without checking if Harper was inside.

Deciding entry through the window might be wiser and cheaper, as a pane of glass would cost less to replace than a new door, he went round to the bedroom, slipping on his gloves to protect his hands before using a rock from the border where the rosemary plants were to break the glass.

The noise was loud and if Harper was inside, she would be certain to hear him. Still, he called her name again, not receiving any response. Reaching inside to fully open the window, he cleared the windowsill of glass and clambered through.

Outside, Bailey barked and whined.

'Wait here. I'll be back in a minute,' Luke urged.

It took him seconds to establish that Harper wasn't in the cottage, but he could see that she had been. The remaining bits of broken-up furniture were gone and the rug was pulled back in the small inner hallway, exposing a trapdoor that he hadn't noticed on his previous visit. The fact it was ajar had his gut tightening. Was Harper down in the cellar? Had she fallen?

Quickly he raised the door, shining the torch on his phone into the hole. Stairs led down and he could see a faint light at the bottom.

Wasting no time, he headed down to find her.

There was another door in the wall ahead of him, beside a bookcase, part open, and that was where the light was coming from.

'Harper?'

Please don't let her have done anything stupid.

He stepped into the harsh white room, taking in everything at once. The bed, the lights and the tripod, the gurney, the desk with the laptop on it, and the creepy-looking plastic cubicle. What the fuck was this place?

It was the bed from the photo that Harper had found. The one with the woman posing seductively.

One of Charlie's lovers.

Nothing in this room screamed seduction. It was too clinical for that.

Just what had Charlie been up to?

And had Harper been down here? If so, where the hell was she now?

Even down here he could hear Bailey barking frantically, and knowing finding Harper was more important than learning more about what this place was, he headed back upstairs.

She wasn't here, but she had been. And Justin was certain he had seen her get into the car with the bartender from the Black Dog. He could call the pub, ask to speak with him. They would be open by now.

Deciding a face-to-face conversation was better, just in case anything sinister was going on, Luke let Bailey into his car and headed back to Norwich.

* * *

Isaac's stomach dropped when he spotted Luke O'Mara walk into the bar. Why the hell was he here?

It had to be coincidence. This was a pub and it wasn't Luke's first visit. There was no way he could connect Isaac to Harper. Maybe he was meeting up with a friend for a drink.

It was possible he didn't even know Harper was missing.

Telling himself to stay calm and that there was nothing to worry about, he plastered what he hoped was a pleasant smile onto his face. 'What can I get you?'

Luke didn't waste any time getting to the point. 'I'm looking for Harper Reed?' The suspicion that Isaac would know her whereabouts was written all over his face.

Why would he assume that?

Dread skittered down his spine. Had he somehow fucked up? It wasn't possible.

He feigned a confused expression, about to ask 'who', because, as far as everyone should be concerned, he knew Harper only as an occasional customer. He wouldn't be expected to remember her name.

'You gave her a lift yesterday,' Luke continued, before Isaac could thankfully deny any involvement. 'Where is she?'

So he knew about that? How the fuck?

'Up at Waxham,' Luke pushed, his tone tense.

Shit. He really did know. Had they been seen?

Quashing down his panic, Isaac smoothed his confusion into a smile. 'Oh, yes, of course. Sorry, I don't really know her by name. I recognised her when I saw her walking along the road and stopped to offer her a ride.'

There, that was good. He sounded convincing.

'Are you her boyfriend then?' he added, wanting it to look like he knew nothing about Harper. In truth, he was fully aware of who Luke was, what he did for a living, and where he lived. He had watched him with Harper on the cameras he had hidden in her house, wanting to cut the man's throat for touching his property. It was only because he didn't want to raise suspicion that he hadn't gone after him. Isaac had already attacked Adrian and killed Gavin for what they did to Harper. If he killed her boyfriend too, the police might start making connections.

'To where?' Luke demanded, ignoring the question.

'Um, home.'

'You dropped her off home?'

'Yes.'

'Her and the dog.'

'Yes!' Sweat was beading on Isaac's upper lip. He hoped it wasn't noticeable.

'So how did Bailey, her dog, get back up to Waxham then?' Luke demanded. 'I found him at her cottage.'

Shit. Think quick.

'Which is where I dropped her.' Isaac forced another smile, even though the collar of his shirt felt too tight against his throat. 'I assumed the cottage *was* her home. I'm sure if you speak to her, she can confirm this.'

'I can't do that,' Luke said tightly. 'Because no one knows where she is. You were the last person to see her.'

'Look, I don't know what to say.' Isaac shrugged, hoping the action came across as helpless rather than disinterested. 'She was fine when I left her. Maybe she just wanted some time alone. I'm sure she'll show up.'

Luke didn't seem convinced.

Luckily, Isaac was saved from further questions by a large group who came into the pub, heading straight to the bar. 'I'm sorry I can't help you,' he said, by way of ending the conversation.

As he served the newcomers, who thankfully wanted to place a lunch order as well as buy drinks, he was aware of Luke watching him, and he tried his best to act normal, wishing the man would just leave.

His mind was working overtime, trying to figure out how the hell he had been spotted with Harper. He knew this wasn't good. If Luke went to the police, which he was certain to do, he was going to tell them that she had been with Isaac, and they would come knocking at his door.

If they found his basement room...

No, they wouldn't. He had been too careful. All they would

see if they looked in the cellar was his mancave. There was no way they would find the room behind the shelves.

He would have to subdue Harper, though, to ensure she didn't make any noise. He couldn't risk her alerting them where she was.

Of course, it would ruin his fun for a while. He wanted her lucid and aware of everything he subjected her to. But needs must, and it wouldn't be forever. Just long enough to convince the police he had nothing to do with her disappearance.

As he finished serving the group, he realised Luke had gone. A relief for now, but it didn't stop Isaac's skin itching with impatience. The visit had put him on edge and he knew he wouldn't settle until he was back home.

Karen was on a break, but as soon as she returned, he decided he would tell her he didn't feel well. He would make his excuses and knock off early.

He needed to check on Harper and reassure himself that everything was okay. And then he needed to make sure he was prepared, just in case the police showed up tonight.

* * *

The kid was lying, Luke was certain of it, and he had planned to go straight to the police, but as he got in his car, his phone started vibrating. He snatched it from his pocket, hoping it was Harper and dismayed when he saw his friend Damon's name on the screen.

'Mate, I can't talk right now,' he answered by way of greeting.

'Oh, oh, is everything okay?'

'Yes, it's just...' He hesitated. Damon was his closest friend and he could use him as a sounding board right now. 'No, actually it's not.'

Damon's response was instant. 'Tell me what I can do to help.'

'It's Harper. She's missing.'

Luke told him everything and Damon listened patiently, chipping in now and again to ask questions. Although he hadn't seen Harper since that first time their paths had crossed at the beach, he knew her and Luke had been dating, and like Luke, he agreed her disappearance was out of character.

'Where's the dog now?' Damon asked.

'Penny's looking after him while I came down to the pub. Why?'

'I just wondered how he would react around this bartender kid. If he has done something to Harper, the dog isn't going to react well to him.'

He had a point, but Bailey wasn't here.

And the bartender was leaving, Luke realised, watching him walk out of the pub, zipping up his coat. The pub had only opened an hour or two ago. His shift wouldn't be over already.

He was definitely leaving, though. Climbing into a black Toyota Corolla. The same car he had picked Harper up in.

Where was he going?

'Luke, are you still there?'

'Yeah, sorry. The bartender's just left the pub. I'm going to follow him.'

'Don't do anything stupid, mate.'

'I won't,' Luke promised, switching his phone to hands-free. He watched as the Toyota pulled out of the car park before starting his engine and heading out in the same direction, careful to keep his distance.

It was early afternoon and the roads were steady with traffic. Enough to help disguise the fact he was following, but not too busy that he risked losing the car.

'So what's the plan then?' Damon's voice boomed out of the speaker.

'I don't have one.'

'You've got to have a plan.'

'I want to know where he's going. He's left his shift early and I want to know why.'

'Okay, but then we make a plan before you do anything. Together. Agreed.'

'Yeah, sure.' Luke took the same turn onto the southern bypass. 'Agreed.'

They exited at the Brundall roundabout, heading through the village and then going through Strumpshaw, the Corolla eventually turning into a remote lane in Cantley.

Luke cruised by the exit to avoid suspicion, before turning the car around in the entrance to a field and following. He kept his speed low as he looked for the car.

When he spotted it parked in the driveway of a large, old detached house, he pulled to a halt a little further along the lane.

'We're here.'

'Where's here?' Damon wanted to know.

'Cantley. I'm guessing this is where he lives.'

'So what's the plan now?'

Luke hesitated. He should call the police, but it bothered him that the bartender had acted so guiltily and that he had left the pub shortly after being confronted. 'I don't know,' he admitted. He could hardly break into the guy's house.

But if he did have something to do with Harper's disappearance…

He thought back to the cottage and the cellar room he had found, unsettled that it might somehow be connected.

'Tell me exactly where you are,' Damon told him. 'I'm coming to find you.'

42

Never one to break a routine, for fear it would bring him bad luck, Isaac checked in on his mother first, unlocking her door and taking her a cup of tea.

She had no idea he was home early. In fact, today she was unaware he was her son. Not for the first time, she had confused him with his father. Something that niggled at him. He preferred it when she didn't know who he was at all.

'Would you like me to bake you a cake?' she asked. 'I can send Isaac down to the shed with a slice?'

Pacifying her, he told her that would be lovely and hoped that when he next came back to check on her, she might have morphed him into someone else.

In the kitchen, he washed up her cup, then took a plastic bowl out of the cupboard, opening and emptying a can of tinned peaches into it. A treat for Harper before he drugged her.

Taking the bowl with him, he headed down into the cellar.

* * *

Harper was already learning to dread the sound of footsteps.

Earlier, Isaac had brought her breakfast. She only knew it was morning because that's what he had called the meal – a bowl of what looked like and certainly smelt like dog food. To humiliate her further, he had forced her on her hands and knees and made her eat from the bowl like an animal.

She had spat the first mouthful out, disgusted, despite the fact her stomach was cramping from hunger.

His response had been to withhold the plastic bottle of water.

'Five mouthfuls of food and you can have a drink,' he had told her gleefully, and to her utter embarrassment, she had begged and pleaded with him to give her the cup.

Eventually, realising he wasn't going to give in, she had obeyed him, each mouthful threatening to come back up.

'How I wish Charlie could be here to see this,' he had commented, taking pleasure in her misery.

Harper was beginning to understand Isaac's relationship with her husband a little better. He had been the underdog in their partnership, being forced to defer to Charlie, a man he had seemed to admire and despise in equal measures. This was his form of revenge. She was the ultimate prize.

If she hadn't gone into the Black Dog Inn, if their paths had never crossed again, would he have left her alone, or would he have eventually come for her?

She couldn't bring herself to ask the question, fearful that she had brought this on herself. If only she had chosen a different pub for her dates.

Isaac had let her have the water and she had emptied the bottle greedily, wishing there was more.

Part of her wished he would use his knives or whatever other tool he planned to kill her with. Just get it over with. She couldn't stand being down here, freezing cold and tormented like this. Forced to eat dog food and pee in a bucket.

And now he was returning. The familiar sound of the door scraping back. What fresh horror was he bringing with him this time?

The light went on and she shielded her eyes as they tried to adjust.

'I've brought you a treat. Lunch,' he told her, holding up another bowl.

Harper didn't want it. She would rather starve.

Hugging her knees to her chest, she watched him warily as he approached.

'Come on, now. It's nice. Peaches in syrup.' He set the bowl on the floor beside the mattress.

She glanced at the food, wondering what the trick was. It looked like peaches, but there had to be a catch. Although she could still taste the dog food from earlier and desperately wanted the food, she didn't trust him.

'On your hands and knees,' Isaac ordered.

She scowled at him. 'No.'

For a moment, they stared at each other as he seemed to size her up, wondering how far she might push this. Was she making a mistake? One he would relish punishing her for?

'Believe it or not, you have things quite good at the moment. I can make them so much worse for you.'

Harper shuddered, but refused to move. She watched as he picked up his remote control, using the valuable second his attention was turned away to reach for the eyeshadow brush she had hidden away, closing her clammy hand around it.

'I'm going to ask you one more time to get on the floor and eat your lunch. If you don't, things are going to get very bad for you.'

If she could get close enough, she might be able to use the sharp end of the brush to hurt him, but if he shocked her, she knew she would likely drop it.

Reluctantly, she crawled off the mattress towards the food.

She could smell the peaches and her mouth watered, making her stomach rumble.

There didn't appear to be anything wrong with them.

'Eat the food, Harper.'

Tentatively, she lowered her head, syrup coating her chin as she tried to eat them.

How she hated him for what he was doing.

She managed a couple of mouthfuls, then tried to get up. Was the end of the brush sharp enough to stab him in the throat? But even if she tried, she had no idea which part of his throat would inflict the most damage, if any at all.

'Back down. I want that bowl licked clean.'

Doing as told, her mind worked overtime. If she was going to get out of this room, she had to help herself.

The door was ajar, but even if she managed to get through it, what would she find on the other side? Besides, she wasn't going anywhere unless she found a way to free herself from the collar.

Isaac still held the remote. If she could get hold of it, he wouldn't be able to shock her. It would be a start.

She dared another glance up at him and, to her horror, watched as he pulled a syringe needle from his pocket with his free hand. That was how he had kidnapped her, by drugging her in the car. What was he planning to do to her?

'Henry? Would you prefer chocolate or carrot cake?'

The unfamiliar voice had Harper glancing towards the door.

An older woman had stepped into the room, her grey hair unkempt. She seemed confused as she looked at Isaac, completely oblivious to the scene she had just walked in on. And Isaac's face was a picture of shock as he stared back at her.

'Mum, what are you doing down here?'

This was his mother? Why had she called him Henry?

'Help me. Please,' Harper begged. 'Your son is keeping me a prisoner down here.'

'Shut up,' Isaac snapped, as his mother finally seemed to register her presence.

'Henry? What is going on?' She took a step further into the room, her face crumpling. 'Are you cheating on me?'

The next few moments seemed to play out in slow motion, as Isaac's mother burst into tears, fleeing the room.

'Mum!'

He sounded stricken, seeming to forget Harper was even there, and as he started to go after her, she acted on instinct, wrapping her arms around both of his legs and tugging hard, causing him to lose his balance.

As he fell to the ground, both the syringe and the remote slipped from his fingers, the case smashing and batteries rolling out. She had hoped to attack him while he was on the floor, but he had already rolled over, the shock on his face turning to anger.

'You fucking bitch.'

He crawled towards her and she scrambled backwards, still trying to keep a grip on the brush. She was barely on the mattress when he caught hold of her ankles, dragging her towards him and crawling on top of her.

'Like it rough, do you?' he snarled, pinning her down with his weight.

Harper thrashed beneath him, screaming out for help, desperately hoping his mother might hear her and raise the alarm, as he ripped at the top of the red dress.

Managing to pull her arm free, she took aim with the brush, stabbing the sharp end towards his face. The first time, she grazed his cheek, but his surprise that she had a weapon had him pausing. The second swing, before he could react to that fact, caught him clean in the eye.

The yowl of pain as his hands went to his face shifted his weight, giving her enough manoeuvrability to wriggle out from under him, and she glanced in panic around the room, knowing that the wound she had inflicted was not life-threatening. She was still chained up and he was going to be mad as hell.

'Somebody help me, please!' As fresh fear rippled through her, she grabbed the slack chain attaching the collar to the wall and yanked hard, even though she knew it wasn't going to break.

Isaac was already on his hands and knees, one hand covering his injured eye, the roar he gave telling her how much trouble she was in.

Yanking Harper to her feet, he turned her to face the terrifying-looking table at the other end of the room. 'If you want to play games, how about I strap you down on my rack over there and show just how much fun that can be?'

Harper had seen the video of the woman tied to the monstrous torture device, and she would never forget the screams as Isaac stretched her limbs.

Even though there was no way for her to escape, she thrashed against him, kicking and screaming, shocked when he threw her back down on the mattress.

Then she saw why.

He was going for the syringe again where it lay on the floor next to the broken remote.

What was he planning to do to her while she was unconscious?

She glanced down at the slack chain attached to the collar,

about to renew her pathetic efforts to free herself, when it dawned on her it was a potential weapon.

Her only weapon.

It wouldn't work. She wasn't strong enough.

Still, she had to try.

As he crouched down to scoop up the syringe, she slipped the slack chain over his head, catching him completely off guard as she tugged it tight against his throat.

His free hand went to his neck and he attempted to shake her off, but she held on, pressing her knee against his back and refusing to let go, her fingers looped through the links and feeling as though they were about to break as she pulled as hard as possible.

He struggled and gurgled, dropping the syringe as he used both hands now to try to free himself.

Acting on instinct, not sure she had the strength to hold on much longer, Harper took a chance. Releasing one hand, she reached for the syringe, her fingers making contact and closing around it. Her grip had loosened, though, and Isaac thrashed violently against her, knocking her backwards as he managed to wrench himself free. He was choking and spluttering, trying to catch his breath, but Harper could see he was already recovering.

Before he could get to his feet, she launched herself at his back, clinging on tightly as she jabbed the syringe into his neck.

It didn't seem like it had affected him, though, and he grappled with her, shoving her to the ground, and climbing on top of her, picking up the chain and pulling it taut.

He started to smile, but it never fully made it to his face, and instead he blinked heavily, staring at her, before the chain in his hands went slack and his eyelids dropped shut.

With his weight pinning her down, Harper wasn't able to dodge his fall as he landed heavily on top of her, and she lay stunned for a moment before her brain kicked into gear, aware the drug would only keep Isaac unconscious for a short while.

She still had to find a way to free herself.

As she attempted to scramble out from under him, she heard footsteps.

'Harper?'

A male voice called her name. One she recognised.

Luke.

At first she was certain she was hallucinating. He wasn't here.

But then she watched him step into the room, his eyes widening in shock and pausing for the briefest second before he went to her, helping to push Isaac's dead weight onto the mattress and pulling her into a tight hug.

'I thought I had lost you,' he whispered against her ear.

Harper couldn't speak, still numb with shock at everything that had just happened.

'Jesus fucking Christ.'

Another male voice had her looking up.

In the centre of the room, Luke's friend Damon was glancing around as he took everything in.

'Is he dead?' he managed at last, looking at Isaac, who was now slumped face down on the bed.

'I drugged him,' Harper managed, as Luke released his grip on her to check Isaac's pulse.

'He's out cold, but not dead. We need to call the police.'

'And get this thing off of me, please,' Harper pleaded, tugging at the collar.

As Luke nodded, Damon's jaw dropped, realising the metal contraption was shackling her to the wall. 'I'm on it,' he assured Luke. 'You make the call.'

'Where's Bailey? Is he okay?'

'He's fine,' Luke told Harper, pulling his phone from his pocket. 'I found him up at the cottage. He's back at my place.'

His place? With his wife, girlfriend? She didn't ask the question. It was the least of her concerns right now.

The first trickle of relief crept through the numbness. Was the nightmare really over?

'Seriously, Harper, this place is fucked up.' Damon was shaking his head, still shocked as he hunted for a tool that would break through the chain. 'Are you okay?'

No, she wasn't. It was going to take her a long time to get over this, but he didn't need to know that. Instead, she nodded and turned her attention to Luke as he made the emergency call, remembering how they had first met at the beach.

'You came to my rescue again,' she told him, trying to keep her voice from cracking.

The tips of his mouth curved as he regarded her with a steady blue gaze, but then he shook his head, gesturing to Isaac's limp body. 'I don't think you needed rescuing. You saved yourself just fine.'

43

Nothing could have prepared Harper for what was to come and over the following days her life was upended.

As the story broke about the bodies at the cottage and her ordeal at the house in Cantley, she had no chance to recover, and her life seemed like it was an endless series of interviews with the police.

Quite what would have happened if Luke and Damon hadn't shown up, she dreaded to think, and she was grateful that after encountering Issac's distraught mother – who had told them her husband was cheating on her with one of his whores in the basement – they had gone into the house to check the situation out.

Isaac was arrested, and for weeks after, he and Charlie had their names plastered all over the press, as victims were uncovered in the horror garden under the rosemary plants. And poor Mrs Collins, who had no coherent idea of what kind of monster her beloved son was or about the prison he had created beneath her house, had been moved into a care home.

Meanwhile, speculation on social media was rife, and the vultures circled.

There were those who sympathised with Harper and everything she had endured, while others created their own narrative, despite not having the full facts, accusing her of being involved. They doubted her innocence, convinced she must have known the truth about her husband and his accomplice, and the theories continued to grow wilder, with some going as far to say Isaac was the victim and Harper had framed him.

Meanwhile, she had her own trauma to deal with, and the home that had once been her sanctuary started to feel like a prison, with reporters and ghouls camped outside. To make it worse, the police had found spyware cameras in her house. Isaac had been watching her in the place where she had thought she was safe.

Eventually, she could take it no more, renting out the house and fleeing with Bailey. Luke had wanted to go with her, but it wasn't fair on him. His career was here in Norwich, and she had insisted he stay behind. She had learnt the truth about his living situation and realised now that she had jumped to conclusions. It had no bearing on her decision to leave. She simply needed to get away for a while.

At first, she stayed with Megan and Tom, trying desperately to get her life in some kind of order, unsure if she even still had a career. She had spoken with her agent and publisher, and by mutual agreement they had decided to delay the release of her next book. But did she even have the heart to write now? Her genre was romcom. Gentle-paced love stories with laugh-out-loud moments and happy ever afters. She had lost hers and each time she tried to return to the keyboard, she felt like a fraud.

As Megan's bump grew, Harper felt in the way. They didn't have room for her and Bailey long term, though Megan would never say that, insisting they could stay for as long as needed. Harper knew her friend was in shock at what had happened and the secrets that had come to light about Charlie. Megan wanted to protect her, but it was time for Harper to stand on her own two feet. Besides, people were figuring out where she was and it wasn't fair on her friends to stay any longer.

Heading to Cornwall, she rented an Airbnb just outside of Padstow. A sweet little terrace painted pastel pink with shutters on the windows. The money she had coming in from her house paid for it, plus there was enough left over to give her the luxury of having a time out. To the locals she befriended, she started going by her middle name, Isabelle, to avoid any uncomfortable conversations, basking in the anonymity it gave her. And with her days free, she went on long walks with Bailey, attempted – with limited success – to teach herself to cook and even tried painting, learning she had a talent for faces, but animals and scenery less so.

Megan was the only one she stayed in regular contact with. Her agent, Adam, reached out a couple of times, as did Justin, after she had messaged him to thank him for the part he had played and to apologise for her behaviour that fateful afternoon on the beach.

And then there was Luke.

Despite telling him to move on, he was insistent that he would wait for her.

Did Harper want that?

She had started to fall in love with him, still perhaps was, but the revelations about Charlie and then her ordeal with Isaac had changed her.

While it would have been easiest to lean on Luke, let him run away with her and help her recover, she had realised it was something she had to do alone.

Her marriage to Charlie had been a farce and she had lost her identity along the way. After he had died, she had become a shell of her former self. It was important that she rediscover herself before even contemplating another relationship, be it with Luke or anyone else.

Gradually, his calls and messages became few and far between, then eventually they fizzled out completely.

It made her heart hurt when she thought of him, but it was fairer to let him move on. He deserved happiness too.

As summer turned into autumn, the old familiar urge to write gradually returned. Harper knew she had a new book in her; she just wasn't sure what it was.

But then she sat down at her Mac and the words started pouring out.

Her story, her life. The romance of how she had first met Charlie, then how it had soured, taking a much darker path.

And it gave her a chance to lay her demons to rest with Alicia. For so long after Charlie's death, she had despised her former friend. But Alicia had been no villain. She had sacrificed her own life to stop Charlie's killing spree, even if she hadn't known at the time what kind of monster he was.

This one was personal, cathartic, a true non-fiction account that was not meant for publication, but then, during a conversation with Adam, she told him what she was writing and he asked if he could see it when it was complete. At first, Harper had said no, but as she neared the end, the yearning to tell the world her version of events grew stronger, and after he had read it, Adam was certain it would be a bestseller.

It would mean reopening old wounds and pushing herself back into the spotlight, but this time she was better prepared. Her time away had helped her. She was ready. And she would include an apology to Alicia for doubting her, dedicating the book to her late friend.

She moved back to Norfolk the following spring, sixteen

months after she had escaped from Isaac Collins and his torture cellar, and her first visit was to lay flowers at Alicia's grave. Spending time talking to her friend and telling her how sorry she was for what had happened was therapeutic.

Her plan was to put the house on the market. The cottage was no more, and after the remains of nine bodies had been removed from the garden, the place had been razed to the ground. It was the best thing for it.

Selling the house would sever her last tie with Charlie, but she had yet to decide if she would stay in the county or have a fresh start somewhere else. Megan had given birth to a little girl, Ava, and Harper was her godmother. She could return to London, be closer to her friend, but it depended on whether there was anything still here for her.

She was back volunteering at the animal shelter a couple of days a week, but there was nothing else to tie her to Norfolk.

The temptation to reach out to Luke, just to see how he was, was strong, but it also wasn't fair. She had walked away from him and he would have moved on. He was probably in a new relationship.

Still, it didn't stop her visiting Salhouse Broad most days, and she knew part of her hoped she might bump into him, just to get closure.

That happened nearly two months after her return as she sat on the bank, enjoying the warm weather and watching Bailey paddling on the water's edge.

'Harper?'

She glanced up, at first blinded by the sun and unable to focus on the figure in front of her, even though she recognised his voice.

As she sheltered her eyes from the sun, he dropped down to

sit beside her, a widening smile on his face. 'I didn't know you were back.'

He looked good. Really good. The sun picking out shades of copper in his dark curly hair, and the vivid blue of his irises, as he locked eyes with her, had her heartbeat quickening.

'I moved back in April,' she told him, not adding how much she had wanted to call him, just to see how he was.

'You're looking really well.'

There was a time when compliments had left her feeling self-conscious, but not any more, and she knew he meant it, from the way he was studying her appreciatively.

'Thank you.' She smoothed a hand over her slightly shorter blonde hair, tucking a strand behind her ear. 'Cornwall was good for me.'

'I'm glad.' He paused. 'I read your book. Alicia would be proud of you.'

Harper managed a smile, a little choked up. Her book had exceeded all expectations, going on to be a huge bestseller, and she had donated much of the money to the families of Charlie's victims. It was the least she could do. 'Thank you.'

They were silent for a moment, unasked questions still hanging in the air.

'So, how are things with you? Still living in Penny's base-ment?' she joked, pleased when he grinned, creases fanning from his eyes and reminding her that the ripple effect of what had happened had touched him too.

She remembered that day she had learnt about his living arrangements. She had still been in hospital at the time and it seemed almost silly, thinking back, that he had been nervous about telling her, worried she might overreact.

But that had been after Isaac, when his revelation had been

dwarfed by bigger things. Would the old Harper have responded badly?

She honestly didn't know. Only that she was a lot more chilled these days.

'I finally bought my own place,' he told her. 'In Thorpe St Andrew. It's a fixer-upper, but I haven't got around to doing much of the fixing up yet.' He scrunched up his nose, making her laugh.

'Perhaps you'd like to see it some time?' he suggested casually, looking down at the grass briefly before locking eyes with her again. 'You could come over for that dinner I promised you.'

Hope warmed inside of Harper. Was he offering her a second chance?

'You're not married then?' Her question was asked lightly, but they both knew what she was really asking.

'Not even dating anyone.' Luke fell silent for a moment, and when he spoke again, his tone was serious. 'I never forgot about you, Harper. I knew I needed to be patient. That you weren't ready and you needed time. That if it was right, you would come back to me.'

He had waited for her?

Taking the initiative, she reached for his hand, linking their fingers.

Her story didn't end with Charlie and Isaac. She wasn't destined to be the widow of a serial killer or the almost victim of one. She deserved her happy ending and she was going to make sure she got it.

Squeezing his hand gently, she gazed up at him and smiled. 'I'm ready now.'

ACKNOWLEDGEMENTS

I pinch myself every day, so grateful that my lovely editor, Caroline Ridding, reached out to work with me. Signing with Boldwood Books is one of the best decisions I have ever made and that is thanks to Caroline Ridding and the rest of the brilliant team. There are so many of you now, but a special mention to Nia Beynon, Niamh Wallace and Claire Fenby, and of course our brilliant founder, Amanda Ridout. My thanks also go to Jade Craddock and Gary Jukes for helping to get my book into shape, and to the rest of the editing/proofing team.

To my family (including Beev pets) and friends, thank you for your continual support. Allison, Bev, Tracy, Daniella and Jo – thank you for everything you do helping me with my reader group on Facebook. And to my beta readers on this one – Tina, Jo, and Andrea. Thank you for your honest and constructive feedback. The points you raise are always relevant, plus you give me faith at the times I doubt myself. Thank you.

I also want to mention the lovely folk at the Walled Garden Cafe in Little Plumstead for hosting my book event in April. It was such a success and that was in big part thanks to all of the staff. Thank you also to Plumstead Road Library for inviting me to do to a talk, and to Matthew and Maria Brown for championing me locally.

Thank you also to my fellow writers for helping to keep me sane – Trish, Val, Tash, Amanda, Charley, Judith, Diane, Jessica,

Sarah, and everyone else – plus the wonderful bloggers and my brilliant readers.

As always, the locations I write about are real, but some of the buildings are fictitious. To those familiar with Norwich, the Black Dog Inn would nestle between The Rushcutters and The River Garden on the Yarmouth Road, River Green area of Thorpe St Andrew. One of my favourite spots.

I often ask my reader group for help in naming the made-up places. Huge thanks to Julie Lacey for coming up with the Black Dog Inn, and to Aileen Davis for suggesting IntoYou for my fictional dating site. It was lovely to meet both of you at my launch and Aileen needs a special mention for travelling all the way down from Northumbria and also for wearing a Beev T-shirt.

Finally, a mention to my beloved Lola puss, who became seriously ill as I was writing this book and sadly passed away on 16 February 2024. Lola was my shadow, my writing assistant, my book poser model, and my best friend for almost seventeen years. By the time this book is published, it will be almost eight months since I held her in the vets as she took her last breath. I miss her terribly every single day. To those of you with furbabies, please hold them close and give them all a big kiss from me.

ABOUT THE AUTHOR

Keri Beevis is the internationally bestselling author of several psychological thrillers and romantic suspense mysteries, including the very successful *Dying to Tell*. She sets many of her books in the county of Norfolk, where she was born and still lives and which provides much of her inspiration.

Sign up to Keri Beevis' mailing list here for news, competitions and updates on future books.

Visit Keri's website: www.keribeevis.com

Follow Keri on social media here:

facebook.com/allaboutbeev

x.com/keribeevis

instagram.com/keri.beevis

bookbub.com/profile/keri-beevis

ALSO BY KERI BEEVIS

THE

Murder

LIST

**THE MURDER LIST IS A NEWSLETTER
DEDICATED TO SPINE-CHILLING FICTION
AND GRIPPING PAGE-TURNERS!**

**SIGN UP TO MAKE SURE YOU'RE ON OUR
HIT LIST FOR EXCLUSIVE DEALS, AUTHOR
CONTENT, AND COMPETITIONS.**

SIGN UP TO OUR
NEWSLETTER

BIT.LY/THEMURDERLISTNEWS

Boldw∞d

Boldwood Books is an award-winning fiction publishing company seeking out the best stories from around the world.

Find out more at www.boldwoodbooks.com

Join our reader community for brilliant books, competitions and offers!

Follow us
@BoldwoodBooks
@TheBoldBookClub

Sign up to our weekly deals newsletter

https://bit.ly/BoldwoodBNewsletter

Printed in Great Britain
by Amazon

48746553R00195